Concerto

JD SPERO

BOOK 2 OF THE *f*ORTE SERIES

Xchyler Publishing,
an imprint of Hamilton Springs Press, LLC
Penny Freeman, Editor-in-chief
www.xchylerpublishing.com
1ⁱ Edition: 1 December 2017
Cover Illustration by Penny Freeman
www.pennyfreeman.com
Interior Design by M. Borgnaes
www.electric-scroll.com
Edited by Penny Freeman and MeriLyn Oblad
Published in the United States of America
Xchyler Publishing

For my boys,

AJ, Adam, and Chaz

" Go green ! "

Concerto

JD Spero

CHAPTER 1

The trail on Skene Mountain has narrowed as the brush has grown in. Cobwebs cling to my eyelashes. Branches smack my sides in a kind of corporal punishment. But I keep moving.

It's been over two years since I climbed this hill. I've been avoiding it. If Brenna, my BFF, weren't beside me, I'm not sure I'd be able to do it.

Hiking today has a two-fold healing focus. One: distraction. Jason's leaving for his summer program at Rhode Island School of Design tomorrow . . . and staying there for his freshman year of college. If I keep moving, I won't have time to think about how much I'll miss him. Why does love have to hurt sometimes?

Two: find my magic again. Revisiting the past and the place where my music and my magic changed everything will hopefully lead me to some trace of inspiration.

Since that night at the cave when I destroyed Aquamarine—the toxic, highly addictive performance-enhancing drug—I haven't felt a hint of magic when I play.

There's still music. On my piano, I roll out sick melodies even if no one's listening. It's not an option. I have to play. It's part of my life, my every-day. But it's just music. That's it. Never any magic. Not anymore. I didn't think it would bother me, but it does. Since I discovered my music had power, it's been hard to appreciate only the song.

concerto

We pause, short of breath from the hike.

"Am I really that out of shape?" Brenna laughs.

"Been a while since volleyball season." I balance-beam on an overgrown root. "Don't worry. You'll be walking everywhere in the city this summer. You won't even realize you're exercising."

It's hard not to be envious. Brenna secured a slot in the summer drama program at NYU's Tisch School of the Arts.

She reads my mind. "You'll love Boston, Sami."

My smile comes easily. She's right. Getting accepted into the summer program at Berklee School of Music is a dream come true. Bonus: Jason won't be that far away.

"And who knows," she says, "maybe you'll find your magic there at Berklee."

"Maybe."

The sky is clouding up, though no rain was forecast. We forge ahead in silence, and I'm grateful Brenna's giving me time to prepare. Turns out I need it. When we step into the clearing, it looks like a war zone.

The clearing had always been a flat part of the mountain, a grassy plain framed by tall pines. A secret plateau not visible from town. On the far side of the clearing was the cliff wall. There, an inverted V-shaped cove opened to the cave where the mother rock of Aquamarine lived. The looming wall of granite seemed to reach the heavens but led to the crest of the mountain. Mom says there's a gorge on the other side, but I've never seen it. Doesn't much matter now. The cliff wall seems to be gone, like a giant excavator came in and scooped it away.

Instead of a green, grassy plain, the clearing is full of debris and dust. An occasional scraggly weed pokes through—offering hope, maybe, or a false sense of it. Most

of it is scorched, like a wildfire ravaged the area or a bomb
went off nearby. Oh, wait. There was an explosion. Quite of
few of them. That was me, my magic, that set it off two years
ago. There's no cave anymore. None that I can see. It's like
a giant sliced a chunk of the granite and served it up as pie.
Fallen trees and upturned roots block where the cave used to
be.

I linger near the tree line, mentally clinging to the trail's
entrance—my escape—like a security blanket. Squatting
down, the ground smells like campfire remnants—a stale,
carbon-y odor that turns me cold.

Bits of bark and stone get caught when I sift ash through
my fingers. Deep into the powdery layer there's darker,
richer soil. It may be a lost cause, but if there was even a
sliver of Aquamarine left, it might tap into the power of my
birthmark, my Nevus spilus. A ghost of the feeling is there,
if only in my memory. The zing of magic into my piano-
playing hands had been like an electric shock. After sifting
a few scoops, I find only charred earth and tiny black stones.
And my birthmark is quiet. Almost numb.

"Oh, Brenna. It's no use. My magic seems lost."

"Have you really not felt a thing since . . ."

"Nothing."

"It can't be over." Brenna's casual tone almost stings.
"It was too powerful. I mean, you were *Dion*."

Dion. My Nevus spilus was the marker. It was the proof
I was Dion, the only one with power to take away Aquamarine's magic and its harmful effects to Goshenite and Fasha
alike. In doing so, I put to rest a decades-old rivalry between
artists and athletes that has since changed the dynamics of
our entire town. For the better.

But not without its side effects. And I'm standing in the

middle of it. I destroyed this space.

Ash particles are airborne from my sifting, making me cough.

"Do you ever think about her?" Brenna asks quietly. She doesn't have to say her name; we both know who she's talking about: Coach Payne. Our volleyball coach who had given out Aquamarine like Gatorade in hopes of maintaining the school's astounding championship record. Up here, on this mountain, she'd tried to stop me—and was swallowed up in the cave in a burst of flickering, multicolored lights.

A shudder staggers through me as I imagine the worst. "I try not to."

"It's not your fault." Brenna holds my gaze until I nod. But it's hard to think of Payne's disappearance as just a kind of collateral damage. What kind of monster am I?

"You did what you had to do," Brenna says, knowing my thoughts once again. "You had no idea what would happen. You had no idea Coach Payne would even be there. She made her own choices."

Still, I feel guilt on a whole new level. A sick feeling pools in my stomach. This mission is growing more hopeless by the second.

Brenna walks farther into the clearing, arms crossed, kicking odd-shaped rocks that seem to weigh nothing. Fire debris. She's on a mission, determined to help me find whatever it may be to trigger my magic again. Her steadfast friendship amazes me.

Oddly, I fight a sudden pang of loss for my childhood friend, Lauren—who I finally got in touch with six months ago, after almost two years of silence. I had gone old school and sent an email. It was newsy and fun, but I did admit to missing her. Her response two weeks later was mostly an apology for taking so long to write back—the words "I miss you, too" must have fallen away into cyberspace.

Brenna shoves away some larger branches as if opening a door. "Sami, check this out."

What could she possibly see in that nest of dead trees? "What do you mean? What's there?"

"Come here. See for yourself."

The fallen brush has made a canopy of shadows, one that Brenna steps into and almost disappears. I hesitate. But I trust her.

Stepping into the darkness, a damp chill folds over me. The brush and rubble beneath my feet make for uneven ground. The air is dense and unmoving. It seems a bad omen. A bug the size of my fist buzzes over my head and I yelp, wanting out. Wanting to be saved. But I can't get my footing—and I start to panic.

"Where are we?"

Brenna points to a huge pile of rubble. Freshly broken stone, its powdery ash almost glows—striking and pale against the shadows. It's the only thing I can see in here.

"What is that?"

"That's what's left of the cave."

My jaw drops. The cave. The mother-rock of Aquamarine.

"What happened to it?" The question is pointless and doesn't need an answer. What happened to the cave was me—my magic. When I played the electronic keyboard that day, I shattered this rock. Tiny explosions. One after another, like fireworks, until all the rock turned to ash. The entire cliff wall crumbled like an avalanche had hit.

I'd never seen the aftermath. Now I'm not sure why I was so eager to come up here.

concerto

My lips part, trembling, and I clutch the T-shirt at my chest. "I don't recognize it." I'm shaking my head—deny, deny, deny. I don't want to recognize it.

"Sure you do." She gestures to a wide fallen tree covered with moss. "That old tree? That's where you played your keyboard. And this"—she sweeps her hand toward the tower of rubble—"this was the cave. The cave where—"

"Don't say it. I know what happened. I was there."

"Sorry. I was just trying to jog your memory. I thought it might help . . ."

Brenna's voice warps and fades as vertigo hits—

All at once it comes rushing back. It's like entering a time warp. My ribcage tightens and my breath becomes strained.

A weird out-of-body thing strikes. My vision goes fuzzy. My stomach drops. I'm falling. Free fall down a well into a pool of firelight—a kaleidoscope of reds and purples. A faint whistling sound can be heard. Fear clogs my throat. It takes my air. A chill surrounds me, a ghost's embrace . . .

She's here.

I can feel her presence. Her aura emotes. It's frantic. There's despair, a clinging hope. Unyielding wrath.

Coach Payne is here.

Survival instincts kick in, but my arms fail to lash out. I tuck into myself instead. My attempt to cry out is a whimper.

My body is clenched, wracked with anger—until I feel something release within me. And I'm no longer afraid—though the energy in the air has shifted.

Eyes open. The uneven rubble swirls at my feet. I sink onto the boulders, the sharp rock edge nearly cutting into my sit bones. It's a welcome pain. Snaps me back to the present. I lower my head and try to process what just happened. I can still feel her presence, like a hovering fog. My heart hammers in my chest.

"Sami?" Brenna's voice reaches through the haze. "You okay?"

"I'm okay." I get up and stumble out of the canopy of shadows, desperate for light. Fresh air. Back in the clearing, my eyes dart around, taking stock of my surroundings. I grind my foot into the earth, testing the solid ground. Daylight reigns. The sky is overcast beyond the treetops. My lungs fill with oxygen—air that smells of soil.

Of *soil*, not ash.

Like the first hint of spring after a long winter. Something has shifted in the clearing. It looks the same but feels different—like nature has awakened somehow.

Sweat gathers on my upper lip. I slowly unfold myself, a renewed energy lifting me up. I'm not trapped at the bottom of a well. Coach Payne is *not* here. It's just me and Brenna. It was a slip of my subconscious, maybe. My memory playing cruel tricks.

"I'm okay," I say again—for my sake more than Brenna's—clasping my shaking hands together.

Still, something is freaking me out. Another moment to catch my breath—and when I do, oxygen runs to my fingertips and toes. My mind races to process what happened, and a chill runs the length of my spine. I'm not sure if it has anything to do with feeling Payne's presence—*Was she really there?*—or my proximity to what used to be Aquamarine, but my birthmark is on fire.

A whir of excitement fills my chest. I breathe it in again, that smell of spring, and I know it's happening. My magic is coming back.

CHAPTER 2

"Congratulations, graduate," I read aloud from the giant balloon. I sound as genuine as I feel, which is not very. Jason's thank you is a feather of a kiss along my cheek. The G-rated version. I get it. His parents are right here. Still, some lip action would be nice. Or even a hug.

By the time Brenna and I got back from our hike this morning, I had to hoof it home and rush my shower and primping so I wouldn't be late, leaving me no time to process what happened up there on the hill. My birthmark keeps nagging at me, though. Like it's trying to tell me something. Or eager to get back to work.

The party's in full swing. Jason's landscapes are strewn along the fence in a makeshift gallery. His backyard's abuzz with laughter and conversation. Jason's dad mans the barbeque while his mom passes out devilled eggs from a dimpled tray. Harry Connick Jr. croons from the Bluetooth speaker on the picnic table. "Ready for RISD!" is spelled out in yellow frosting on the vast sheet cake.

"Quite the par-tay," I mumble, missing him as if he's already left for Rhode Island.

He squeezes my hand, but he's distracted, looking everywhere but at me. "There's someone I want you to meet," he says.

I recognize the colorful woman from what Jason's told me—and she's all but out of place here in Skenesboro. Aunt

concerto

Gaye from Boston, spinster extraordinaire, owns a fine art gallery on Newbury Street. Her statement red glasses match her lipstick and are striking against her buzzed silver hair. Her necklace of chunky turquoise beads matches the swirls on her long swingy skirt. I like her instantly.

"You must be Sam." Gaye says Sam with a soft *a*, like they would in England. "I've heard all about you." She pulls my hand from Jason's and sits me in the chair beside her.

Jason's smile is for me alone and makes me feel shy.

"Go," I tell him, knowing he's got to work the room. Or yard. Still, my heart droops when he turns away.

Tomorrow, he'll be gone. Everything just got real. All hope sags. What am I thinking? Without Jason, it's pointless. My magic, my music doesn't have a chance.

A sigh escapes before I can catch myself.

Aunt Gaye sips her ginger ale through a straw. "Jason tells me you'll be in Boston this summer."

"Yes. I got accepted into the summer program at Berklee School of Music."

"Ah, we'll be neighbors." Gaye's eyes light up. "And you'll only be a short train ride away from Jason in Providence. What luck."

Some luck. "Right." The word is a whimper, a sound bite of nagging doubts weighing on me. Jason and I haven't had "the talk" yet, but I know it's coming. I have my entire senior year to endure here at Skenesboro High. How could I insist he wait for me? He'll be in college. Not just any college: Rhode Island School of Design! He'll be chumming with other sophisticated artist types. Smart, talented girls who share his passion for his kind of art. What kind of desperate, possessive girlfriend would I be to tell him he couldn't be free to date one of them if he wanted? Ugh—the thought literally makes me sick.

Gaye remains cheerful, though. "I understand Jason leaves tomorrow. What about you?"

That knot in my gut cinches tighter. "Later this week. Wednesday, I think."

"And look here." Her palms go skyward. "You have to share your boyfriend with all his family and friends on his last day at home. What a shame."

What a shame is right. That hopeless feeling creeps back.

Aunt Gaye takes another gurgling sip, looking up at Skene Manor—Brenna's home—in all its mysterious glory. One of Jason's landscapes mirrors the view. With one major exception.

"That's not how it looks anymore." My words are bitter.

Jason's version shows an untainted Skene Mountain— with fluffy, healthy green trees. That's how it looked before I did a number on the cave up there, and the hill still shows its scar. Burnt earth. Singed trees. In a giant amoeba-shape on the side of Skene Mountain. The streak of dead earth is visible for miles.

It looks so different from a distance. Did Brenna and I hike all the way up there just this morning? It seems like ages ago. The ever-present ash, the stale campfire smell, and Brenna's discovery of the cave. . . . My birthmark is still warm from that strange out-of-body thing that happened. Staring up at the scar makes me wonder: Was it all my imagination? Was that really Payne's spirit I felt encircle me?

The memory is like indigestion.

Now that we're down on terra firma, it seems so far away. It makes me question whether getting my magic back would be a good idea. As poor Skene Mountain stands to

concerto

prove: my magic tore things apart.

"Don't beat yourself up about it," Gaye says, gesturing to the scar. "Some would say it has more character."

I hide my surprise, wondering how much she knows. Does she know about Aquamarine? Does she know who I am, or was, as Dion? Jason wouldn't have told her everything, would he? I risk a glance her way. Her eyes stay on the mountain.

"I'd like to fix it, though. Make it green again." I sound like an Al Gore groupie, and an embarrassed laugh follows. "Gosh, that would be some bumper sticker."

"Ah, green is good, Sam. Green is good." Hmm . . . maybe Gaye's an Al Gore groupie? To my relief, she doesn't get preachy. "You still play piano, I trust?"

"Um, yes. I do."

She nods. She shakes her empty soda can and turns to me. Her intense brown eyes are eager and sincere.

"Not enough to just play, though, is it? You'll be doing something useful with that gift, I hope." She taps my birthmark, as if ringing a call bell. It's a friendly touch, but still takes me off-guard. It's like she knows my soul—and for some reason she has my implicit trust. Something passes between us, and I want to tell her everything.

"Something useful—yes. I don't want to just play music. I want to do something with it. I want to use my piano . . . to make a difference."

"How could music possibly make a difference in the world?" The question is a challenge—or a vote of encouragement. Either way, it's like she knows the answer. I'm suspended, waiting for her to finish. It dawns on me that Jason's Aunt Gaye might be my next mentor. I study her, hoping she'll go on, desperate for someone to give me direction.

But she's waiting on my answer.

"I'm . . . not sure." I break eye contact, chickening out. It's only been a few hours since I've had a hint that my magic is returning. How could I know what to do with it already?

Still, Gaye waits.

I revert to my summer course description. "I was looking into music therapy?" I hate it when my voice upswings like that.

"Ah, aiding the healing process through music. That's a nice sentiment." She smiles warmly. "That's good. That's a start. But it may only be the start of something bigger." She holds her arms out—embracing the Adirondack Mountains from afar.

My mouth fills with cotton. Her words awaken something in me—that smell of soil still fresh in my olfactories. Gaye's not looking at the scar anymore, she's gazing west—to the layers of rolling hills that seem an endless watercolor. A view that still takes my breath away. Reveling in its summer prime, its lush emerald landscape is in full bloom. Gaye's right: green is good.

Something bigger.

My years in Skenesboro have made me think small. Of course! There's a whole world out there that might need help, that might need my magic. Following Gaye's line of vision, I see the mountain range in a new light. It feels—I don't know—personal somehow.

Gaye fills the silence with a contented sigh, mirroring my feeling. We share a smile, and a warmth fills me.

I try to think of more to say so she won't leave my side. "Do you play an instrument?"

"Me? No, no. I'm busy with my gallery. But music intrigues me. I do believe it holds a sort of power."

concerto

Her eyes bore into mine. I go tingly inside.

"Especially your piano, Sam. Your music has proven to be quite powerful. You'll have to learn to control it."

The pulse of my birthmark ramped up a notch just thinking about what my magic could do. It's hard to keep eye contact as she's speaking. Aunt Gaye is right. I'll have to be careful. Aside from destroying Aquamarine, I have no idea what my magic is capable of.

"You know about my magic." My words are a whisper.

"I do. And I know you struggle with what you've done." She waits, but I have nothing to say. That peaceful feeling ebbs.

Gaye takes my hand. "Sam, you do realize you did an extraordinary thing?"

"I know, but—"

"But nothing. It had to be done. With every earthly thing, there's always a little bit of bad that comes with good. It's called balance. And it keeps our world turning."

Gaye's crafting bumper stickers again. I screw up my eyebrows at her.

"Sam, there was an imbalance of power here in Skenesboro that was hurting people. It wasn't your average athlete-artist high school rivalry; it was Fasha against Goshenites. Magic was involved on both sides—fueled by a natural mineral. A natural mineral that had to be destroyed. You didn't only cause destruction. You restored balance here, whether you realize it or not."

My birthmark buzzes in Gaye's hand. She clamps down on it. Her eyes drift back to the mountains. "It was a step in your journey, a small step. After all, this is a small town. Your magic could make a difference on a larger scale. It's time to think bigger."

She lets go of my hand, pats my pad of freckles. "Boston's a good place to start."

CHAPTER 3

Party guests long gone, Jason and I finally have some time alone. In front of the family room TV, I click through channels and fiddle with the volume, but the remote's a prop. Jason's arm around me feels charged, and I know he feels it, too. The clock tells me his parents might still be awake. If we have to wait much longer to make out, I might burst. Clutching his hand that's draped near my shoulder, I thread my fingers into his. Turning toward him, I ready my lips, which—to my astonishment—are quivering. Why am I nervous?

He's leaving tomorrow. It's really happening. It's what they call a cold, hard fact.

I swallow it down and think about something else. "Aunt Gaye seems really neat."

"Neat?" Jason laughs. "What—are you using old lady adjectives because she's an old lady?"

"I'd never describe Gaye as 'old.' She kind of seems— I don't know—mystical. Like, she has inherent powers or something."

"Oh, yeah?" He looks bemused.

"I'm serious. It's like she could see into me."

Jason's slow smile doesn't have anything to do with Aunt Gaye. He leans closer, whispers, "I love it when you talk magic."

"Don't you think? Has she ever—"

concerto

He stops me with a kiss. Not a G-rated one, either. At first, I mumble through, trying to make my point, which quickly becomes pointless. I relent. I've been waiting all day for a kiss like this.

I'm going to miss him so much.

I hook my arms around him, savoring his warmth, his taste. Stars burst behind my eyelids as we sink deeper into the kiss. I feel it to my toes and all through my body, like everything's lit up inside. I pull him closer, and he follows, pressing his body against mine in waves with an eagerness that I've never seen in him before.

Then, I'm pinned—sandwiched between him and the couch. It's going too fast. It's like he wants to inhale me. I wrench my mouth from his and take a gasping breath.

I manage a laugh. "Jason, Jason, hold on."

He moves to kiss my neck, and those starbursts are back. It takes utmost fortitude to blink them away.

"Jason, stop." I mean to shove him off gently, but he thumps to the floor. "Oh! Sorry! Sorry, sorry."

"What's wrong?" he asks, a hungry, unseeing glaze to his eyes. He works to catch his breath, the flush in his cheeks slow to fade.

No answer will be a good one. A tangle of emotions runs through me, and I regret pushing him away. My lips ache to kiss him again, but that pit in my gut won't quit.

Today, reality came crashing down: he's leaving. And we haven't talked about it. We can't put it off any longer. I try not to whine. "Can we talk?"

He throws his head back with a silent laugh. "You. Are. Killing. Me."

"Jason, really. We have to talk about it."

"About what? Aunt Gaye? Her magic? Or yours? The

magic you can't seem to find?" He rolls his eyes. "We've kind of covered that. A few times, I'd say."

I catch my jaw dropping. The eye roll? Really? I bury my hurt feelings. "No. I want to talk about us."

Sigh. "What about us?"

"Jason. You're leaving. You're going to college in Rhode Island."

"So?"

"I have another year here . . . over two hundred miles away."

"And?"

That earns him another shove. "Jason, don't be a doofus. You know what I'm saying."

He's softens all over, back to his old self. The lust monster is gone. "No, Sami. I don't. I don't see how that matters."

I jump off the couch. "Are you kidding? You don't see how that matters? You're leaving tomorrow. I'm leaving in a few days. We're going to different places. Everything's changing!"

"Hey, come on, now." He's on his feet, too, and holds my shoulders. "You're right. Things are going to change. We've both been accepted into awesome programs. This is the good kind of change. We can't be afraid of it. Things are always changing, but it doesn't mean we have to make a decision to change us."

My tears are winning. "But—"

"Stop worrying. It's all going to be okay." He leads us back to the couch.

"How do you know that?" My words are warbled, and my face crumples in sorrow.

"Because there's more to us than *us*. We're more than

concerto

'Jason and Sami.' And you're not just an amazing musician. You have goals that are bigger than most would dare to even think about. Sami, I can't wait to see you get there."

That gives me pause. I haven't had a chance to tell Jason what happened up on Skene Mountain earlier today at what used to be the cave. And how Aunt Gaye's words awakened something in me.

Something bigger.

All signs point to my magic coming back—and on a grand scale. It's both terrifying and thrilling. Normally, Jason would be my go-to in noodling this out. But after the eye roll, do I dare share this with him?

I need to see where he truly stands first. "What if I'm wrong? What if the best I can do is just . . . play?"

"There's honor in that." His words are soft. He sweeps my hair off my neck and moves closer.

"Honor in music for . . . what? Art? Entertainment? I don't think—"

"And I'm not just a painter," he says. "Granted, I don't have a lofty goal like you do." He says "lofty" with the same tone as the eye roll, making me cringe inside. "But that's what college is for," he goes on, a faraway look in his eye. "Who knows what I'll learn at RISD? It'll open doors for me in ways I can only dream about."

He's just reinforced my argument. "Right!" I slide away from him. "And I don't want to be the one holding you back."

He closes the space between us. "Holding me back? Sami, it's our love for each other that makes it possible."

That triggers more tears. It's not the first time he's said he loves me, but it's the first time he's said our love is important. I'm a puddle of emotion.

20

"Did I say something wrong?" His grin is nothing short of impish.

I laugh-snort. My nose is running. I sure know how to impress my boyfriend.

"Thanks," I say when he hands me a tissue. "I still feel like we need a plan."

He snuggles me on the couch, and I melt against him. He kisses my hair. "Let's take it one step at a time. I don't know about you, but I'm kind of psyched there's only a short train ride between us this summer. A hop, skip, and a jump from Boston to Providence."

Doubt creeps back. "But that's only a few weeks—"

"Five weeks. There's our five-week plan."

The moment is gone. If we made out now, I'd cover his face with snot. Lovely.

We silently face the TV, which shows a commercial for Ka-Bingo Bathroom Cleaner. Its jingle becomes the soundtrack of his closing argument: *there's our five-week plan.*

The tissue Jason gave me is soaked, and my nose won't stop running. On my way to the bathroom, I resign myself to his plan. Our plan. I guess it's okay. But something keeps nagging at me—his eye roll. I fight a sinking feeling it means something more, marking a shift in our relationship.

After going through a half dozen tissues in the bathroom, I'm distracted from my red-nosed reflection by a big potted plant in the corner. It's a wonder I hadn't noticed it before; it's huge and almost entirely blocks the window. Bold and beautiful, its dark, paddle-like leaves feel waxy to the touch.

"What kind of plant is this?" I call to Jason.

"Huh? Oh." He chuckles. "Believe it or not, it's called a rubber tree plant."

concerto

"Rubber tree?"

"Yeah. Apparently, they used to make rubber from its sap. Or whatever."

"You're kidding," I say, too quietly for him to hear over the drone of the TV.

The leaves are almost heavy. It's like I can feel the sap inside. On impulse, I lean into the plant and take a whiff.

There's that smell again: soil.

Squatting down, I press both hands into the white-speckled potting soil, feeling damp earth seep between my fingers.

My birthmark zings. And fireworks begin . . . all big, blue lights behind my closed eyelids.

In my mind's eye, the electric keyboard's in front of me, and I'm back at the clearing on Skene Mountain. As I play, it comes back to life. Those scraggly weeds green up and sprout through the ash. Trees swell with moist sap as leaves bud and unfurl in an accelerated springtime. Rock minerals rebuild before my eyes, curving to form a cave on the side of a healthy wall of earth. My music being magic again but in a different way.

Gaye's words ring through: *you restored balance here.*

Yes! I neutralized a toxic mineral. I changed an element of the Earth. If I could do that, I can change other things about the Earth. Right? What if I used my magic to somehow make things grow?

"Sami, are you gonna stay in the bathroom all night?"

The spell is broken. I'm back in Jason's house, bonding with a rubber tree plant. He must think I've lost it.

"Coming." I wash the dirt off my hands, but I can't wash the smile off my face.

The romantic comedy he's chosen is about to start. I settle onto the couch next to him. Throughout the flick, I laugh at all the right times, but I'm not really watching. I can't stop thinking about my magic and what it can do.

Restore balance. On a larger scale. Something bigger. As Gaye said, Boston's a great place to start.

CHAPTER 4

Mom's poring over the orientation packet while I study the menu. We spent the morning moving me into my digs at Berklee. Now we're rewarding ourselves with an early dinner at a local favorite café. It's been so busy, I haven't thought much about what happened the other day on Skene Mountain. I haven't had time to miss Jason, even. My growling stomach won't let any other thoughts in.

"You have to be in the auditorium in two hours for the welcome wagon," Mom says.

"It's called Orientation, Mom."

"And tomorrow classes start. Why start classes on a Thursday, though? Short week. Probably to ease you in."

Mom does this sometimes. Answers her own questions. It's like I'm along for a ride as she converses with herself. I smile inside, realizing how much I'm going to miss her.

The waitress delivers our Mediterranean appetizer plate.

"And this is kind of cool—this Showcase thing?" Mom reads from the packet. "Each Friday, they host what they call 'Showcase nights.' Oh, it's like a talent show. You can sign up for fifteen-minute slots to perform music—solo or in groups. Are parents invited? That would be so totally rad."

I nearly inhale an olive pit. "Um, no. I don't think so." I might miss Mom, but that doesn't mean I want her hanging around campus on Showcase nights.

concerto

Mom shrugs. "I probably couldn't make it down anyway."

"I'm still getting used to the fact that I have my own room," I say, grinning widely. That was a pleasant surprise when we arrived on campus this morning. I'd been prepared to meet a roommate—pushing aside nerves that come from being an only child and unaccustomed to sharing my space. But due to the small enrollment in the summer program, everyone gets a single.

"Are you sure you feel safe?"

"Yes, I feel safe." I slurp up a marinated artichoke. "Honestly, I wasn't thrilled with the idea of having a roommate."

Mom looks pointedly at her silverware. "Are you planning to invite Jason up to visit?"

Oh, she's sneaky, alluding to my virtue like this. "We talked about me going down there, to Rhode Island. But it's not like either of us need a chaperone, Mom."

"I know. Anyway, you'll get a roommate when you officially get to college." Mom rubs her forehead—hard—like she used to when she'd get those awful Aquamarine-induced migraines.

"Don't tell me you have one coming on." I had hoped they were a thing of the past.

"No, it's not that."

She still looks miserable. She hasn't touched our appetizer plate. I scoop hummus with a triangle of pita and hand it to her. But she doesn't take it.

"What's wrong?"

She gives me a sideways look. "I think you know what I'm going to say."

My mouth freezes mid-chew. "Seriously?"

"What? You don't know what might be here. What if"—she lowers her voice—"you find something here that could hurt you. Something like Aquamarine did. And it affects you—your talent and your health. It makes me nervous."

"Mom, I'm not going to"—I make air quotes—" 'experiment with substances.' "

"Why are you smiling like that?"

My laugh comes out on its own. "I'm not. I don't know. It's silly, is all."

"It's very serious, Sami." She's using a tone I haven't heard for over two years. It's like fingernails on a chalkboard.

"Oh, come on. It's been years. Ancient history. Chapter closed. End of story."

Mom opens her menu and pretends to read it. My pita offering remains untouched on her tiny plate. Her mouth is clamped shut. She's not happy, I can tell. I study my own menu and hum a made-up tune to assure her everything's fine.

"Oh, be quiet," she snaps.

That makes me laugh again. "Mom, really. Have some faith. I'm a big girl. Remember, I grew up in New York City." It's my turn to lower my voice. "And I single-handedly neutralized the magic on Skene Mountain." I flash her a grin. "I think I can take care of myself."

Mom's not smiling. "You're not invincible, Sami."

That makes me stop. "I never said I was."

"We've had a few good, quiet years, but you still need to be careful. Don't get comfortable. You are still Goshenite. You are still Dion. It will always be within you."

She's got my attention now. I lean in. "What will always

concerto

be within me?"

She shifts uncomfortably. Her words are so soft I almost have to read her lips. "You know. That force. Or power. Or magic. Or . . . whatever."

Electricity tingles up and down my body. Excitement bubbles to the surface, and I want to squeal aloud. Mom doesn't know I've found a hint of my magic. And how it might be able to help natural imbalances in the world. Somehow. The question now is how to tap into it. I'm hoping Berklee will help me figure it out. Could it be dangerous? I'm not sure. But I've got to think bigger than Skenesboro. As Gaye said, my work there was a stepping stone.

My next words are careful. "I understand. I'll keep myself safe. Promise." I hold her gaze so she knows I'm sincere.

We move on to other, gentler topics, and somehow, I make it through the meal without Mom realizing what she's triggered. She walks me back to campus just in time for Orientation.

We give our goodbye hugs. As she gets back into the car to head home, I head into the auditorium. But that's not where I want to be. Not now that I know for sure my magic is still there—always has been!—and is literally at my fingertips.

Getting to the piano studio is now an urgent need. I have to play. I'm convinced something will reveal itself.

All of the summer program students—I've been told there are fifty-seven total—sit in the main auditorium off Mass Ave. Not two minutes into the spiel, I realize there's no AC in here. I fan myself with my orientation packet in a vain attempt to cool off. The heat drains the life out of me. I task myself with texting Jason to boost me up.

Orientation time!

Woop. Delivered.

Staring at my screen, I wonder what Jason's doing right now. He might be in class, I suppose. It dawns on me it would be a good idea to swap schedules.

U in class? Send me ur sched. [smiley face] [smiley face]

Woop. Delivered.

Jason's not answering. Sigh. Must be in class. Bummer. Now I really do have to pay attention.

They're going over the meal plan. All meals are provided except on Saturday and Sunday. It seems most of the students are somewhat local and plan to go home on weekends. Worry pokes at me: Could I go to Rhode Island every weekend? Would Jason want me there so often? I bite my lip. My piano might be my only company on Saturdays.

Piano. The mere thought makes my fingers itch. When will Orientation be over?

A professor enters from stage left, and I have to blink her into focus. She's like an apparition. Surely, the heat's getting to me. The woman is completely white. As if she is made of gossamer, it's unclear where her flowing white dress begins and ends. Her hair is a stark platinum. Her skin is albino pale—like our old neighbor in New York, the one with the violin strapped to her back. Despite the heat, I shiver inside. The professor introduces herself as Ms. Aleia, but from here on out I will think of her as "the white woman." I make a mental note to keep away from her.

concerto

"I'll be teaching Music Therapy and Psychology of Music," the white woman says in a wispy voice.

My ears perk up. Those are the very two classes I signed up for. I erase my mental note regretfully. It will be hard to keep away from her since she's my teacher.

"There's more to music than meets the ear," she says. "By the end of this program, my students will experience an entirely different and surprising side of music." Her grin is full of yellow teeth, and all at once she seems human. I like what she's saying, and I find myself intrigued with the idea of her "different and surprising side of music." She may even be a mentor for me. I inch forward in my seat, hoping for more. But she gracefully exits stage right, silent as a ghost.

Another teacher comes on stage to introduce his class—History of Instruments—but I've checked out. I'm eager to talk to Ms. Aleia one-on-one. I can't wait for classes to start tomorrow. And to get to my piano. Tonight. I'm going right to the studio after this. Restlessness makes my legs twitch. Maybe it's a trick of the mind, but my birthmark seems to throb.

Blah, blah, blah . . . Another teacher is introduced. And another . . .

Heat builds as the clock ticks on, and my ambition slows to a crawl. A yawn takes over, making my eyes water. My mind wanders. My gaze droops. Am I melting? I gaze at my cohorts seated in front of me. A dozen or so back-of-heads blurring together.

Then, something familiar makes me sit straighter, and I fumble with my packet before it drops. It's the hair. Wavy dark hair curling at his shoulders. Head tilted in such a way—listening. Lean, broad shoulders. He's the only one not fanning himself. He holds himself with a cool confidence I've seen only once before. Could it be?

No. I shake the thought away. Miles—my Miles—is in New York City. Why would he be here in Boston? At the Berklee summer program, no less?

By reflex, my cell is out and I'm thumbing through my contacts. LAUREN, then MILES, in consecutive, pixelated rows. It's been almost three years since I moved away. Longer still since I spoke to either, save for that surface-y email exchange with Lauren. Yet they're both still in my phone. Funny; back in New York, I'd thought Miles had broken my heart in choosing Lauren over me. But that bruise healed years ago. The pain that's lingered for three years is for Lauren. She chose Miles over me. That hurts worse.

I highlight his name to delete it, but something won't let me. I should be paying attention, anyway. I click off my screen, fetch my packet from the floor, and refocus.

"Tomorrow, classes begin," says the guy onstage. "If you haven't already done so, please be sure to . . ." His voice drones in Martian language. The packet he holds up is warped in his grip. He points at it and says something else, but I zone out, staring at those dark curls a few rows ahead of me. It's like they've hypnotized me. Then olive-skinned musician's fingers comb through them. My ribcage tightens. I know those hands. Those fingers—those hopelessly talented fingers—peeled me an orange so many years ago. R.E.M.'s *Orange Crush* zings through my head as the memory smacks my senses.

Miles?

I lean forward to make sure. If he'd just turn an inch my way, I'd catch his profile and . . .

Wait. What's with all the guesswork? The program!

concerto

I've been fanning myself with the answer all along. I scan the names of students listed on the inside. There it is in clear black and white: Miles Eichen.

Holy crap! It's him. It's really Miles.

OMG! And I thought it was hot before. It's Sahara-hot, now. My mouth feels like I've inhaled sawdust. I'd kill for some water. The rest of the presentation may as well be in Swahili.

My heart is racing. My mind, too. Should I hide? Should I say hello? Should I run out of the auditorium, unregister from the program, and hop on the next bus to Skenesboro?

I close my eyes and count to ten. Force a yoga breath.

Maybe it wouldn't hurt to say hello.

Maybe it would.

Never know until . . .

Whoa—presentation over. People are getting up, filtering out. My knees are knocked by shovers too hurried to say "excuse me." I'm stuck in my seat while a group of girls in short shorts pass to the aisle. I crane to see around the half-nude butts, trying to keep an eye on those dark curls.

Too many people are in the way. By the time I'm out of the aisle, there's no sign of Miles. Is that really him? Maybe someone else has the same name? Gosh, why do I even care? I have a boyfriend. Miles who?

Right . . . Miles who . . .

Maybe it was a dream. A heat-induced dream. Isn't that a thing?

Oh geez, now I definitely need my piano.

CHAPTER 5

It's peaceful in the studio. Professional soundproofing works both ways, and I'm grateful for a break from the first-day, moving-in chaos. And the strange serendipity of seeing Miles here, in my program. It still feels like a dream.

Sliding onto the piano bench, my hands position themselves, and scales pour out automatically. With closed eyes, I let go of expectations and let it take me, meditating on the sound. The world slows to a crawl so I can process what's happened the past few days . . .

The out-of-body thing on Skene Mountain.

The smell of soil—like the promise of springtime.

My birthmark coming alive, nudging me alert.

Meeting Aunt Gaye. *Restore balance.*

Saying goodbye to Jason.

Mom's words. *It's still within you.*

The white woman's *different and surprising side of music.*

And Miles.

Miles Miles Miles.

Scales become chords, which roll into a familiar soft melody—one of my favorites I've secretly coined *Adrift*. My inner ear tuned in for any hint of a higher power at work, i.e. magic. My breath matches the rhythm and sounds like ocean waves. In, and out. Everything falls away except the music. This.

concerto

Focus now.

It's still within you.

I need to own it. Make it work for me. Find the right channel for it.

Images appear on the screen of my closed lids. A bird's-eye view—as if on a helicopter ride—I soar over mountain ranges and sparkling lakes and vast farmlands. Our Earth. Our beautiful planet. I want to protect it. I want to restore it. But how?

The melody shifts. I follow, listening closely. It's more aggressive, yet still fluid and beautiful. Images shift, showing a less beautiful part of our planet. Melting polar ice caps, the island of trash in the Pacific Ocean, devastated rainforests . . .

A hard brick crumbles inside me, and emotion swirls. My breath gets ragged. Holding back tears, I pause to shake out my hands. The stillness in the studio now feels sticky and no longer brings me comfort. Stretching my arms, I do a few neck rolls.

Back to work.

Piano fills the room again. I zone in on each note, each chord. Each moment is a slice of beauty. My arms heat up as a surge of energy reaches my fingertips. Focusing on the breath, trying to find that rhythm again, I concentrate.

The tempo picks up. My fingers pop with each note struck, as if the keys are mini trampolines. It's passionate and forceful—resonant of Mahler or Dvorak. My jaw clenches. My arm muscles pulse and begin to ache, but I keep going.

Please. Show me my magic. Let me feel the power in my music again—and channel it for something good. Let me make a difference.

The images now coming into play are familiar but strange. Past meets present, and I'm faced with a different kind of distress. Black hair curling at his broad shoulders. Those impossibly talented fingers. That olive skin. Those ice-blue eyes.

Miles.

On a seashore. Pristine blue water. Miles flashes a grin and turns to face the wind. It makes his clothes billow and his dark tendrils dance. The camera zooms out to show we're standing on a beach. He's pointing out at sea, saying something—but there are no words, only music. He laughs and waves me over, closer to the surf. Closer to him.

Waves gently fold onto shore in a comforting rhythm that no longer matches my breath—which is caught in that tender place between the inhale and the exhale. Like I've forgotten how to do it.

It takes a moment before I register the silence; my music has stopped, too.

I open my eyes to the dense, impatient silence of the studio. It smells like an airplane cabin. A film of sweat covers my forehead, pricking my scalp.

Why did Miles appear with my music? That was totally unexpected. Unwelcome, even. I blink a few times to get rid of him. He is not part of my plan. A shiver runs up my arms, and I hug them close. Of course, it means nothing. I try to shove away all thoughts of him. But it's no use.

And what were we doing on a beach? One that is clearly unpolluted. No balance to restore there. Am I completely off-base with what my magic can do?

So much for finding my power in this session.

Disheartened, I scamper out of the studio, now craving fresh air. I'm outside on Boylston Street, staring at traffic,

concerto

breathing in the urban smells that remind me so much of my childhood in New York City. A walk will clear my head.

It's dark, and the moonlight is overpowered by street-lights, storefront neon, and traffic lights. When I pass by Copley T Station, train rails screech, and a burst of hot air floats out towards me. It carries the faint odor of urine and locker-room sweat. Nearby Mass Pike roars with the ebb and flow of traffic. I smile, imagining it the city's ocean. The energy fills me. One of the first things Jason ever said to me was about New York City being "dusty." I couldn't help but be offended. It's not dust, it's grit—and I love it. It's real and raw and true.

Wish u were here.

Woop. Delivered.

Sometimes I fantasize about Jason and I getting our own apartment in the city. We'd walk everywhere and use one of those big wheelie baskets for groceries. I wonder if Jason would love the city as much as I do.

But I love living in Skenesboro, too. Don't I?

I pass by the fancy stores, door after door offering more and more extravagance the farther I go down Newbury Street. Should it bother me that I feel more at home here in Boston—after only a short time—than I did in Skenesboro?

Jason hasn't answered my text. He's been unusually quiet since he left for RISD. For some reason, that's not what bothers me most. What bothers me is the image I can't shake. Everything I love about this city, I loved about New York. A few years in the mountains upstate can never change that.

With every sound and smell that hits my senses, I'm reminded of Miles.

Miles.

I loop around and head back to campus by way of Boylston Street, letting memories of my old friend play out with an open mind. Jason and I have no rules about having friends. And that's all Miles ever was: a friend. There's a reason he showed up during my session tonight. The fact that he appeared near the ocean must be a sign. Maybe he's part of the plan after all.

Maybe he can help me.

CHAPTER 6

The first few days of classes at Berklee: not so great. I'm not sure what I expected from a college course, but there are a lot of lectures. It's not clear what exactly I'm supposed to do with all the information coming at me.

The girl seated next to me smells smoky-sweet and has a diamond stud in her nose. Miles isn't in any of my classes. The white woman is our teacher. She seems to have only one volume: barely audible. And her eyes. They weren't noticeable from the stage, but now that I have a good look at them, they give me the willies. They're so pale—almost colorless. A lot like Coach Payne's.

I do my best to laugh away that thought.

There are more important things to think about. This program is exclusive. I have to take advantage of it. I have to get as much out of the next few weeks as possible.

Despite my internal pep talk, my mind wanders as the clock's pace slows to a standstill. Thoughts of Jason are front and center, of course. Miles is there, too, which surprises me, creeping in at the corners. Flirting with me. Teasing me.

I do my best to laugh that away, too.

Compared to midweek, the student lounge is a ghost town. It's Friday, but there's no Showcase the first week, so most students have left for the weekend.

Jason expects me tomorrow. Why didn't I plan to go to

concerto

Rhode Island tonight? As the lounge empties, so does my motivation. Maybe it's not too late to catch a train—although Jason and I haven't even talked about it. As if on cue, my phone buzzes in my pocket. Jason's name and picture appear on the screen. My heart lifts. I swipe to answer, but—

"Hey there." It's a voice behind me.

I've already swiped. Blood rushes to my cheeks. "What? Hello?" I say into my phone. "Wait, hold on."

My phone hangs in my palm as I swivel toward the voice.

It's Miles.

The real Miles. In the flesh. And he looks like someone out of a J. Crew catalog. My eyes drink him in. Khaki shorts and denim shirt—his voluptuous locks flirting with his strong shoulders. A messenger bag crosses his chest, framing a hint of rippling pecs. He's Miles 2.0, new and improved from the eighth grade. His glasses have been upgraded to square black frames. Those and his tanned skin make his blue eyes pop. His face has grown thinner. The shadow of his shave grazes his well-defined jaw. My stomach does a few backflips.

"Oh, hi! Wow. It is you." I'm squealing. Too loud. Rhode Island is listening. I hold up a finger and hunch into my phone. "Can I call you back? Thanks." I tap red before registering Jason hadn't said a single word. Gosh—did I just hang up on him? It's okay, I tell myself. I'll call him back in a sec.

"Sami." Miles says my name as if he owns it.

"Miles! I can't believe it." On tiptoes, my arms are around Miles' neck before I think better of it. He's taller than I remember. With Jason only five or so inches taller than me, I'm not used to hugging this kind of height. It feels foreign—

in a good way. He smells like the sea. Salt air and warm sand. Like he just stepped off the beach. The image from my session the other night soars back to mind.

He hugs me back, pulling me in. His messenger bag buckle dents my ribcage.

We dislodge, and I wave my phone around like it's stuck to my hand. "So, what are you doing here? I can't believe you're in this program. Here. In Boston."

"I could ask the same of you." His smile is thin and devilish. "Last I heard, you escaped upstate, to the mountains." He finger-combs his hair. A rogue curl falls over his brow. My pulse hiccups.

Pshaw. "Escaped, right. As if. I was heartbroken to leave New York. You, of all people, should know that." It comes out too easily, defying the three years of happiness I had in Skenesboro . . . with Jason.

"Me, of all people," he repeats.

I swallow hard, feeling slightly disloyal.

Neither of us say anything for an agonizing moment, and I all but trip over my own tongue to fill the silence. "So, tell me. How have you been? How's Lauren?" As soon as her name's out, I want to take it back.

Miles' eyes go wide.

Why would I go and mention Lauren in the first five minutes of conversation with Miles? I don't really want to hear about their love life. It's been years since they started dating—pouring salt on my broken heart. I'd lost my two best friends. My only friends. But then I moved upstate, which may as well have been Timbuktu. For all I know, they could still be together. Obviously, the sting is still there for me. My face is burning.

"Lauren? I guess she's okay. I wouldn't know." Okay,

concerto

mystery solved. They're not together anymore. His smile vanishes, and I'm left to wonder: is he still in love with her, or was it just a passing thing between them?

"Sorry," I say.

He shrugs his smile back. "It would be cliché to say 'it's complicated.' Let's just say, Lauren is one complex chick."

That throws me a little. Lauren? The girl I grew up with who loved music and dancing and laughing and being silly . . . until she decided to pour all her energy into practicing her beloved cello. The last word I'd think to describe her would be 'complex.' But, then again, it's been years. I don't know her anymore.

I don't know Miles anymore, either. But I'm drawn to him in a way that feels dangerous.

"I have a boyfriend," I blurt. Defense mechanism? "Back home."

Miles pretends not to hear. Or, better yet, he didn't actually hear. But I'm squirming in my skin. I fight the urge to face-palm. Why am I being such a dork?

No matter, he's still grinning. "We should get together one of these days. You know, to catch up."

My phone buzzes. Without checking the screen, I know it's Jason.

"Yeah, definitely." I show him my phone apologetically. "Sorry. Gotta take this."

"Really good to see you, Sami."

It kills me to turn away from Miles, but I have to. I can't even tell him how good—really good—it is to see him, too. I step into the snack shop in an attempt for privacy, cradling my phone to my ear.

"Did we get disconnected or something?"

My words to Jason are hushed. "Oh, we must have.

42

Sorry." Does he hear the twang of guilt?

"You set to come down tomorrow?"

From the shop window, I see Miles reclining on a campus couch, reading something on his iPad. His grip on the device is almost tender. My pulse kicks up a few notches. It's for Jason, surely.

"Yes. I can't wait." It's true. I can't wait. So why, through our whole conversation, are my eyes glued to my childhood crush through the shop glass?

Jason makes his voice overly husky, "Why are you whispering?"

"Me? Whispering?" Miles' foot—propped on the other ankle—bobs casually as if music's playing. Jason's still talking, and I'm not listening. I tear my eyes from the shop glass, but Miles' image sticks in my subconscious.

A display of Berklee trinkets and souvenirs stands near the register. Following an impulse, I pick out a silver keychain that shows the Boston skyline.

"I got you a present," I say at a higher-than-normal volume, grasping onto something solid that proves my heart is with Jason. I hand it to the cashier and reach for my wallet, feeling myself smile for all the right reasons. I'll give it to him tomorrow, and everything will be put right.

CHAPTER 7

We'd agreed I'd catch the earliest train possible to make the most of our time together. But I was so worried I'd miss it, I barely slept. Hopes of catching some Zs on the train fall away. I'm just too eager to see my guy.

The train screeches to a halt at the Providence stop. Jason's waiting for me on the platform—hands in his pockets, looking sheepish and adorable. We share a smile through the glass, and my heart whirs as I rush to meet him, nearly forgetting my overnight bag.

The entire train ride down, I envisioned this moment with such yearning it hurt. Even though it has been less than a week, already a hole has formed inside me. One that only he can fill. Thankfully, thoughts of Miles are put in their place. Far away.

But falling into Jason's arms feels different than I expect. His clothes smell like chicken wings. His kiss carries the harsh tang of tartar-control toothpaste. It takes him a few moments to actually look me in the eye. That hug I'd been craving—needing—seems anticlimactic.

"You're here," he says, smoothing my hair. But I know he senses it, too. After all, I've carried that plastic train car smell with me. And that Altoid isn't masking the everything bagel breakfast I grabbed at the station.

Still, we forge ahead. Jason takes my hand and leads me to our ride—a car that makes Mom's dinged-up sedan look

concerto

like a Mercedes. The guy standing next to it looks like he just rolled out of bed. His thick, dark hair touches the sky, and his clothes have bedsheet-pressed wrinkles.

"This is Kurt."

"Hi, Kurt!" My voice is way too loud.

"Ugh. I need coffee," Kurt says, and we pile into the car.

From the backseat, I'm struck by the easy banter my boyfriend has with this zombie-like driver. They speak in half sentences and chuckle simultaneously about who knows what. Something holds me back from joining in. It's not like they're really talking about anything. And, as Kurt mentioned, he really needs a cup of coffee.

Kurt doesn't ask for my order at the Dunkin Donuts drive-thru. He pays from the loose change in the ashtray—and the steaming Styrofoam cup is huge and striking against the beat-up maroon interior of his junker.

My view out the window does little to hold my interest, but I zone out to avoid the inside jokes going on in the front seat. "Later," Kurt blurts after he drops us off at Jason's dorm. And then he's gone. It should be a relief, but resentment lingers. I feel like I've missed the punch line.

Jason brings me to his dorm room. His roommate, Tiko, is at least awake enough to say hello. His dark, friendly eyes disappear with his huge smile. He gives me a little bow and then shakes my hand—blending Asian and European cultures in a single greeting. "I've heard so much about you!" he chirps with a hint of an accent that sounds musical to me. I could listen to him talk all day. But he excuses himself bashfully, making a point to tell us he's made plans to sleep elsewhere that night.

With Tiko gone, we're finally alone. And a weird panic strikes. Isn't this what I've been waiting for? Why do I feel so—awkward? Wandering around the small room, I take in little pieces of Jason's new life as if visiting a stranger. It feels sterile. There are hardly any personal artifacts on either side. Two sets of bedroom furniture fit in like Legos.

Only when Jason clicks on his desk lamp do I see a 4x6 picture of us—a selfie near the canal Jason must have had printed from his phone. It's not my favorite shot; I'm not a fan of selfies, really. My nose looks way too big in them. I'd rather see our cliché prom pose displayed. But Jason's smile is proud as he studies the photo. I hope he sees mine as happy, too.

Then I remember: "Oh, I have a present for you." I give him the silver keychain with Boston's skyline—which is still warm from my pocket. He runs his finger over the design, which now looks cheap and touristy.

"Thanks." He puts it in his desk drawer, where I know it will stay. He'll never use it. Why couldn't I have picked out something cooler?

I slump onto his bed. He sits at his desk and swivels the chair to face me.

"So, what do you want to do?" His hands are on my lap, rubbing my thighs industriously, like he's trying to warm me.

"I don't know. What do you want to do?" Really—why would he ask me that? He's hosting me, after all. Hasn't he thought about this? "What've you got planned?"

We both sense it's not the time to make out. But why? Haven't I been dying to see him? Why don't I want to jump his bones right now? Why do I wish—of all things—that Tiko were back in the room?

A shrug. "I guess I could show you around campus."

Another shrug. "Okay."

concerto

For the next hour, he's a tour guide. We see the student lounge and the auditorium, the Met where he eats and hangs out with his friends. He points out various buildings with feigned indifference, greeting a handful of students he doesn't bother introducing me to. He lights up when we get to the studio, though. We spend another hour or so in there. Jason speaks animatedly about all the projects he's working on. It's impressive. After only a few days, his growth is evident. Once again, I'm spellbound by his talent.

Our time at the studio seems to have cured whatever awkwardness lingered between us. He threads his hand into mine, and we walk along the Providence River, talking about nothing and laughing about nothing. This. This is what I've been missing. This is what I've been waiting for. Finally!

We head up Canal Street—

"This canal runs through Providence?"

"Yeah. Doesn't it feel like home?"

The next time he holds me, he feels like home. We smooch a little bit until our grumbling stomachs tell us it's way past lunchtime. We grab something at a divey burger joint and head back to the dorms, wanting naps.

It's dark when I wake up. My burger lunch is a brick in my stomach. It takes a minute to realize Jason's not curled next to me anymore. I hear voices talking in the hallway. I scrub sleep from my eyes and stumble to the door, feeling like I've missed a deadline. Something stops me from opening it, though. Jason's out in the hall, and I can make out at least two other voices—one, a girl's. They're making plans. For tonight. That hitch in my stomach has nothing to do with a greasy burger. I hurry back to Jason's bed as he opens the door.

"Hey, you're awake." He smiles. "I thought you'd sleep

the night away."

"Who were you just talking to in the hall?" I hate my suspicious tone.

Jason doesn't miss a beat. "Oh, a bunch of us—I mean—they're going to a concert at Brown tonight to see the Old 97's. We're invited. I think we should go."

"Brown University?"

"Yeah. It's right around the corner."

"Old 97's? What's that?"

"It's—they're a band. A really good one, too. Gavin got me into their music. It's awesome. And . . . they're pretty famous. It's kind of a miracle they're doing small gigs still."

"Who's Gavin?"

Jason's cheeks puff with a sigh. "Sami, if you don't want to go, just tell me—"

"No, it's not that—"

"But I don't know what else we're going to do. I think it sounds like a pretty good deal." He stomps to his closet/cubby and changes his shirt, his face tight with irritation.

Why is he irritated with me? I'm here to see him, not some band with a bunch of strangers. Why can't we do something just the two of us? Go to a movie or check out the Providence nightlife. Why—on my only night here—are we going on a group date?

Still, I hear myself say, "No, we'll go. It sounds fun."

"Wow. You sound excited." For the millisecond he meets my eye, it dawns on me he might not want me here. The feeling rises up in my throat like bile, and I tamp it down before it takes over.

This is Jason, Sami. Your boyfriend who loves you.

"I am." Despite my best acting efforts, Jason knows

concerto

that's a lie. "I just need to brush my teeth." Oh, geez. How romantic.

We meet about five other students outside the dorm. Jason introduces me by name only. Not that I gave him a script, but how hard would it be to say: *This is my girlfriend, Sami?* He runs through everyone else's names so fast there's no way I'll remember any of them. Except Sydney. She's here, looking adorably studious in her retro glasses. I recognize her voice from the hallway earlier.

At first, there's hope she and I might bond together, girl-power style, as the boys start their nonsense banter. No such luck. She's right there with them. I can't even follow their conversation. I soon find myself trailing behind the whole group.

We're at Brown, nearing the concert entrance, when Jason remembers I'm there. "You okay?"

As if I'm the one with the problem. "Yeah, are you?" My sarcasm sounds angry. That tight irritation crosses his face, and he turns away, handing me my ticket as an afterthought.

Thus starts a lively game between the two of us that goes on for the rest of the night. I pull back, waiting for Jason's attention. He ignores me, not giving in to my passive-aggressive behavior. The fact that I'm not part of the fun doesn't seem to bother him. He laughs with his new friends, even sways with the music, a.k.a. dancing! I can hardly believe it. He never once danced with me back home. Not even at prom!

It's so dark and the music is so loud, it's like I disappear. It sucks. I want to join them, I really do. But I can't. The more he ignores me, the more I fade into the background until there's no hope of reemerging.

An ugly feeling takes root in my stomach. It keeps me up most of the night as Jason sleeps soundly next to me. Another sleepless night makes for a trying next day . . .

Maybe the visit has taken on a life of its own, but the morning continues to be weird. Jason acts more like a babysitter than a boyfriend. Part of me wants to catch the early train home before anything else bad can happen, but Jason insists on taking me to breakfast.

My hunger, the driving force that gets me to the restaurant, turns to nausea when I see none other than Sydney saving a table, waving us over.

"Where's everyone?" Jason asks her.

Everyone? Did he plan another group date . . . for breakfast?

We sit. We order. I simmer like Super Bowl chili. Anger chokes me, making it impossible to eat. Sydney is friendlier than last night, asking me about Berklee and my music. At least Jason told her about me. But my terse responses don't welcome conversation. My mouth tugs into a frown that won't go away. I have no interest in making friends with Sydney—a girl who apparently came here to meet my boyfriend for a breakfast date. I barely make it through without exploding.

Jason's not happy with me.

"You could've made a little more of an effort, you know," he says on the way to the train station.

"I could've?" A bitter laugh. "You're one to talk."

The silence thickens as we pull into the station. This is it. This is the tipping point. Our last chance—his last chance—to salvage this visit. Jason comes around the car toward me, and I brace myself, unsure exactly what I expect or want him to do. He gives me a searching look, which I

concerto

return in kind. A few awkward beats and he leans in for a half-hug, which becomes a pat on the back.

A freaking pat on the back.

I board the train, not knowing if I want to puke or cry or scream at the top of my lungs. That ugly feeling from last night morphs into the Kraken—snaking into my intestines. It stays with me the whole way back to Boston. Until the darkness turns to sadness, and quiet tears distort my view out the window.

What happened? How did it get so bad? Where did things go so horribly wrong? I replay our time together, wishing we could have held on to that tenderness we shared as we walked along the Providence River. It's partly my fault, sure. Still, Jason could have made room for me.

CHAPTER 8

Sorry about the concert.

That's the text I wake up to, back in my own dorm at Berklee. Four simple words attempt to erase a weekend-long fight. Inside, I wrestle with his apology. Part of me wants to stay mad, but I hate fighting with Jason.

Sorry too

Make it up to u next wk. promise

K [heart] [blowing kiss] [floating heart]

I linger in bed, relieved, enjoying the easy flow of oxygen in and out of my lungs. Until I realize my music therapy class starts in only ten minutes. I must have forgotten to set my alarm last night.

I get to class on time, un-showered, with my mind somewhere between Boston and Providence—a niggling doubt about my magic hovering over everything. If the last forty-eight hours have proven anything, it's that I'm a regular teenage girl. Far from magical. Far from Dion. Should I even bother trying?

Ms. Aleia sways behind her podium as if she's rocking a baby to sleep. Her long white skirt billows on either side like sheer curtains in the wind. My notebook is open but remains blank.

concerto

"Music therapy has been integrated into our healthcare system in recent years, much like pet therapy or touch therapy for the critically, chronically, or terminally ill. It may seem like a relatively new fad, but it's not—although it's fairly new in the US."

My pencil is primed but remains unmoving. History of Music Therapy is proving to be kind of a snoozer.

"After the First World War, music therapy was used to help with shell shock. And then to treat combat exhaustion in veterans of World War II. But, it was hardly a new strategy."

The smoky-sweet smelling girl sitting next to me with the nose ring is typing away on her Mac, and I see her hands are covered in tattoos. Strange I hadn't noticed that last week.

Ms. Aleia goes on: "In ancient times, shamans used music as an essential part of healing practices. It was a common belief that music and dance were medicinal."

I turn to my neighbor. "Oh, great. Like an exorcism?"

She glares, her green eyes shadowed with thick charcoal lines.

I turn away and pretend to take notes. But in the next moment, darkness covers my notebook. With the lights off, Ms. Aleia starts a film clip. It's of some sort of tribal ceremony with lots of drums and half-naked people gyrating. I'm chewing my pencil so hard, I nearly taste lead.

When the lights come back on, it's like I've been awakened from REM sleep. I barely notice class has ended until my stud-nose neighbor packs up her things.

"You have a photographic memory, I take it?"

If she bothered to look at me, she'd see total confusion. When I don't answer, she adds, "Your notebook. It's blank."

"Last I knew, I was registered for music therapy, not witchcraft." She doesn't laugh with me. "My name's Sami."

"I'm Poppy." Her tone is scornful. I can guess why. She seems way too badass to have such a girly name.

"Like the flower?" Another glare. She mumbles something under her breath—a curse, maybe—and turns away. "Whatever."

What am I doing? I've offended the first potential friend for me here at Berklee—again—and after that disastrous weekend in Rhody, I desperately need a friend. "Wait." I touch her shoulder, and she recoils. "I'm sorry. Let's start over."

She shrugs, but she's frowning hard. Moody. Even her hair is angry—choppy short with grown-out highlights. With her dark clothes and dark aura, she seems more Goth than I ever did—regardless of what my Skenesboro friends used to say. She's a puzzle to figure out; I'm drawn to her.

"I like your tattoos." I tap the Nevus spilus on my hand. "Some people think this is a tattoo. Or dirt. But it's a birthmark." I want to tell her it's magical, but she'd think I was nuts.

"They're not real tattoos," she says. "They're henna." She hitches her bag over her shoulder and makes to leave.

I stay with her. "Did you have a good weekend? I hear this place kind of empties out. Did you stay in the city?"

A shrug. "I work."

"Oh. Where?"

"What is this, twenty questions?" She folds her arms. "At Henna on Newbury—right around the corner."

I marvel at the design on her hand. "Is this your work?"

She rubs her hand like I used to do with my birthmark and nods. To my surprise, she actually blushes.

concerto

"I really like it."

Her jaw relaxes into a kind of smile. "You should stop by sometime, and I'll do one for you."

"Really?"

"They're temporary, if you didn't know."

"I'd like that." My smile is big enough for both of us. I think I've made my first friend at Berklee.

Things will be okay here—whether my magic's a part of it or not. I just need to give it a chance. "Hey, are you signing up for Showcase this Friday?"

"I'm not a stage performer."

"You could do a group thing. Maybe we could do it together. What's your instrument?"

Her laugh sounds like a wrapper crinkling. "I'm not a traditional musician. Not my thing. I'm not technically in the program. Just cleared to take a few classes because I'm interested in therapy. Tactile therapies."

"Like henna?"

She tilts her head, sizing me up. "Kinda."

I instinctively caress my birthmark. "I like that."

CHAPTER 9

I must've blinked away the week because suddenly it's Friday. The first full week of classes was an absolute blur thanks to Ms. Aleia, who assigned a term paper—term paper!—due by week's end. Friday, end of day. Honestly, if I thought I'd be spending all my time in the computer lab rather than the piano studio here at the renowned Berklee School of Music, I might not have applied in the first place.

All my precious practice time vanished. My hope to channel my magic had gotten sucked into this paper. It was so all-consuming, I didn't even have time to firm up plans with Jason for Saturday. Hopefully, he still wants me to come down.

I get to Ms. Aleia's office at 4:50 p.m. and drop my tome onto the growing stack of papers there, hardly registering she's conferencing with another student. The slap of my paper gets their attention, and I see the student is none other than Miles, who I've avoided—consciously or subconsciously—the entire week.

"Oh, hi," I say, my face heating up. When's the last time I washed my hair? Why didn't I put on lip gloss before leaving my room? Really, it takes less than a second to apply lip gloss.

"I guess it's that time." Miles smirks in my direction. "Are you going to Showcase?"

"Showcase?" My voice is squeaky. "Oh, yeah. That's

concerto

tonight, right?"

"Yeah. In, like, an hour."

"I guess . . . yeah, I guess I'll go."

"Meet me in the student lounge. We'll go together."

Before I get to answer, Miles leaves, nodding a goodbye to Ms. Aleia.

"Thanks for your paper, Samantha," Ms. Aleia says. "Would you like to talk me through your topic?"

"Thanks, but no." I backpedal out. "I really have to go."

An hour. *Ahh!* Just an hour to shake off that term-paper haze. I have to primp for Miles . . . and get in touch with Jason about my coming down tomorrow.

Hey! Term paper finally DONE!! Still want me tmrw? [winking smiley]

SEND

No time to wait for a response. I fly through a shower—opting for dry shampoo to save blow-out time. I glop on some mascara and lip gloss. Back in my room, I pull on my skinny jeans and a white crop top. I fluff out my hair and use a curling iron to get that wavy waterfall look. This isn't a date, but the buzz of nerves in my stomach says differently. The mirror tells me I'm trying too hard. I opt for flip-flops and decide at the last minute to yank my hair into a ponytail. There. Casual. Friends. Non-date-like. Perfect.

On my way out the door, I grab my phone and—

Call me . . . reads Jason's text.

Showcase starts in ten minutes. Miles is waiting for me in the student lounge. Can't call Jason now. Nervous thumbs dance at the keypad . . .

Call u in 1 hr? On way to show

Before sending, I reconsider sharing too much. He doesn't need to know why, does he?

Backspace Backspace Backspace Back-Back-Back-Back . . .

Call u in 1 hr? [smiley]

SEND

Woop. Delivered.

Notifications OFF, legs ON, sprinting to the student lounge.

Miles is definitely bringing sexy back—wearing a graphic tee and jeans. When I get closer, the scent of jasmine cologne is there—and I find myself yearning for that beachy smell that connected him to my vision at the piano.

"There you are," he says, studying me.

"What? What are you looking at?"

"The past three years must've been good for you."

"What's that supposed to mean?"

He touches my elbow just so. Warmth rushes to the surface, from my toes to the tips of my ears.

"Come on. It's starting soon."

We sit side by side in the auditorium, and when the lights go down it's like a wall of heat extends from the armrest between us. Paying attention to the amateur musicians proves a near-impossible challenge.

A pianist, formally trained. Probably considered an expert, but missing passion.

A saxophonist, who seriously lacks some necessary sex appeal.

A vocal duet—all wrong. Opera meets folk.

concerto

And some others who are pretty good. I mean, I think they are. Not really sure. Because all my attention is absorbed in that wall of heat between Miles and me.

It's over in about an hour. It's dusk when Miles and I step onto Mass Ave. There's a moment suspended between us—and I'm not ready to say goodbye.

"What'd ya think?" I ask.

He grins comically. "It was good. Right? I mean, they were all super talented."

"Sure."

"But, I dunno."

I nod. "Yeah, I know."

"You do?" He laughs.

"I do!" We're laughing together now. It's silly. We're not making sense, but we understand each other.

"Hey, I'm gonna try out this burrito place. Caf is closed. You know, because—Friday. Wanna join?"

"Oh!" My hand goes to my chest. "Me? Really?" I catch myself. "Yeah, I guess I could. I'm kinda hungry."

"You're kinda hungry?"

That smile is back. It's making me go goosey inside.

"Yeah, kinda . . . hungry."

There we go again. Except this time, laughter doesn't erupt from our smiles. In words, it's nothing. But the subtext is everything, and an unspoken energy connects us. Like when he peeled the orange and sang *Orange Crush* so many years ago. I'm warm all over as he leads us to the burrito place on Mass Ave. But this is what we talked about, right?

We should get together one of these days. You know, to catch up.

That's all it is: old friends catching up.

Over our heaping, steaming burritos, we do just that. He

tells me about his classes: History of Music City, which fo-
cuses on influential cities like New Orleans, Nashville, and
Detroit. He's also taking History of Musical Instruments, in
which they'll build woodwinds out of hollow logs and string
instruments with nylon. I'm envious of his class schedule.

He tells me about his parents' divorce and his father's
move to Boston's North Shore. *Aha, so that's why Boston.*
He also brags about his wide-ranging expertise as a musician. He's had a certain knack since childhood, but what he
claims now seems downright miraculous.

"Let me get this straight," I say. "Violin has always
been your thing, so it makes sense that you can play all the
strings. But brass and woodwinds, too?"

"Like I was born to."

My last bite was too big. I hide my mouth with a napkin.
"You're full of it."

"Wait until the next Showcase. Matter of fact, I'll leave
it up to you. You can choose which instrument I play."

A thrill goes through me with this promise to do something together in the future. My huge bite is under control
now. "Ooooh, what should I choose? What's the hardest besides violin? Maybe French horn?"

"I also dabble in percussion." He drums the table.
"That's always fun."

"What about piano? You know, some say it's the easiest
to learn in the beginning but the hardest to master in the
end."

His grin has turned cocky. "I never want to face an instrument I can't play."

"That's a lofty goal." I'm careful to avoid Jason's tone
with the word.

"Oh, that's just the beginning. Playing is one thing,

concerto

making it meaningful is another."

I pause. It gets quiet all around us. His words could easily be my own. "Yes. I know what you mean. I feel the exact same way."

We've hit a new plateau. I can feel it. Hope and panic surge in equal parts.

I play it cool. "So, what's your plan? Like, how do you want to make it meaningful?"

He kind of wiggles his eyebrows. "Topic for another day."

Another promise for more.

Of course, I can't wait to tell him my plan for my music. He might be able to help me. I've had that gut feeling since the other night. Part of me wants to share my vision at the piano: he and I together on a beach, the waves lapping, the wind caressing our skin . . .

He must be connected to my magic or can help in some way. How would he react if I told him all this? Knowing Miles, he'd be up for the challenge. Is it wrong to feel excited? Friends help each other, right? There's no shame in that.

Something holds me back, though. It's not the right time.

We stuff ourselves with surely the yummiest burritos in North America. He doesn't mention Lauren, and I don't ask about her.

"Your turn," he says. "Tell me everything."

It seems like a lifetime since I left New York. How to describe my life in Skenesboro? I can't very well tell him about Aquamarine and the magic. Or . . . Jason. I stick to my volleyball.

"So that's why you're so toned." He slides the back of

his hand along my triceps. Goose bumps surface. "These are the arms of an athlete."

There's admiration in his voice. Like he's star-struck.

Table turned! All at once, it's easier to be with him. It's like the playing field's been leveled. Or, maybe, he finally sees me as more than just a friend.

My heart is so high, I can't take another bite. Good thing there's nothing on the table but empty wax paper wrappings and our drink cups. Who knows how long we stay there? Time zips by when you spend most of it laughing. It's dark when we leave. Which, I'm hesitant to admit, makes it feel like a definite date.

Miles takes out his phone. "I need to add you again. Lost all my contacts when I lost my phone last year."

My phone number sounds strange on my tongue, or maybe I'm reeling from the most promising promise to see each other again. I check my phone for the first time all night under the auspices of adding him, though we both know he's in there.

My screen lights up as I press the home button.

And the brakes screech—

Four missed calls from Jason. Three texts.

Three hours ago:

We need to talk tonite

One hour ago:

Where r u ???

Ten minutes ago:

Helllllooooooooooo??????

CHAPTER 10

Oh, no. Jason's got to be pissed. I said I'd call him in an hour, like, four hours ago. I need to call him. Now.

But Miles insists on walking me to my dorm.

"No, really. I got it. It's right there. Room 203." Why did I tell him that? He doesn't need to know my room number.

"Suit yourself." He pivots away.

Part of me wanted him to insist. "Bye!" I call to his back.

He answers with a backwards wave. Doesn't even turn around. Just keeps walking. Even his walk is irresistible. Maybe five paces until he's around the corner. Whatever. Why do I care? Miles doesn't fit anywhere in my life anymore. It was nice to catch up, but that's it. What did I expect? He was a childhood friend turned mega crush turned total heartbreaker. Why would someone like that affect me after so many years?

Still, I watch him walk with that confident swagger until he's out of sight.

And only when he's gone do I let myself freak out.

Jason!

I race into the dorm and up the stairs. My key must be broken. Yes, this is room 203, and yes, this is my key. Still, it takes eons to open my door.

When I flick the light on, it's too bright. And too quiet.

concerto

Shame falls down around me. Part of me wishes I hadn't responded to his text at all. Part of me doesn't want to call him, even still. I tap Jason's name from my Favorites list.

As it rings—and it rings for days—I realize I have to pee. *Oh, great.*

Voicemail.

"Jason here. Not. You know the deal." *Beep.*

Light and airy. Light and airy. "Hey, babe. It's me. Um, sorry I've been MIA. Crazy term paper. I don't even want to talk about it . . . So, call me. Still okay for me to come down tomorrow? That was the plan. But that was a while ago. Oh, never mind. I'll throw you a text."

What a stupid, rambling message.

My legs are squeezed together. My bladder aches. But I have to reach him. Now.

I open a new message.

[heart] [blowing kiss] Tmrw?? [train] [heart]

SEND

I fling open my door with a loud groan and dart to the loo. That's what they call it in England. So much cooler than saying "bathroom," or worse, "toilet."

Bathroom acoustics are irresistible. My song is one word on repeat: "loo, loo, loo—!"

The mirror shows a pretty decent version of me. Everything is basically in place. Some wispies have escaped my ponytail and I could use a refresher on the lip gloss, but my mascara has stayed put and my cheeks have a natural, rosy hue. I skip out into the hall, feeling bubbly. Part of me yearns for the studio. I could fill in all the quiet of campus with a late-night session at the piano. My heart picks up. Maybe my magic will appear. Maybe a plan will materialize.

The text waiting for me when I get back to my room isn't what I expected.

It's from Miles.

Stealing u tmrw

His message blinks neon. Miles is stealing me tomorrow? My grin is huge. I read it fourteen times before thinking of a response. Hmmm . . . "I'm going to Rhode Island to see my boyfriend" is way too cumbersome to text. How about "Going to RI. Sorry." But . . . where does he want to take me? Curiosity gets the best of me.

Oh? To where?

I swear, the text wrote itself.

His one-word response: *beach*

Wha-a? An eerie, Black Mirror feeling comes over me. That image from my session last week. OMG. It's coming true. Why would he . . .

I'm beyond intrigued. But of course, I need to decline the invite. Question is, how? Something witty. With an emoji. Um, thinkthinkthink . . . My thumbs are on the keys when my phone dings.

A text—from Jason.

Classes tmrw. Free Sunday?

His words read red. My thumbs mad-tap:

Classes on SATURDAY???????

Dots roll on way longer than his response merits.

concerto

Come Sunday?

I grit my teeth. Even if I could catch the express from South Station, it would still take me about an hour from Berklee. That would be two hours round-trip. For only, what, three or four hours with my boyfriend? I wouldn't even be able to sleep over.

This time, he answers my call.

"What's up with classes on a Saturday?"

"Where have you been?" The way he emphasizes "you" sounds accusatory. Or maybe it's my conscience.

"Oh. Showcases are every Friday. Didn't I tell you that? They're kind of a big deal. Anyway, what the heck—classes on a Saturday? That should be banned."

He sounds far away. "It's a one-day seminar. Meets pretty much the whole day. But it's, like, the best instructor. I was lucky to get a spot."

"Lucky. Right."

"Don't be like that."

"Sorry." I sigh the word. "I just miss you. That's all."

"I miss you, too. It might be a push to come all the way down just for one day. I get it. But, hey. Next weekend, I'm all yours."

I tamp down my disappointment. "Okay. Next Friday, I could come right after classes."

He doesn't answer right away. "Yeah, that would work." He sounds distracted.

Why did he hesitate? Doesn't he want me to come down? "Is there something going on next Friday?"

"No, no. Just a bunch of us are going to see this band in Newport. But, I mean, I guess you could come with us."

My thoughts cloud over like a storm rolling in. That

same ugly feeling from my first visit takes root in my gut. Is he putting me off?

Then, I remember Friday is Showcase night. Miles wants me to choose which instrument he'll play. My next breath is breezy.

"Actually, we have Showcase here again next Friday. I'll just come Saturday morning."

His words are quick. "You sure?"

"Yeah, yeah. Sure."

The pause that follows is so long, I wish I could see his face. "No. You know what? You stay put. I'm coming to you."

"Really?"

"Yeah. You came here last. It's only fair. Besides, I have some making up to do, don't I?"

I just love this guy. "Maybe."

"Maybe, right." I can hear his smile, and it doesn't matter that our plans have changed.

He changes the subject. "Hey, have you seen Aunt Gaye, by the way?"

"No, why would I?"

"What do you mean? Her gallery is right around the corner."

"I know, but I figured she didn't need me poking around."

Big, groaning sigh. "Sami, she wants to see you. She's expecting you to stop by."

"Okay. Well, next time I'm down there, I will."

"Besides, she told me she'd keep an eye on you."

"Oh, really?"

Another long pause. I wish we were in the same room so I could smooch him or nuzzle into his neck. I don't know

concerto

what to say now.

"So, I guess we'll talk later." It dawns on me that this might be our first phone conversation that's lasted more than forty seconds. There's no heart emoji to end it smoothly. How do you say goodbye to your boyfriend *on the phone*?

"Right. Talk to ya."

"Okay. Bye."

The phone is an empty shell in my hand. I hurry to send him a few heart emojis. That fills it in a bit.

My yawn takes me by surprise. I'd thought about going to the studio, but now I want my bed. I'm pulling off my clothes when my phone dings, catching me half-naked.

It's Miles: *Lvg @ 10. B ready*

Now I feel very naked. That yawn is a distant memory as my pulse races. It's like I'm on a tightrope. I have two guys contacting me through this device. My old childhood crush, who happens to be here in Boston with me in the same program. And my boyfriend, my love, who's in another state. What's the old adage? *Out of sight, out of mind*. Ugh. Not good. What about—*Absence makes the heart grow fonder*? I like that one better.

Still, something tells me nothing good can come of texting either one of them right now. I shut down my phone deliberately, but that last text glows brightly behind my closed lids.

Lvg @ 10. B ready

And it keeps me up most of the night.

CHAPTER 11

We're just friends, I keep telling myself, sitting in the passenger seat of his Camry as Miles drives north on I-95.

"It's a Saturday in July," he announces. "Time to get out of the city. Get some fresh air."

The windows are open and the radio's booming, so Miles has to shout. He taps the steering wheel to the music, his eyes smiling behind his Ray-Ban Aviators.

The sky is a flawless bright blue. Sunshine has painted joy on everything we pass. I swim my hand in the wind, watching its reflection in the side view mirror. I can't remember the last time I felt so . . . free.

"How far is it?" I ask.

"About an hour. It's the best-kept secret: one of the best beaches in the world is just an hour north of Boston."

I yank at the elastic where my bathing suit pinches, wishing I had planned on changing when we got there. My suit makes uneven bumps through my sundress, hardly emphasizing my slight curves. Miles wears a patchwork plaid bathing suit, topped with a white linen button-down. He looks all Cape Cod. Not the city boy I remember.

We merge onto a lighter-trafficked highway and up go the windows. Miles surprises me by clicking off the radio, too. He sighs in a way that sounds sad.

"I haven't talked to Lauren for over a year," he says, as if she'd been a conversation thread.

concerto

As much as I'd wanted to know, I'm not ready to talk about her. "Oh?"

"We kind of had a falling out."

Falling out? Does he really want to talk about their breakup? "That's too bad," I say after a few beats. "What about?"

"It's kind of a long story. But there were real feelings there. On both sides. No matter what she says now." He checks the rearview and shifts lanes. "You in touch with her at all?"

Something stabs at me. Is it jealousy? Is he trying to get back together with her—through me? "Aside from a brief email exchange a few months back, I haven't spoken to her since I left the City."

"I remember. She was really broken up about that—you leaving. And then," he flicks his hand at the dash, "nothing."

My mouth drops open. Lauren was upset about my leaving? About our friendship ending? I had no idea. "Phone works both ways." It comes out more bitter than I intend.

Miles doesn't seem to notice. "That's one of the reasons I was psyched you were here. You're one of the few people who get it, I think."

"Get what?"

"Lauren. Me. Us. The three of us were inseparable when we were younger."

Huh. Interesting version of history. "Is that how it went?"

"You don't think?"

That's how he remembers it? "I think we were all friends until you and Lauren became inseparable."

"I think we were all friends until you moved away," he challenges.

Whoa. It's like a punch in the gut. I've never thought of it that way. All this time, I blamed them for our friendship ending. They started dating, and I was an instant third wheel. My move was a coincidence in timing. Wasn't it? It shouldn't be so hard to remember . . .

Maybe it's better not to. "Whatever," I say the word kindly. "It's not worth arguing about. Old news."

We drive for a while, the hum of tires on pavement the only sound. In the quiet, I piece back the months and weeks which led to my move upstate. My feelings for Miles grew into a scary romantic hope, then he and Lauren got together, then they stopped hanging out with me, and then I moved . . . . Or, did I push them both away during that three-month window when our apartment was selling and we were packing and I was mad at the world because I wasn't able to go to LaGuardia School of the Arts?

OMG. I pushed them both away—directly into each other's arms.

Why rehash ancient history like this? Why should I care? I have Jason.

I shift my thoughts to him. The morning sun beats down on the windshield, heating me despite the AC in the car. It's a delicious warmth. I'd like to drift off to sleep but don't want to be rude. My eyelids start to get heavy when Miles says, "You had a boyfriend up there in the mountains, you said?"

Oh. Is this the do-you-have-a-significant-other conversation? I ignore his use of past tense. "Yeah. Jason . . ."

"Mountain man." He swings his arm like a lumberjack, laughing alone at his joke.

"What's that supposed to mean—'mountain man'?" Is he dissing my guy? He doesn't even know Jason. "It's not

concerto

like we all live in the trees up there, you know."

I wasn't trying to be funny, but he thinks I'm hilarious. He makes a bullhorn with his hand and yodels a Tarzan call. It's so loud it fills the car. Now I'm laughing, too.

When we finally turn off the highway, all laughed out, Miles puts down the windows again.

"You can smell the ocean from here."

I stick my head out as much as my seatbelt allows. He's right. The air is thick with salt. I close my eyes and let it wash over me. The scent grows stronger as we drive. Gulls circle overhead. We're getting closer. Anticipation makes my knees jiggle. Miles doesn't talk, and I'm glad for it.

We pull in next to a cream-colored cottage framed by dunes of sea grass and, beyond that, the ocean. Oh my, it's like the whole world opens up.

"Here we are."

The cottage looks like something out of a fairy tale. It could be made of vanilla taffy. "Where's here? Whose house is this?"

"It's my dad's. He's not here. Might join us later."

Later? I swallow a hiccup of eagerness. What's going on later?

Miles grabs his duffle from the backseat. I follow him into the taffy cottage. It's like going back in time. The décor is done up '70s style, plastic and artificial leather. Almost everything is white. But the real eye candy is through the bay windows and sliding glass doors—where ocean is front and center. The view is breathtaking.

Miles' eyes are on the water. His entire aura relaxes. He's quiet for a while, and I start to think he's meditating.

"It's always changing. It's like a living, breathing thing."

Standing next to him, looking out at the rolling tide together, feels oddly intimate. "What is?"

He doesn't answer right away, then his voice gets soft. "The ocean. It's, like, a wild animal. Right now, it's polite and purring. But watch out for its roar. You have to be careful. It commands respect."

Yes, yes, yes! My synapses are firing. Miles is saying what I've been trying to communicate for years now. The ocean commands respect. I love that! Most people don't get it. The Earth is mostly ocean, its footprint growing as ice caps melt. We're living on borrowed land. We need to protect it. Cherish it.

I glance at Miles' profile, his laugh lines slightly hardened by the sun. It's like we're communicating telepathically or something. I sense our thoughts are the same. My hunch has to be right. He must be able to help me. My lips tingle, partially open. I hope whatever I manage to say is the right thing.

"I completely agree," I say slowly, over-enunciating for emphasis. "You're so right." Then, my words speed up. "And I've been trying to figure out how to use my—it's going to sound silly—but if you could've seen what I was able to do up in the mountains . . ."

I'm scrambling for the right words. And I'm jumping ahead. *Back up, Sami. Let's establish the problem before pouncing on a solution.*

I take a breath. "What I'm trying to say is: yes. The ocean is so important."

Miles smiles at me, and my vocabulary vanishes. It would be a lot easier to talk to him seriously if he weren't so seriously good looking. I give him a desperate look, willing him to read my mind.

concerto

"You know what's cool?" He folds his arms. "How the ocean affects the weather. Like, extreme weather."

Wait—weather? That's not where I was going. "Yeah, extreme weather seems a lot more common lately."

"Yeah, but it's cool. It's such a force. Like, raw power. Since my dad moved here, it's been really something. A storm will be out in the middle of the ocean. Something you can't even see. But we'll feel it. You know?"

"Right." Can he hear my disappointment?

"Like, there'll be a hurricane brewing, and these surfer guys will be out there for the big kahuna wave. The wind is crazy and the waves get huge. They don't realize. It's all fun and games until, you know . . . The ocean can kill, too."

"Ah. That kind of respect." I'm thinking rebuilding and restoring balance and he's thinking . . . what? Destruction? I laugh stupidly and grasp a straw. "I was thinking of respect as in something that needs protection. You know, the effects of global warming. That kind of thing."

"Global warming." He looks at me like I'm a little girl. "You're sweet."

Sweet? "No, I'm serious. Some people think these unusual weather patterns don't have anything to do with it."

"Do with what?" He opens the glass doors. And it's as if someone turned up the volume. The waves are thunderous.

"Global warming." My words are swallowed by the sound. "Climate change. Whatever." The last word's a whimper.

He stopped listening, anyway. "Tide's coming up," he calls. "Come on. We gotta get out there."

Now's not the time to be Debbie Downer. He's in vacation mode. I should be, too. It's a beautiful Saturday in July, and we're at the beach.

In the sun, the wind is warm. Miles leads me down the steps to the beach. I take off my flip-flops to feel the sand in my toes. It's like walking in dough. My feet sink with each step into luxurious warmth. I pause, taking it in, while Miles inches toward shore.

Déjà vu.

Just like he appeared to me during my piano session: he flashes a smile my way and points to something out at sea. His lips move, but I can't hear what he says. He waves me over and points again. I hesitate, the familiarity of it all making me woozy, but I go. Closer to the surf. Closer to him.

He leans into my hair. It's like he's soaked up the sun's energy. I can feel it coming off his skin. "Look. It's a seal." His words tickle behind my ear.

I squint out past the rolling foam. Sure enough, a little black head pokes up. He looks right at us. I squeal, delighted, and squeeze Miles' arm on reflex. He holds my hand there and leads us deeper into the water.

"No, no. I don't want to get wet."

A laugh. "You don't want to get wet? At the beach?"

"No, I mean. I don't—"

The surf breaks against my shins, and a shock of cold travels up my body. Another squeal, sounding so girly it makes me giggle. The next wave crashes above my knees—too quickly for me to brace myself. Next moment, Miles' arms are around me. I fall against his chest, and he hugs me close. He's delectably warm. And he smells tangy and briny and perfect. "I've got you," he whispers, almost too soft for me to hear. Almost.

I should unravel from him, step back out of the waves. The hem of my dress is soaked. Goose bumps run the length of my body. I run hot and cold at the same time. Dizzying.

concerto

I have no business letting Miles in like this. Letting him hold me like this. He's protecting me, though. Making sure the waves don't bring me down. It's what a friend would do. Right?

We stay that way for a while, and I let the waves crash me against him. Again and again until my feet are numb and my teeth start to chatter. Miles shivers against me. He brings me to dry sand and wraps me in a towel. The gesture is so tender it nearly stops my breath.

"Thanks," I manage.

He doesn't say anything with words. But the look he gives me is a soliloquy.

CHAPTER 12

My grin hasn't quit since the beach. Part of me is grateful for Ms. Aleia's snoozer class; I can while away the time in reverie.

The rest of our beach day was, in a word, perfect. Miles and I sat in the sand until high tide and the sky changed, filled with pink. We came in and dried off, and then Miles took me around the corner for some famous beach pizza before heading back. We didn't talk much on the drive home. I didn't feel the need for words.

He walked me to my dorm like a gentleman. Gave me a big, G-rated hug goodbye. My goodnight texts to Jason were all about him, hoping his seminar was good, *blah, blah*. He was tired. Didn't really feel like talking. What a coincidence. Me, neither.

I slept well that night. Miles says it's the salt air that does it. Miles says—

Poppy nudges me. "Yo. You still here?"

"Oh, yeah. Why?"

She nods toward Ms. Aleia. "She's noticing. I'm just sayin'. Don't make it awkward, you know? Don't be so obvious."

For the remainder of the class, I try to pay attention. I really do. Still, my notebook remains blank.

"Not meeting your expectations, I presume?"

Class is dismissed. Students are dispersing. It takes a

concerto

moment to realize Ms. Aleia is speaking to me. "Oh, well. I don't know."

"Tell me, Samantha. What is it you came here for?"

Her directness throws me off. "What do you mean?"

She reads from her roster. "You are a pianist, I understand. What makes you interested in music therapy?"

I'm not ready to share. "Well, it's like what you said during Orientation. We'd see a completely different side of music. Something like that."

"And?" Her eyes slide off the roster and go to, of all things, my birthmark. For a moment, I'm speechless. Is she really staring at my Nevus spilus?

"I also believe music can have a . . . higher purpose."

She shifts focus off my birthmark and busily packs folders into her hobo bag. "Salvation through song. That kind of thing."

"Kind of."

"Will you study medicine as well?"

"I had something else in mind."

She pauses, her bag suspended in the air, waiting for me to explain. I bite my lip. My gut tells me to keep it private. But why? Do I not trust her?

Her stare cuts right through me. "We all have our secrets."

"It's not a secret. I'm just still trying to figure it out."

Ms. Aleia pulls her bag over her shoulder. "Well, I hope you come to accept that we professors at Berklee are here to help you do just that." She takes my hand—my left hand—and her thumb grazes my birthmark. "When you're ready to talk, come and find me."

❧

The sun is high, reflecting off the high-rise windows, making the city too bright. Walking down Newbury Street, I squint against the harsh light, rubbing the spot on my hand. Why had the white woman stared at it like that? And why did she touch it? I feel violated slightly—in a way that makes me crave the security of Jason's company. I should call him. Or text him? Why am I at a loss for words? He's my boyfriend. Speaking of obligation, I'm supposed to stop by Aunt Gaye's gallery . . .

"Sam?"

I know that voice. I spin to face her. "Aunt Gaye?" I can't help but be surprised; her gallery is still a few blocks down. A tug of disappointment hits. She beat me to the punch. "I was on my way—"

"My goodness, child, you look like you're in need of a refresher."

She leads me into an air-conditioned smoothie shop. Upbeat music fills the place, along with a yummy, fruity smell.

"How do you like your drink?" Gaye asks.

I didn't realize how worked up I'd gotten with Ms. Aleia and the birthmark thing until my first sip of Mango Spirulina. Aunt Gaye, sitting across from me, looks elegant and untouched by the oppressive heat.

"I've been meaning to stop by and see how you're doing," she says. "Forgive me. It's been an unusually busy season at the gallery."

"Forgive you? Jason says I'm the one who should've come to you. Sorry for that."

concerto

"Oh, forget it." She pats my arm. "So, tell me every-thing."

Everything would include Miles. That, and—what else? I can't think of anything else but Miles. I'm sitting across from Jason's aunt, and still, I'm thinking about Miles. I hedge, sipping my smoothie so hard it goes to my head.

Gaye helps me out. "Do you like your classes?"

"They're okay. Not what I expected, I guess. I'm trying to figure out how to get the most out of the program. I feel like I'm going to blink my eyes and it will be over."

"Five weeks do go fast. Sometimes you need to advo-cate for yourself. If you're not getting what you want, speak up. Say something. Make sure you find it." She smiles.

"I don't know." I shake my head. "Sometimes I wonder if . . . Can I ask you something?"

"Of course, child."

"At Jason's party, you seemed to know what happened on Skene Mountain. With me. And my piano." I wait, but Gaye looks blank. "Do you know what I did? What I was able to do with my piano?"

She inhales deeply. "I do."

"Jason told you . . . everything?"

Gaye hesitates. It's like she's trying to pull an old file. "Oh, sure." Her words are quick. "Jason told me."

I fidget, not sure if I'm annoyed or flattered. "I'm sur-prised he told you. I mean, that was kind of heavy stuff. Not exactly secret, but—"

Gaye's hand on mine is warm and contrasts with the strong AC in the shop. "Listen," she says. "I have a knack for knowing things, you could say. I know how special you are, for example."

"You know about my magic? You know what I did with

Aquamarine?"

Serious now, she meets my eye and it seems to get very still in the shop. "Yes."

"You know about . . . Dion?"

"I know you are Dion; Samantha Frances McGovern, the only Goshenite with the singular power to unravel a rivalry that was ruining a small town. I know what you were able to do as Dion—neutralizing toxins from a mineral people had been abusing as a type of performance-enhancing drug—with your music. It was extraordinary."

Everything about Gaye exudes pride, from her tone to her facial expression. Still, my insides tremble, hearing Gaye recount my Dion victory. Sometimes the memories seem like a dream. Was it really me? Did I really do that with my music?

But now is not the time to reminisce. Gaye leans across the table. "But it's not over. That was only your first mission as Dion." She must see confusion on my face. "You have a unique kind of magic, Sam." She circles my birthmark with her index finger. "This Nevus spilus is more than just a mark or indicator of Dion. It's a channel for your magic. Years ago, Aquamarine and the friction between Goshenites and Fasha triggered it. But that's not the extent of your magic. That, as they say, is the tip of the iceberg. There's more to unlock. As Dion, the supernatural force at your command is more powerful than you can imagine. It's incumbent upon you to learn it, understand it, and use it in a constructive way."

I blink at her, too shocked to speak.

"You are important, Sam. You have important work yet to do."

Unexpected tears sting behind my eyes. Gaye eases

back in her seat, patiently allowing me to process what she's just told me. It should be daunting but, strangely, everything begins to make sense. Relief manifests in a single tear. It trickles down my face untouched.

"So I'm not crazy after all?"

Gaye wags her head slowly, reassuring me.

Fortified, I sit up a little straighter now. "I feel I do, too. I'm not sure how exactly, but I know how important it is. I can feel it. That, in itself, is powerful."

"I'm sure it's overwhelming."

My voice is small. "I'm going to need help, though. Can you help me?"

Gaye's smile is mollifying. "I thought you'd never ask. Tell me what you're thinking."

All at once, Gaye seems different. She even looks different. Like, there's a glow about her. "It's going to sound crazy. Promise you won't laugh."

"Child, I've seen my share of crazy in my years. Trust me, I save my laughter for the good stuff."

"Okay, here goes." Shoving away any reluctance, I begin. "Rather than use my magic to destroy something, I want to use it to rebuild."

"Rebuild what?"

"The Earth?" My eyebrows go sky high.

"Is that a question? Are you asking me?"

"No, no. It just sounds silly, saying it aloud."

"Not silly. And I would never laugh at something so vital. Go on."

"I'm studying music therapy, but I want to use my music to . . . heal the Earth?" Gaye looks blank, so I ramble on. "I mean, you said it yourself. I returned balance to Skenesboro by changing an element of nature. And you said

I needed to think bigger. So, I'm going to use my music to revive, or repair, the Earth."

Gaye's eyes round out. "Repair? What part?"

"Not sure. There's so much that needs help, right? I mean, look at what's happening all over the world. The rainforests dying, the icebergs melting . . . There's a lot that needs rehabilitating. And in that way, I can restore balance to the Earth. I should be able to do that—or, at least help in that. Right?"

"Based on what you've been able to accomplish in the past, I would think so. But only you can find out for sure."

My energy dwindles as I realize the enormity of it all. But I can almost see the gears turning in Gaye's mind. "So, that is why you're studying music therapy. But instead of a person, your patient will be the Earth."

Huge breath of relief. She gets it! It feels good to be heard. "Yes. And I have an inkling that my magic is coming back. The problem is, I'm not sure how to get the power to work like that. As you said, I'll need to figure out how to control it. But I'm scrambling. I mean, the whole Aquamarine thing was kind of instinctive. I didn't even know I was capable of magic. But now, it's different. How can I get my magic to cooperate and do what I want it to?"

Gaye holds her chin and makes a humming sound.

She's got to hear about my visions. I lean in to whisper. "I thought if I concentrated on my piano and my music, the answer would show itself. The other night, I had a piano session and a vision came to me—but it was all wrong. Or, I took it as a sign but it turned out it wasn't." My vision of Miles on the beach was only a precursor to our date or whatever, not a sign he'd be able to help me. "So, I don't know where to go from here."

concerto

"Or,"—she flutters her eyelids—"maybe it's happening already and you don't realize it."

"Doubt it."

"Why do you doubt it?"

I clasp my hands together, prayer-like. "Because I would feel it. I know how it feels."

Gaye reaches across the table and presses her thumb directly on my birthmark. Unlike the sensation when Ms. Aleia touched me there, Gaye's touch feels wholesome and seems to fill a void.

"Keep trying. You, of all people, can do this."

I shake my head. "Okay, but what I'm setting out to do: It's bigger than me. It's bigger than Dion. I need to find someone who—I don't know—knows more about the Earth and science and stuff."

"The Earth and science and stuff?"

Even when I laugh, Gaye still doesn't. "How about your teachers? Do you think they could help?"

"I have the same teacher for both my seminars. She's kind of strange. In a good way, I guess. Mysterious. She's always in white, which matches her super pale skin. And she, like, whispers—"

"Aleia." All the cheer drops from Gaye's face.

"You know her?"

"Let's say we go way back."

Gaye looks so sad and serious, I try to lighten the mood. "Oh, don't tell me there's an ancient rivalry between you two."

Gaye doesn't return my laugh. Then she switches the subject. "I don't suppose you've seen Jason at all?"

"Once. I went the first weekend. Now it's his turn. He's coming here on Saturday."

"Oh, good. So, you'll be here for Showcase?"

Gaye surprises me again, knowing about Showcase night. Then again, she seems to know everything.

"Would you mind if I come to watch?" she asks. "It's been a while since I sat in that auditorium. And there are so many old friends I'd like to see."

"Not at all." I finish my smoothie in one marathon sip, not caring about the imminent brain freeze. Maybe it will offset the shock that Aunt Gaye is somehow connected to Berklee and Ms. Aleia.

"As far as 'the Earth and science and stuff'—you and I can figure that out together. I have no worries about that, child." She winks and pushes up from the table. "I'll be there Friday. Save me a seat."

CHAPTER 13

Poppy isn't in class the next day. It's like a rebuke, her absence. I pay a bit more attention as a result and manage to jot down some notes. But it's still all theory, and I can't help my disappointment. Maybe it's a combination of Poppy's reproach and Gaye's encouragement that gives me the guts to speak up. As soon as class ends, I approach Ms. Aleia.

"Can I ask you something?"

She doesn't answer. Just stares at me.

"Can we learn how to actually perform the therapy? I mean, when can we practice?"

"Don't you already play piano? I'm not here to teach you how to make music."

"Sure, but I was hoping to learn how to use the music for therapy. You know, instead of the history of music therapy."

She clamps her colorless lips. "This class is an overview. It's an exploration of the ideology, the philosophy behind this delicate kind of therapy. On that note . . ." She hands me my graded term paper. "Your work here was decent, for high-school level. You're going to have to dig a little deeper in the next few years for college-level assignments."

A big B-minus in purple ink graces the top of my term paper. I roll it into a tube to hide my grade.

concerto

"I'd like to dig deeper by getting out there and practicing. Is it possible we could, or I could, learn actual skills to perform music therapy in some way?"

She hands me a business card with a ghost of a smile. Her voice gets low. "I hold office hours. Even during the summer. Shame you haven't sought me out before now."

The card feels electrically charged in my fingers. "You mean, you want me to come to your office hours? And you can, like, tutor me or something?" Gosh, I sound like an idiot.

Ms. Aleia looks at me for a long beat and then nods once. As she turns away, her pale skirt twirls and kicks up an aroma of something familiar. It takes me by such surprise I'm frozen for a moment. The classroom is empty now but I can still smell it.

Ocean air.

❧

Lunch in a college cafeteria has such a better vibe than high school. There aren't bulky trays. Everything's à la carte. And no one seems to care how popular you are. Actually, it seems that the more nerdy you are, the better. I think I'm going to like college. Waiting for a made-to-order turkey wrap, I wonder whether Jason's having lunch now, too. And what he's ordering. And who he's sitting with . . .

Poppy is conspicuously absent from our usual table, but I head for it anyway, when Miles steps into view. "Looking for me?"

I shake the heat from my face. "Oh, hi. I was looking for Poppy, actually."

"Ah, the one with the nose ring and the attitude?"

"She's pretty cool, actually, if you get to know her."

"Why would I want to get to know her?" He looks at me so intently I feel shy.

He leads me to a table in a neutral zone. Where he usually sits are two boys who seem to be Miles' clones—with the same black square glasses and longish hair. Not nearly as handsome, though. They shoot me daggers.

"We have something important to discuss," Miles says.

"Really? What's that?"

He points at me playfully with his plastic fork. "You, my friend, are supposed to choose what instrument I play on Friday night."

"Oh, that."

" 'Oh, that,' " he mocks. "Dude, it's Tuesday. I need some time to practice."

"You do? I thought, since you're a prodigy and all that, you wouldn't need to practice. You know, 'there's no instrument you can't handle' kind of thing."

He chuckles. "Play fair, Sami. Just tell me what you want me to play."

"Maybe I should keep you in suspense. Until Thursday, say."

"That would be cruel and unusual."

"Would it?"

We're flirting. Shamelessly. I can feel it in my toes. Our table may as well be sitting on a cloud. The two guys, Miles' twinsies, have left their table. Miles is unfazed. All his attention is on me. His grin hasn't quit, even through his meal. Even the way he eats is sexy, for crying out loud. My stomach is so hyped up, I can't eat. And I was famished when I first came in.

My eyebrows wiggle. "I wouldn't want to be cruel and

concerto

unusual."

"Well, don't be cruel." His lips are slick with oil from his sandwich. "I kind of like your unusual."

"Do you?"

I manage a bite. My turkey wrap is so dry, I nearly choke before I get my bottle of water open. When I finally get it down, my eyes are watering. Blinking in rapid succession is in no way an intended eyelash flutter, I swear.

"You okay?" He's laughing, covering his mouth with the back of his hand. He holds his sandwich the way he'd hold an instrument. With a gentle confidence. Gosh, his hands are beautiful. "You tell me when you're ready," he says quietly, looking down at his tray.

I clear my throat. "Piano." I'd decided a while ago.

"Piano?"

"The easiest to learn—"

"The hardest to master."

"Right."

He shrugs. "Okay. Got it." He gets a faraway look in his eyes, surely planning his big performance already. I consider another bite of my turkey wrap, but now I'm gun-shy. I settle for potato chips, which are so salty I drink the rest of my water in two seconds flat. And I'm still hungry.

"So I was thinking," he says, licking salt off his lips. "This Saturday is going to be a *scorch-ah*, as they say here in Boston. Wicked hot. Perfect beach day. What do you say?"

I wish I had something to put in my mouth so I didn't have to answer. I peel off a part of the tortilla and chew on it. "Um . . ."

Miles' eyes go wide. "You don't want to go?"

"Oh, no. It's not that." *The beach sounds absolutely*

heavenly. "It's just that . . . I kind of already have plans."

"Someone came along with a better offer?" He winks, and I want to crawl under the table.

The words are impossible to say. "Someone's coming to visit."

Miles holds a chip in the air, waves it around like he's painting with it. "Oh, who's the mystery guest?"

Gosh, I don't want to tell him. Why, though? Why don't I want to tell him? Heat crawls up my neck. My scalp starts to sweat.

"Jason," I blurt. "The—boyfriend—I told you about from Skenesboro."

"Ah, the mountain man." There's no mirth in his laugh.

I start to protest, but my defense would sound too . . . defensive. "He goes to RISD. He was going to come Friday but he's got a concert to go to in Newport. Which is fine, though, since there's Showcase. And I'll be there to cheer you on while you play your piano masterpiece."

The pause that follows is loaded bigger than TGIF's potato skins.

"Lucky me."

"Sorry." He has no idea how sorry I really am. I'm ashamed of how sorry I am. Why the heck do I want to go to the beach again? Jason's coming to visit!

"So, things are serious with this mountain man?"

Sweat gathers in odd places. "Well, yeah. I mean, you know how it goes. When you're with someone for a long time, you have your ups and downs." Why did I just say that? *No downs, Sami, only ups!* Still, that first visit has left a bitter taste.

"I do know how it goes." The firm line of his jaw relaxes. "With Lauren, it was like I was given a different lens.

concerto

It's like she changed the way I saw the world. Or maybe that's what love does to you." He palms his neck, bashful. "When things were good, they were great. When we fought, though, it was like the Earth stopped spinning."

My lips part, an unexpected relief washing over me. "Yes. It's awful."

"I take it your Earth has stopped spinning for the moment?" His eyes are sorry, sincere—and it dawns on me he truly cares about me. Probably always has. And I went and moved away all those years ago and abandoned a true friendship.

Tears bubble up. I sniff them away and nod, looking down at my dissected turkey wrap. I stare at it, wondering how I ever felt hungry. My stomach is a huge hollow log.

His touch on my arm surprises me—in a good way. Like Gaye's the other day, it seems to fill a void. "You just need to see him. As soon as you're together, face-to-face, everything will click into place."

I'm already shaking my head. "That's just it. The last time I went down. I don't know . . . It was weird. Everything felt off."

Miles is quiet for so long, I'm forced to meet his eye. And the look he gives me cuts right to my core. "I don't know what to say. Except: I've been there. I'm sorry you're going through it. But we have to believe that it will all work out somehow."

I smudge away a tear. "It's hard to have that kind of faith."

"Don't I know it." He stares off into the crowd, like he's searching for her. "But we have no choice, do we?" He meets my eye again, and there's something else there: unfiltered desire. It makes my kneecaps quiver. My heart goes to my throat.

"We can't give up."

He's not talking about me and Jason or him and Lauren, but us.

CHAPTER 14

Miles has got me all flustered. My steps through the maze of corridors are rushed and clumsy. It's like he's reached in and taken a piece of my soul. How is he able to do that?

I'm desperate to hear from Jason. He hasn't texted all day.

Hey luv u

Woop. Delivered.

It's, like, dead in my hand. Stupid phone. I should throw it into the Charles River. Why won't he freaking text me? Notifications OFF. It's better to be off the grid than wait for his call.

Music is the answer. If there's one thing that will keep me grounded, it's my piano. I run-don't-walk to the studio, feeling all at once the lapse in my practice time. It's blissfully empty since classes are still going on. Wasting no time, I sidle up to the keys and start before I've caught my breath. And I can feel my heart sliding into place.

Glorious sound fills the room. I sink into the music and let those nagging questions run through my mind.

What's this thing with Miles turning into? Why am I letting it turn into a thing, anyway? What's wrong with me? I have a boyfriend.

Yet, Jason's barely reached out since that first visit. He

concerto

answers my texts and sometimes my calls, sure, but he never starts anything. Is he really so busy he can't be bothered? Mom once told me that, as a rule, guys think long-distance communication is reserved for emergencies only. Well, hell if this isn't turning into an emergency. Can't he sense it, too? Can't he feel the distance growing between us? Will his visit this weekend make everything right? It's hard to imagine.

I'm staying offline for a while. It's his turn to squirm. I'm pouring my energy into my first love: piano. That'll show him. And Miles. And Ms. Aleia. And everyone else who feels like confusing me this summer.

Before making a conscious effort to craft a tune, I hear a Mozart medley coming from my piano. Gradually, my breath comes easier. I let those nagging questions float away. I shut everything out and zone in on the music only, closing my eyes. I'm not even expecting any magic. I'm not expecting to see anything—

But it's like the vision was expecting me.

Light against black. Fireworks—bright neon red—cut through a dismal gray sky. Only they're not your standard, organized Independence Day starbursts. They fall in clumps, or long arms, helter-skelter from all corners of the sky . . . and last less than a second. A flash.

Oh, wait—these can't be fireworks. It's lightning. A creepy, strange kind of lightning. Falling in twos or threes, like claws reaching for an itch. Red pillars of light fill the sky—a warning signal—but as they get bigger and brighter and more frequent, I know there's no time for a warning. The danger is here.

My eyes pop open. I slap my trembling hands on my lap. Afraid to move, I blink a few times to clear what has settled behind my closed lids—those frightening images.

What was that? I've never seen lightning so aggressive, so violent. And the color—it was so unnatural. And so polar opposite of the magic blue light of Aquamarine.

A feeling of dread rises from the base of my spine.

Something feels wrong. This isn't my magic I'm seeing. It's like I'm observing another force at work—an evil force that's working against me. It seems to hover over me for the rest of the day and into the night—a dark cloud over my head. It's nearby, here in Boston, bearing down. The sky shows me no answers but I'm determined to figure out who or what's behind it. And because I'm Dion, I will. Gaye says I've barely scratched the surface of what my magic can do. Whatever evil force this is won't stand a chance.

CHAPTER 15

The dark cloud has got me feeling skittish about nearly everything. My vision last night during my piano session left me with the distinct feeling there is an evil force working against me, and it's hovering ominously over my every thought.

Poppy isn't in class the next day. That's two days in a row. Paranoia sets in. Paying attention in class is more than a challenge. The subject matter seems immaterial.

Ms. Aleia lectures about how music therapy affects the brain: "Patients with neurological ailments or traumatic brain injuries have responded favorably."

She speaks so quietly. And seems bored. It's like she's not even interested in what she's saying. What they say is true: excitement is contagious . . . and so is boredom. My blank notebook has become a prop. My hope is that Ms. Aleia is saving her gems of genius for her office hours.

"According to psychologists," she adds in a skeptical tone. Wait—isn't she a psychologist? Her business card doesn't list an official job title. It does say her office hours don't start until later this afternoon, leaving me a two-hour window to dodge that dark cloud.

After class, I venture onto Newbury Street and head for Aunt Gaye's gallery. It's about time I see it. And I'm craving her soothing company.

concerto

In just a couple days, Jason will be here with me, walking by my side. Thoughts of him dissolve that dark cloud some. I wish he could be here with me now.

But he's not in my notifications, and I have to scroll to remind myself of our last text exchange. It was fine, I guess. When we last talked, he did say he had some making up to do. It's all good, I think. I'm trying to be understanding. It's hard to be patient. His non-contact brings a whole different level of foreboding. I tuck my phone back in my pocket without texting him. Maybe later.

Miles isn't in my notifications either, which should bring me relief. He doesn't belong in my notifications. He's not my boyfriend. Yet, at lunch yesterday, he seemed to get me. And I really need someone to get me right now—especially when the rest of the world seems hell-bent on confusing me.

A half-block from Mass Ave, I see Henna on Newbury, where Poppy works. Of course, if she can't make class she wouldn't be at work. Still, someone there might know how she's doing or where to find her. Gaye's gallery can wait, I suppose.

The place smells like incense and cloves. It's filled with hippie-like clothes, chunky beaded jewelry, and what look like tribal drums and other handmade instruments. I tap the call bell next to the little sign: *Please ring for service*. While waiting, I check out the goods in the glass case. Pipes and glass baubles and—are those voodoo dolls?

"How can I help—"

She must be as surprised to see me as I am to see her. "Poppy, you're working?"

"Sami, you're . . . shopping?"

"No, not shopping. Looking for you, actually."

"Okay. So, you found me. Now what?" She folds her arms. "Are you going to turn me in?"

"Why haven't you been at class?"

Her arms fall to her sides. "Boss lady is sick. Like, going through radiation sick. She needs me to man the shop. I'm too much of a sucker to say no."

"But what about the program?"

A one-shoulder shrug. "I told you I wasn't officially in the program. So it's not a travesty to miss a class here and there."

"To me it is. And you've missed more than one class. I haven't seen you for two days at least."

Poppy's hard edges smooth. She almost looks pleased that someone misses her. "Well, I can't see making up the work after missing all this time. It's a short program to begin with. You know?"

"But Poppy, you have to come back. There's got to be someone else who could man the shop."

She looks at me sideways, and those edges are back. "Really, Sami? Why do you care?"

"I could use a friend right now. You're, like, my only friend there."

"Oh, please. You were barely there anyway."

"What do you mean? I haven't missed one single class."

"In body, maybe, but not in mind."

I gape at her. "Judge much?"

"Oh, forget it. You're here now. I prefer to live in the moment." She comes around the counter and takes my free hand in hers. She gives a sly wink. "Let's sling some henna."

Well, this is unexpected. Poppy insists on painting my

concerto

left hand, claiming my birthmark "offers intrinsic opportunities" to amp up the design. It feels sacrilegious or something to do henna over it, though, so Poppy promises not to cover it, but incorporate the mark as part of the design.

"Is it going to hurt?"

"Not at all. I don't use a needle. It's more like a pen."

"Should I close my eyes?"

"I just told you it wasn't going to hurt, bonehead."

We laugh together, which relaxes me a bit. She prepares the pen-like cone. To my relief, she starts on my pointer finger, away from my birthmark. She works slowly, giving me tips on how to care for henna as she goes.

"It takes a half hour for the henna paste to fully dry. So don't touch it or anything."

With the first henna mark on my finger, I already feel badass and way-cool like Poppy. But I'm still nervous.

She makes small talk. "So, how's Miles Eichen?"

"What do you mean?"

"Oh, are we going to play that game, then? Okay, so anyone with eyes can see the chemistry between you two. You guys grew up together, I heard?"

"You heard?" People are talking about us—about me and Miles. I'm so preoccupied I hardly feel the henna go on. "What are people saying?"

"Just that. And that you're hanging out."

"Which means 'going out.' We're not, though. We're not going out."

"Chill, whatever. It's cool. So, you're just hanging out, then." Her grin is one step from mischievous.

"I have a boyfriend." Why are the words hard to say—even to Poppy?

She shrugs, keeps her head down. "He's playing Friday

at Showcase. I saw him on the signup sheet. Don't know what he's playing, though."

"Piano—*ow*!" Lightning shoots up my arm. I snatch my hand away. "Ouch!"

"Don't smudge—"

"I thought you said it wasn't going to hurt!"

Poppy looks stunned. "It doesn't."

"Um, yes it does. You just . . . burned me. It still stings."

"No, it doesn't. It can't. There's nothing that could burn you." She stands and studies me more closely, trying to see my hand that I'm shaking at my side—careful not to touch it against anything. "Wait. Let me see." Poppy takes my hand. "Holy crap. Your birthmark."

"What about it?"

She doesn't answer. It's like slow motion as I look from her shocked face to my wounded, hennaed hand. My jaw drops with a gasp. The design on my pointer finger looks like tiny bird's wings, overlapping in a cohesive flow past the knuckle. It's gorgeous. And shocking . . .

As the design flows down my hand toward my birthmark, it appears to be stunted, stopped in its tracks. No—singed—like a burnt end of a rope. Around the dark circle of freckles—my Nevus spilus—is a ring of neon blue.

All lit up.

"Holy Magoo," Poppy says. "I've never seen anything like this."

Panic creeps up my throat. "Sorry, Poppy. I've got to go."

I run, breathless, directly to the piano studio at Berklee, holding my hennaed hand away from the rest of my body

concerto

like it's germ-ridden. My birthmark continues to glow, pulsing, angry—it's almost more pain than I can bear. By the time I get to the studio, I'm completely freaked out.

What's happening to me?

Still, there's undeniable excitement, too. That wakeup call on Skene Mountain was a tease compared to this. Mom's words echo: *it's still inside you.* Oh yeah, it's definitely inside me. And it's looking for a way to get out.

I ready myself at middle C, breathing through the pain. *Play. Just . . . play.*

My hands are shaking, and the effort it takes to play music seems unreachable.

One note. Start with one note.

As soon as I depress a key, my birthmark flares. Blue light—not red, thankfully—fills the studio in a quiet burst as music begins from the piano.

But I'm not the one playing.

Where is the music coming from? Is this a trick? Is this a player piano? Maybe my hearing has gone wonky. Or maybe it's playing in my head, like I've resurrected a suppressed memory.

But no. It is me. I am the one playing. The blue light feels like home, so different from the red lightning yesterday. This light energizes me—no, more than that. It comes from me. It's part of me.

Studying my hands, though, these hands that have played ever since I can remember, they seem like someone else's. I watch them move over the keys with command. Is it muscle memory? But the tune isn't something I've played before. It's completely unfamiliar. It's complex and passionate and something I would have had to practice for months before mastering. But, strangely, I'm able to play it without error.

What's going on?

Inexplicably, I'm not afraid. Somehow, it feels right. It feels like this is supposed to happen. I try to relax and force my eyes closed. As the song plays out, I listen carefully, sure there's a message for me there.

Like a flash, an image comes through: a storm hitting a port city. What city is this? I don't know it. It's getting pummeled by rain and severe wind. It grows more intense and violent every second. The images get more disturbing as the music plays on. Quite a storm—it would be categorized as a major hurricane. Extreme stuff I've only seen on the Weather Channel. Windows implode. Trees crash into homes. Waters rise by the second. People are screaming. Running for their lives . . .

In a moment, the music stops. I'm hyperventilating into my hands. Tears start in my eyes. What was that? Some kind of view into the future? This isn't the kind of power I wanted. My music is supposed to help heal the Earth, not help destroy it. I'm full on crying into my hands now, which seem guilty. My birthmark is quiet, but sore.

I look around the room, desperate for answers, when I spy a small, white rectangular paper that had fallen out of my bag onto the floor.

Ms. Aleia's business card. Her office hours end in a half hour.

CHAPTER 16

"Ms. Aleia!" I burst into her office without knocking.

She gives me the once-over, impassive, as if she'd seen me coming. "Heavens, you could start a fire with that heavy breathing." She closes the door behind me, trapping me in her tiny office, and waves at the chair.

But I'm too agitated to sit.

"Something insane just happened. I was in the studio, and I was playing this song. Only it wasn't me playing, really, it was a force, or something and—"

"Samantha." She's frowning, her eyes downcast. "What's on your hand?"

I'd almost forgotten. "Oh, that's just henna. But listen, this song was just coming out of me and—"

Ms. Aleia grasps my hand, cutting me off. She runs a bony, pale finger down the tiny bird's wings design on my finger. When she gets to my birthmark, she circles it with her fingernail. A shudder of disgust runs through me.

"That tickles." I take my hand back. It more than tickles, but I don't want to hint of its power.

"Samantha, what were you thinking? Defacing yourself like that?"

"Defacing? No, it's just henna. It's not a real tattoo. It comes off."

Her face flushes. She's out of breath suddenly. "You must be extremely careful. You can't place tribal marks or foreign etchings or . . . Middle Eastern symbols on your body. Certainly not on your hand. Your hands are for playing music and not playing with henna." There's no color in her face at all. Is it possible she looks even paler than before?

"No, it's fine. It's not done with a needle or anything. It's temporary."

"Are you so naïve, Samantha? Henna is known to cause dermatitis." She leans into my face, showering me with bits of saliva. Her words come out, rapid fire: "Swelling, inflammation, redness, itchiness, scaling, blisters, scarring. Tell me you didn't feel any side effects?"

Her office, like Coach Payne's closet of an office, is too small for me to back away. Claustrophobic. Painful flashbacks flood me.

"Sorry, Ms. Aleia." I clutch my gut. "I'm not feeling so well. I'd like to go to my room. I think I need to lie down."

"Of course you do," she sing-songs. "Because you were fooling around with henna."

"No, that's not it." I try for the door, but she's blocking it.

Seconds tick by on her desk clock. She folds her arms in slow motion. "You came in here all hot to tell me something. What was it?"

It's crystal clear: Ms. Aleia is not any mentor of mine. I can't tell her this. I can't trust her with anything. "Nothing," I hedge. "I mean, I was playing piano and . . . felt inspired."

"In a music therapy kind of way?" She's sneering at me. "Maybe you could play your way to feeling better?"

OMG—she's mocking me. Where did that come from?

She laughs silently and leans against her desk, giving me just enough space to squeeze past her, open the door, and get out.

❧

Back at my dorm, I want to curl up and go to sleep, but I want a shower more. And Jason. I miss Jason more than anything.

My shower is as hot as I can stand it. I want to scrape a layer of skin off. I scrub the henna, which comes off, but the stain remains. I'm fraught with anxiety. Is it true? Is it bad for you? Is it responsible for playing that song? Did it cause that—what was it—hallucination?

That image still haunts me: a massive hurricane devastating that seaside community. So many unknowns: Why did the image come to me? What city is it?

And—why does Ms. Aleia care if I do henna?

I'd told Mom I was a big girl who could take care of herself, but I don't know what the heck I'm supposed to do. Gaye's encouraging words are far away. I feel like I have to do something. But—what? How?

Out of the shower, I wrap myself, still wet, in a snuggly robe, wanting only my bed. This kind of exhaustion rivals what I felt during volleyball training. I grab my phone.

Can u talk?

Jason doesn't respond. I wait three minutes before texting again.

Miss u. Cant wait til Sat

Writing the words brings tears to my eyes. I feel so far away from him. And all this confusing stuff keeps happening. To fill him in, where would I begin? I stare at my phone, willing those dots to appear that tell me he's responding.

concerto

Nothing. And then, nothing.

I fall into bed with my hair wrapped in a towel. Crying myself to sleep seems like a good option. *Come on, tears. Take me away. . . .*

Knock, knock, knock.

Blinking my clock into focus, I see that I'd been asleep for almost an hour.

"Hold on," I say, scrambling out of bed. Should I throw on some clothes? Lip gloss? The door is open before I'm awake enough to decide.

It's Miles. My hand goes to my chest, cinching my robe at my sternum.

"Oh. Hey."

"Hey." He pushes into my room and sits on my bed, on my sheets that are still warm from my sleeping body. I'm overly conscious of being naked beneath my robe.

"What's up?" I instinctively take the towel from my hair. Judging by Miles' expression, it must reveal a lovely rat's nest.

"What are you doing?" he asks, a primer for *Want to do something with me?*

"I'm . . . I was sleeping."

"Quite the nap. But it's not even seven o'clock. Are you in for the night or what?"

"I-I don't know." The fog clears. Something clicks. "Hey, did you tell anyone anything . . . about us?"

"Um, well, let's see. Maybe." He reclines on my bed, propping an elbow on my pillow. "Like, what would I tell 'anyone' about us?"

He's touching my sheets. And my pillow. It feels all too cozy and familiar. He shouldn't be here. Heat builds under my robe. Moisture gathers under my boobs and armpits. It steams off me in a spring-fresh Ivory scent. "I mean, did you tell people we were hanging out?"

"Aren't we?"

My sigh must stink like sleep. "You know what I mean."

"No, I don't." He reaches into his pocket. "I brought you something."

He puts a box, a beautiful glass box, in my hands. It's slightly bigger than a ring box and is edged with shiny gold piping.

"Oh!" All that heat under my robe transfers to my face. A giddy laugh bubbles out, and I turn it into a joke. "Hey, what's the idea? It's empty."

He opens the top via the tiny gold latch, letting his strong, bronze fingers linger over mine. "It's for you to fill."

"For me to fill? With what?"

He stands, and the box is between us, which he holds with me, his fingers interlaced with mine. My mouth goes dry as other parts go wet.

"Seashells. What else?" He leans close. So close our lips almost touch. He smells like warm sand. It's intoxicating. "Come to the beach with me on Saturday."

CHAPTER 17

Showcase night. Sitting in the auditorium, it's like I'm a tiny flea lost in dog fur. Inconsequential. Not like Miles, whose stardom will shine brightly tonight. Inside my stomach is a trapped hummingbird. He's got to stop doing this to me.

Come to the beach with me on Saturday.

The scent of his words lingered on my lips, feeling more intimate than if we'd kissed. Pulling away, ignoring my total-body trembling, I was careful not to make any promises. How could I? Jason's coming to visit. And even though I told Miles that earlier this week, he was insistent.

"I told you I have plans."

"Plans can change, though." His grin was devilish. "Plans change all the time."

He wasn't backing down, so I gave him a glimmer of hope. "I'll think about it." My smile made the glimmer more like a beacon.

But there's nothing to think about. I'll tell him—firmly!—after the performance tonight. Jason is coming. He would be here now if he weren't going to that concert tonight in Newport. But yes, my boyfriend is coming to see me. End of discussion.

Maybe that's what's causing the nerves.

People pour into the auditorium like it's a Taylor Swift

concerto

concert. The energy is contagious. Waiting for the performance to start, I'm reminded of Brenna's plays back in Skenesboro with a mixture of nostalgia and melancholy. They were so impressive. Year after year, more and more elaborate: Brenna's screenplay and Jason's set design. It made me so proud to know them—my best friend and boyfriend. That pride fills me now and weighs on my heart. It's been two weeks since I've spoken to Brenna, who's deep in her program at Tisch by now. If it weren't frowned upon, I'd text her this moment to see how she's doing. She would love this. Maybe she could visit one of these Fridays and come to Showcase. The Chinatown/NYC-to-Boston bus is super cheap.

Poppy and Aunt Gaye both asked me to save them seats. Questions swirl for both. For Poppy: why did I have such a reaction to henna? I haven't seen her since running out of her shop when my birthmark went electric. Part of me wants to talk to her about it, part of me hopes she doesn't remember it.

For Gaye: what's her connection to Ms. Aleia?

Speaking of, Ms. Aleia peeks out from the velvet curtain—a wisp of stark white against the vivid red. Safely hidden in the crowd, I study her. The determined look on her face, as if this performance means more than music. Maybe she's the stage manager? Her words from Orientation come back to me.

There's more to music than meets the ear . . . By the end of this program, my students will experience an entirely different and surprising side of music.

It had inspired me before. Now it makes me uneasy.

Aunt Gaye appears at the entrance, looking ravishing in a sage green cape. I signal to her, and she makes her way to my aisle. As she settles in, I lean in to whisper, "I've been wanting to talk to you about Ms. Aleia."

She busies herself undoing her cape. "I hear Jason's coming to visit tomorrow."

I smile through my surprise. My communication with my boyfriend has been limited to two-word texts and lots of emojis. It's like the relationship has been cheapened to simple cartoons of smiley faces and hearts. My heart is torn between those cartoons and a live, trapped hummingbird that won't quit: Miles.

The fact that Jason's been in contact with Gaye makes me swell with envy. "You talked to Jason?"

"Well, sure. I have to check up on him, too."

"And he answered his phone?"

What the heck? *He never answers his phone.*

"Child, I don't do the texting, so he has no option but to talk to me the good old-fashioned way." She pats my knee. "He's eager to see you."

"I know. I miss him, too." I miss his voice, which Aunt Gaye has had the honor of hearing. I miss his laugh. The way he eats. I miss the way he holds a paintbrush. The cedar smell of his skin. Losing myself in his arms. Being away from him is harder than I thought it would be. And it has everything to do with Miles. Tears unexpectedly fill my eyes. I blink them away, turning my attention to the stage.

Ms. Aleia peeks out again, panning the audience until—I swear—she looks right at me. Out of everyone in the crowd, she's staring me down. I nudge Aunt Gaye and am about to ask her my burning question—*What's your connection to Ms. Aleia?*—when I realize it's not me getting the stink eye from the white woman. It's Aunt Gaye.

"There she is," Gaye says, more to herself than to me.

concerto

Her voice is ruthlessly bitter. "Who's her minion this summer?"

What the heck does that mean? Turning back to the white woman, I notice she is not alone backstage, scouring the audience, glaring at Aunt Gaye.

Miles is with her.

"Ah, a boy this time," Gaye says, speaking of Miles.

My Miles. A protective feeling comes over me.

"I know him," I tell Gaye. "We grew up together in New York." I leave it at that.

"Oh, really?" Gaye sucks air through her teeth.

My eyes stay on Miles. Can't help it. Ms. Aleia is whispering something to him, and his arm is around her. Wait— *is his arm around her?* Why would that be? A stab of jealousy hits me before I rationalize it. *Come on, Sami.* It's like the Jason and Brenna thing. Miles is in the program; he's performing at a Showcase on piano. She's the stage manager. Or director. They're working together. Of course that's what they're doing. Besides, she's, like, a hundred years old. Isn't she?

That's the weird thing. When she first appeared on stage during Orientation, she seemed a hundred years old. Her hair was so white I assumed it was gray. Her frame was so slight, it seemed wracked with old age. Yet, up close, she shows hardly a sign of aging. Her face is porcelain. Her skin unmarked by the sun. Her hair white blond, not gray. Her thin frame dainty, petite, like a child's.

Still, Miles couldn't possibly be into her. Could he?

Even though there are other performers, Ms. Aleia seems solely interested in Miles. She's bending his ear, speaking urgently. Now he's whispering animatedly to her. They're in some kind of heated discussion.

House lights dim, a cue it's about to start. Poppy's still not here.

The first showcase is a flutist. She's wonderful but stiff as a board and could use a healthy lesson in stage presence.

Poppy slides in next to me as they transition performers. Following a hidden impulse, I squeeze her hand. She gives me one of her wry smiles. It cements our friendship somehow.

Next, dance and drums. Amazing stuff. It's like watching a group of street dancers. They use overturned buckets and aluminum trash lids to make their music *à la* STOMP.

"Very cool," Poppy says.

"That's it," I say, feeling inspired. "I'm signing up for Showcase next week."

She gives me the thumbs up as the next performer is announced. By Ms. Aleia. The only performer she's introduced. Of course, it's Miles.

He strolls out to the baby grand in what looks like a black tuxedo from the 1700s—with ruffles running down his chest. It's like he's channeling Mozart. Anyone else would look ridiculous, but he makes it look exotic. Stately. Like, he's clearly at a higher level than any other performer tonight. My heart picks up against my will, despite the fact that Jason's flesh and blood sits next to me.

"I wonder what he'll play." Gaye's tone is snarky.

A nervous laugh flutters out, my eyes glued on Miles. He doesn't sit on the bench straightaway, but makes a grand gesture to the audience. Towards me.

"This is dedicated to one of my oldest and dearest friends."

He winks, and my cheeks burn. Gaye's eyes are on me. I don't dare look in her direction.

concerto

I've hardly collected myself before he begins. It starts soft, in an unusual key, and then grows into a refrain that's somehow familiar. As chords roll out fluidly, the song takes me to another place. As beautiful as Miles is to watch, my eyes close . . . and a nightmare image replays behind my lids.

A storm hitting a port city, pummeled by rain and wind, more intense every second. Windows implode. Trees crash into homes. People are screaming. Running for their lives . . . a major hurricane.

My eyes pop open in alarm—and go to Ms. Aleia, who stands downstage right, watching me—or Gaye—intently. This song.

This song!

It isn't a well-known piece. I've only heard it once before. Miles is performing the same song I played in the studio the other day, after my birthmark went electric. When I played outside of myself, as if possessed.

Miles is playing the exact song.

And the same image comes to me now as it did then: that terrible hurricane.

Miles' playing becomes more impassioned as he crescendos to the song's climax. Aunt Gaye gasps beside me and grips my arm. The look on her face is sheer terror. She only says one word, but it's enough: "Jason."

Oh, my God. Jason's in danger.

CHAPTER 18

Gaye and I manage to squeeze out of the packed auditorium while Miles is still playing. A humid rain shower changes Mass Ave in an instant. It drums onto the street, making it opaque with foam. Steam billows from the concrete as a chill takes the air. Thunder roars overhead. Due south, lightning strikes in a frightening cluster—the storm is coming from there. And Newport isn't that far away. Jason!

Everything erupts in chaos. People are running for shelter, gripping their clothes as if they might blow right off their bodies. We start to run through the rain and instantly get soaked. My hair becomes a mop of wet snakes smacking my face as we keep running, fighting the wind to get to a nearby store's awning for shelter, fear taking our words. Still, I tell myself that summer storms are normal. Thunderstorms in July are not unheard of in the Northeast. *Please let that be all it is in Rhode Island.* But even here . . . it's different. I've never experienced anything like this.

My first call to Jason goes right to voicemail.

Gaye whips out her flip phone to try him. She has no luck, either.

"He must have it silenced or something," I tell her.

"Do the texting." She waves a hand near my screen.

I open Messages but go blank. It dawns on me we're going on mere intuition here. We don't know for sure Jason's in danger. "What do I say that won't be weird?"

concerto

"Are you really worried about being weird right now? You young people are incredible. Just, go. Do it."

We huddle over my screen. My thumbs are itchy over the tiny keypad before tapping the letters.

Call me

Gaye looks at me expectantly. "That's it? That's your texting?" Gaye is red-faced with concern. "Do you think you could be a bit more specific?"

Storm here. Worried about u. r u ok?

Woop. SENT.

"How's that?"

"Better." A few beats pass. Gaye bounces on her heels. "So now what? Why isn't he answering?"

"I don't know. His notifications might be off."

"What's the point of the texting then?" Gaye's hands fly overhead. "It makes no sense. Never mind. Let's call the school."

"Jason's not at campus. He's at a concert in Newport."

"But the school might know something."

"Right. Okay." I open a browser and find the main number for RISD campus.

Something clicks on the line, and the circular ringing on RISD's side seems endless—an unavailable answering service. I click off and notice the tremor of my hands.

"They didn't answer?" Gaye asks. "Why did you hang up?"

With my back to the wind, I tap the RISD website and zoom in, ignoring the sudden pallor of my fingers. No announcements or emergency messages. I make a fist and breathe through a sudden bout of dizziness.

What do we do now?

Gaye grasps my arm. "Oh, my Lord. Put the damn phone away."

I follow her line of vision through the window of a nearby tavern, where breaking news has made a headline:

Hundreds forced to evacuate as sudden hurricane devastates Newport, RI.

Blood drains from my face. I feel like I'm hyperventilating. "I'm going there. Right now. I have to get to South Station."

"Sam, are you mad? You can't go to the site of a natural disaster—in the middle of said natural disaster! Let's get more information."

We push our way into the tavern to see the full news story. My retinas go numb; it's exactly what I saw Wednesday in the studio after my birthmark went electric—when that song poured out of me. The same song that Miles was just playing for Showcase. Wait a sec—

Things begin to click in place—a mental Candy Crush score. This can't be a coincidence.

"Aunt Gaye—"

Her phone interrupts me. Her face lights up in an instant.

"Jason? Is it really you? We just saw on the news—"

My boyfriend. My turn. The phone's in my hand before she can fight me for it.

"Jason, what's going on? It says there's a hurricane." All I hear is wind. It's screeching through the phone. "Jason?" I have to yell. "Are you there?"

He's in and out. Bad connection. ". . . so much water . . . out of nowhere." His voice cracks with emotion.

concerto

"Jason?" I shout over the rush of wind. "I'm coming down there. I'm coming to help. Can you hear me?"

Sirens. A muffled thump against the phone, like it's hitting something. Jason calls over the noise, "Are you—crazy? . . . have no idea! . . . serious stuff, Sami."

"Where are you now?"

"Hotel . . . bunch of us . . ."

"You're with your RISD friends?" Visions of Sydney put a knot in my chest—and I immediately chide myself for it. *Jason's in danger, Sami.*

". . . lost some of them."

Panic numbs me. "What? You lost them?" And here I am worrying he might be with Sydney? And Jason's friends are missing—maybe killed? My head shudders side to side. *No, no, no.* This can't be happening.

A woman screaming. A man—policeman?—yelling instructions. "Gotta go." Jason yells to someone far away. It cuts off mid-word.

Disconnected.

"Jason? Jason!"

The line is dead.

The knot in my chest has invaded my lungs. I'm unable to breathe. I'm shaking all over. A sob chokes my throat. He might as well be in Thailand. What good is living close by if I can't help during emergencies like this?

I slide Gaye's flip phone across the table to her, avoiding her eyes. "So?"

"I could barely hear him. There was so much noise. So much wind. I could only make out a few words. He's missing some of his friends he went down with—" All at once it's too much, and my tears win out. Gaye hands me a handkerchief, and I cry behind it. "I can't be with him now. I feel like I need to be there. I'm so helpless!"

"We're both helpless right now," Gaye says. "But he's alive."

"I think he's in a hotel. Maybe there's a makeshift emergency shelter there? But it sounded so scary."

Gaye covers her mouth and stares at the sodas the waitress delivered while I was talking to Jason. I hadn't realized Gaye had ordered anything, but I'm grateful. A bowl of popcorn acts as a centerpiece.

"I don't even know if he's going to be able to make it here tomorrow."

Gaye looks at me like I've grown horns. "Sam, of course he's not going to make it tomorrow. He'll be lucky if he can make it to RISD. He may have to stay at that hotel for a few days. Depends on whether there's another storm surge."

"What?"

"Never mind. It's just . . . this isn't over. These things are never simple. They're messy. For a long time."

"I know, but I haven't seen him since that first weekend." My voice is whiny. "And that was way awkward. There are only—what—two weeks left to the program? Soon, I'll be back in Skenesboro, and I'll never see him."

Gaye blinks at me. "Oh, please. The drama is getting out of hand. Let's put things into perspective, shall we?"

I dry my eyes with Gaye's handkerchief and take a long drink.

"If only I could use my magic to save Jason right now. If only my music could rescue him. Lift him up out of the storm and back to safety."

"That would be pretty miraculous." She gives me a small smile and then tosses a few neon-yellow kernels in her

concerto

mouth. I can almost taste the salt from across the table. She frowns as she chews and pushes the bowl away. "Cardboard."

Out the tavern's window, the rain is steady, relentless. It seems angry. Thunder drums in the sky. Maddening. It dawns on me Showcase is still going on.

"Aunt Gaye, did you recognize that song Miles played? Is it famous or something?"

She rolls a plump shoulder. "I think it's original, knowing Aleia. But I could be wrong. Why?"

"What do you mean 'knowing Aleia'? How do you know her?"

Gaye takes a breath. "It's a long, sordid story. Why did you ask about the song?"

"It's going to sound weird. But last night, I was in the studio, and I played that exact song."

"Hmm . . . Didn't you and Miles grow up together? Maybe it was something you learned when you were little?"

"No. It couldn't be. Besides, he didn't play piano until, well, recently. But, Aunt Gaye, it was more than the song. When I played, it was like the music came out on its own, like it had a couple years ago on Skene Mountain. Nothing happened this time, though, except . . ."

"What?"

"I saw things. I had another vision."

"What did you see?"

"That's the thing." I lower my voice. "I saw the storm. I saw a hurricane ruining a port city. Like what's happening in Newport."

"You saw the future," she says, without a hint of mockery.

"I guess. As soon as I heard Miles playing, it all came

rushing back, and I could feel it happening." Gaye nods, and it gives me courage. "But, Aunt Gaye, how did you know something was wrong? We both had an inkling Jason was in trouble at the exact same time. What triggered it for you?"

Gaye eats more stale popcorn. It's like a nervous tic. "You know, humans are not the only beings on the planet. And not the most important, either. Or the most powerful, despite what some might think."

"Okay. But I don't get what that has to do with—"

"Remember you asked me about how I knew Aleia? Well, from my past experiences with that woman, I know what she's capable of. I didn't know it had to do with Jason. Not until I looked into your eyes. Then, my gut told me."

"Your gut told you?"

"You have your magic, and I have mine, I guess." Her smile holds secrets.

"Then it's Ms. Aleia who did this," I say more to myself than to Gaye. "Not Miles."

She takes a long sip of her ginger ale. "He can't be completely innocent. I'm not sure what she's up to, but I intend to find out."

I keep checking the tavern's TV for the latest on the storm, but the same headline keeps looping in a red banner across the screen.

Suddenly, Poppy appears at our table—flushed and out of breath. And dripping wet.

"Sami, Miles is looking for you."

My face goes hot. Miles is looking for me?

"Why?" I blurt, grinning like a dope—and unintentionally watch for Gaye's reaction, which is flat-borderline-frown. Which makes me ask her: "What?"

Her eyebrows go sky-bound. "You're asking me? I

concerto

should be asking you!"

Poppy's focused on me. "Showcase is over. Everyone's hanging around the student lounge. Go and find him."

"Why should I? It's not like I'm his girlfriend or anything." I say this for Gaye's sake, and she knows it. Her wrinkled hand encircles mine.

"Go," she says. "Find out what you can. But don't let on that you know anything about what's happened in Rhode Island. Don't say anything about the song. Don't let on that you're Goshenite."

My jaw drops as I look from Gaye to Poppy and back again. Gaye just spilled a huge secret about who I am. Strangely, Poppy doesn't react.

"Don't worry about Poppy. She's one of your kind. You should've figured that out by now."

Poppy's smile is knowing. "I sure figured it out. As soon as your birthmark went wild at the shop. It all clicked into place."

"But, how would you know? Are you Goshenite?"

"Yeah. We're all over. Not just in your little mountain town."

I look back at Gaye, who's flushed with awkwardness. Her shoulders go to her ears. "Not me. I'm just a supporter."

Poppy tugs on my arm, impatient. "We can explain later. You've got to go to Miles—now while it's hot."

"While what's hot?"

"His powers. Magic. Whatever you want to call it."

I wave a lame goodbye to Gaye as Poppy drags me out of the tavern. "He's Goshenite, too?"

"Not sure. He's got to be with another group. But that's what we need you to figure out."

"We? Okay, Poppy. You have to give me more than

that."

Rain pelts us as she leads me down Mass Ave, giving me an exasperated look. "Okay, real quick. Keep Miles on the hook—even if you'd rather date a warthog. We need info from him. And if he trusts you and thinks he can win you over—"

"What information, though? What am I supposed to ask? Gaye said I can't talk about the song, and I can't let on that I know anything."

"Gaye's right. And if you're, like, 'whatever' about his powers, he'll want to show them off to you, alpha-male style. We've got to know what his plan is. Then we can make one."

"Poppy, wait. How . . . Hold on. Have you been working with Gaye? I didn't realize you knew each other."

"Newbury Street is small enough. Like its own little hub. The shops work together on things. Besides, she has the same goals."

"Same, how? What goals?"

Poppy looks annoyed. "To save the world, bonehead."

I'm so shocked, I don't know what to ask next. Poppy doesn't waste a second. "There he is," she says with urgency. "Go!" She shoves me through the entrance. Right into his path.

And Miles practically catches me.

CHAPTER 19

My skin slick from the rain, I slide into Miles' embrace.

"Whoa, easy. There you are." He's like a warm towel. I shiver against him.

"I thought I lost ya," he says, pulling me closer.

I squirm away and look for Poppy, who's suddenly disappeared.

"You missed the show." He gives me an exaggerated frown.

"I was there. I saw the whole thing."

"Not the whole thing. You left in the middle of it. Why'd you leave?"

My eyes widen. "You noticed I left, as focused as you were?"

He lifts my hand for a gentleman's kiss, except his lips don't touch. His breath warms my knuckles. My birthmark spasms, like ants are beneath the skin.

"Of course. I'm keeping tabs on you." He glides his lips over my hand, barely touching. Goosebumps rise. His eyes stay on mine. It feels like he can see into my thoughts. For the first time since our reunion, danger lurks. I take my hand back, rubbing the rain from my arms.

He puffs his chest. "What did you think? I'm dying to know."

Seriously? He's asking me about his piano skills? As if it matters anymore.

concerto

He's waiting. I have to give him something.

"You played beautifully." My voice curlicues. "I was really impressed."

Can he hear how fake that sounds? If he notices my robotic tone, he doesn't let on. He flashes me a spectacular grin and threads my arm into his. He leads me out of the student lounge and on to Mass Ave—where the rain has diminished to a fine mist. Interesting. The storm died down just as Miles finished playing . . .

I frantically search for Poppy among the crowd, but she's nowhere to be seen.

Miles chatters busily as we walk. It doesn't occur to me until we've crossed to Newbury Street to ask, "Where are we going?"

"Ice cream. To celebrate."

"Celebrate what?"

My tone is harsh. Miles frowns. For a moment, he looks like a young boy—vulnerable and needy—and I remember the Miles from my childhood. My heart softens, and I reprimand myself for turning so quickly. I squeeze his arm, which is still linked in mine.

"Sorry," I say. "Of course we need to celebrate. You were amazing tonight."

Switch flipped: he's back to his confident swagger. "Really? Do you think?"

I smile at the pavement. Our steps are off. His gait is too long for me, and our footfalls sound like a drummer's flam. Not like the way it is with Jason. When Jason walks beside me, we're totally in sync. Like we were made to walk side by side. It's a little thing, but it gives me pause.

He holds the door for me. When I pass through, he whispers into my hair, "I have a surprise for you."

My heart flutters despite my better judgment. "You do?"

He nods and steps to the counter. Without asking, he orders mint chocolate chip—my childhood favorite—for both of us. He hands me my cone with a wink. "You didn't think I'd forget, did you?"

My smile is bittersweet. It was also Lauren's favorite. He leads me to a booth toward the back, and I position myself with a view of the door. Although I'm watching for her, Poppy's sudden entrance jolts me. Our eyes meet for a millisecond before she takes a seat near the front without ordering anything. Her look says: *I got your back.*

My shoulders come away from my ears. I take an easy breath. There's an invisible power shift; I can feel it. Now's the time to take charge.

"It's a good surprise." I slurp up a chip. "I didn't know you liked mint chip, too."

Miles studies me and then barks a laugh. "No, my surprise isn't the ice cream, sweetheart. You're going to see my dad. Tomorrow. He promised he'd be there this time. He was bummed to miss you last week."

My eyes are slits. "Miles, I told you I have plans tomorrow. My boyfriend is coming to visit."

He blinks rapidly, like he's caught. "He's not still coming, though, is he?"

"Why wouldn't he?" I chomp my ice cream. This should be good. How could he possibly know Jason's plans have changed?

He's flustered. It's comical how he tries to stay cool and composed. I glance at Poppy, who gives me a slight nod of encouragement.

I don't let Miles answer. "Why would you think Jason's

133

concerto

not coming?"

He smirks. "I was hoping."

"That's it? Just hope?"

He hides behind his ice cream. "I caught a headline at the lounge. Rhode Island is in some deep waters." He chuckles.

"It's not funny."

"I know. It's not funny." He gets solemn, but it's all a façade. "It's very serious. Is your mountain man okay?"

My spikes come out. "You can call him Jason. And, yes. Miraculously, it seems he's okay. For now. I think he's at a hotel. Some sort of shelter. His friends are lost, though. So he's freaking out. And, as you can imagine, I'm freaking out, too."

"Oh, wait—was he in Newport?"

"I told you he was. At a concert."

"Oh, geez. I must've forgotten that. Yikes. How awful." Ugh, he's a bad actor. "Are you okay? This has probably rocked you to the core. No wonder you're a little off."

That makes me prickle. Poppy's gaze is expectant. He's got to give me more than this. "Do you think it's over? The storm or whatever?"

"Oh, yeah. It's over."

"How do you know?" I catch myself. "I mean, maybe we should check the news or the Weather Channel or something."

His tone is strange. It's like he's wrung out. "Trust me. It's done. It was enough."

"What do you mean by that?" *Is he claiming responsibility?* He's businesslike all of a sudden. Maybe pissed. He throws out our nearly-empty cones. Discussion over. Did I cross a line?

"Let's get you back to the dorms," he says almost sadly.

Outside on Newbury Street, a new resolve fills me. I can do this. I can glean information from this guy. I've got his trust. If I play my cards right, he'll tell me everything.

"Yeah. Jason can't come up tomorrow." I say quietly. "But I'm not happy about it."

"I know," he says. "You're worried about your mountain man—Jason, I mean. Even if he's okay. It's hard to be away when something big and scary happens like that."

"The whole thing is beyond upsetting. I've never been through anything like this before. It's terrifying."

"My gosh, it's gotta be. But, let me just say . . . if you can't be with him, you can at least help yourself."

"What do you mean by that?"

"You know. I don't know. Take care of yourself." He half-grins. "Make yourself feel better."

"How do you suggest I do that?"

"Come with me tomorrow. Let's go to the beach. It'll wash your sorrows away."

"You think?"

"Promise."

My skin goes cold and damp. The idea of going anywhere with Miles makes me a little sick. Part of me wants to tell him where to stick it. I mean, if he did cause that storm? If he's responsible for this major thing? Jason could've died. A death toll hasn't been announced yet, but I'm sure it's coming.

But—what if he didn't cause the storm? And what if he can lead me to the answers that Gaye and Poppy are so desperate to find? Poppy's words come back to me: *we need to know what his plan is.* It's not like I can come out and ask him. What if it's all a weird coincidence? He might not have

concerto

anything to do with the storm in Rhode Island.

I know what I have to do. And I'm doing it for Gaye . . . and for Jason. If an evil force is trying to hurt him, I'm going to find out who it is and how to stop it.

It's not my heart but my mind that answers. "Maybe you're right." I shrug for effect. "Okay. I guess I'll go. It can't hurt, anyway. Right?"

He gives me a sideways hug. "That's my girl."

My insides recoil. I'm not his girl. Not now. Not ever. If I'm sure of one thing, it's that.

All I can think about is Jason. If he's found his friends. Whether he needs me, just to talk, even. My excuse to get a good night's rest before our beach day works.

Finally alone in my room, I call. He answers.

"Jason, I can't stop thinking about what's happening down there. It kills me I can't be there with you."

"I can't tell you . . . I wish this wasn't happening." His voice wavers, on the brink of tears. It's eerily quiet in the background.

"Did you find your friends?"

"No." He chokes on the word. "The police are on it. There's a search. They're not the only ones. Eight people have died already."

"What? You're kidding."

"Might be more. It's not over."

"Jason, what can I do? Let me do something. If roads are closed and trains aren't running and I can't get there, maybe there's something else. Maybe make some calls for you? If there's anything you need, say the word and I'll do it. You know that, right?"

"I know. I love you." He says it so fast I almost miss it. "Everything's screwed up. I can't imagine finishing the program. But I also can't imagine leaving Rhode Island any time soon."

I hope he doesn't think I actually expected him to visit. "Oh, I know. I support anything you need right now."

"I know you do."

"Love you."

"I know you do."

Hearing his voice is like medicine, but I feel so helpless it hurts.

Guilt creeps into my psyche. The terrifying thought has crossed my mind: maybe I'm the one responsible for the storm. I'm the one who had the vision the night before. What if I'm the one with the power—my magic turning on me or out of my control—and I unintentionally caused it? I cry against my pillow, hugging it tightly, wishing it were Jason by my side.

Sleep seems impossible, but tears are my sedative. I fall into a deep sleep. My dreams take me on a boat way out to sea. I'm on a whale watch or a deep-sea fishing excursion. The calm waters are soothing at first, and then out of nowhere a storm moves in. With it, enormous, angry waves. It throws me from port to starboard as if I'm a ragdoll. Until suddenly a miracle occurs as only can happen in a dream: I'm lifted out of the boat and up over the storm clouds, flying with seagulls toward the horizon. Someone has saved me— carrying me high in the sky like Superman. Although my dream doesn't show his face, I know it's Miles.

And it wakes me with a jolt.

CHAPTER 20

Such a different feeling heading to the beach this time. To think, a week ago today, I'd been flirting with disaster, flattered by Miles' attention. All those good vibes have been swapped with trepidation. Images of that hurricane loom in the back of my mind, and I suspect Miles is responsible for it. His charm and good looks are still there, but don't have the same effect on me. It's like my eyes have been opened. I won't let myself be distracted.

"Carsick," I complain and pretend to sleep most of the ride up. (Poppy coached me on some avoidance strategies.) Thankfully, Miles doesn't press me. He plays soft music and leaves me alone.

We pull up to the vanilla taffy house, and I swallow down the icky feeling that plagued me the whole trip from Boston.

"Are you feeling any better?" he asks as we get out of his Camry.

My groaning sigh is pure melodrama. "I think I just needed some ocean air."

He eats it up. "I told you! It's the antidote for every-thing." He slings his messenger bag over his shoulder and shortens the space between us. "Soon, you won't be able to stay away."

His breath is minty and brushes my lips like a kiss. Tick-les me everywhere. As he locks his eyes on mine, heat creeps

concerto

up my neck and takes my words. It pisses me off. Why does he affect me like this?

"Miles!" A burly, bearded man waves from the vanilla taffy door. He's wearing a white bathrobe, open to show his bathing suit and oversized gut. It's been half a decade since I've seen him, Miles' father. Not sure I would've recognized him out of context.

"Dad, you remember Sami, right?"

Mr. Eichen gives me a big bear hug. "Sami! What happened? You were an itty-bitty thing. Look at you now! So pretty and tall. You must have all the boys after you."

"Hi, Mr. Eichen."

He leads us to the stairs. "What's this 'Mr. Eichen' stuff? Don't make me an old man. Call me Posh."

He studies me a moment too long. Miles gives me a secretive smile.

"After you," Posh says. My arms hug my midsection as I lead the way up the stairs into the taffy house—acutely aware of my short shorts. Why didn't I think to dress with more . . . clothes?

Inside, Posh has '50s jive music blasting from the surround sound. He does a little dance into the kitchen, making his robe sway like a ball gown. He swivels back, offering me strawberries from a shell-shaped bowl. I take the biggest one in the bunch. It's perfectly ripe and fills my mouth with such sweetness, I feel myself relax.

"Come. Ocean calls," he shouts over the music.

Holding up my tote bag, I gesture to the bathroom. Last week's ride home in a sticky, sandy bathing suit taught me a lesson: never beach without a change of clothes. Posh waves me on and keeps dancing. In spite of everything, his joy makes me smile.

140

As I close myself in the bathroom, the track changes to a ballad. It's an old love song: *I Only Have Eyes for You*. The original, by the Flamingos. Mom used to play it in the car. It's supposed to be heartwarming, but to me, it sounds sad.

In the mirror, natural light from the window shows a constellation of tiny pimples on my chin. It also makes my hazel eyes shine with bits of green sparkling through. Everything's brighter at the beach. Even on a cloudy day. I lather my face in sunscreen, silently giving my reflection a pep talk. *Sami, you're not here to have fun. You are on a mission. Get whatever information you can.*

I frown into the mirror. How?

It's like Poppy and Aunt Gaye are nudging me from afar: *What's the extent of Miles' power? What's he trying to do? What does he want?*

Besides me.

Or not. Maybe Miles doesn't like me in that way after all. Maybe it's something else. Maybe he knows my music unlocks special powers. Or senses it. Maybe he hopes I can help him.

Still. No one—not Jason, not any boy—has ever been so aggressive trying to win me over. He won't take no for an answer, and it sends me reeling. Why me? To get this kind of attention, I would have to be someone special. He would not do all this, whisking me away to the beach two Saturdays in a row if he didn't like me—like, really like me.

That full-of-helium feeling gets to my head. Even now, when I know it's wrong—perhaps even dangerous—I still can't believe he likes me. Now that things are definitely done with Lauren, does he want me to be his girlfriend? After all this time? Or does he see me as an extension of her

concerto

somehow? Gosh, I wish she were here. She could illuminate all the gray, give me the real deal.

But she's not here, so it's up to me to figure it out. I yank my suit out of my tote. There's work to be done. Enough wasting time. I'm not solving any mysteries in the bathroom.

I Only Have Eyes for You gets softer, dissolving into the background. "Geez, Dad, you're going to go deaf if you don't watch out."

As I wiggle out of my shorts, something shifts. Everything gets still on the other side of the door. The music is faint. Miles and his dad are talking in hushed tones. My curiosity gets the best of me. I put my ear against the door to eavesdrop. I'm coming into the conversation midway . . .

"But you missed the mark," Posh says. "I'm not sure what you were trying to do, but you need to be more careful."

Miles talks more quietly. It's hard to understand him.

"Didn't she direct you? It's supposed to move inland. I don't know what you were thinking."

Who's "she?" Ms. Aleia?

Another mumble from Miles. It goes on and on. I press my ear so hard against the door my earring nearly impales me.

The next thing from Posh comes out strained, as if he's talking through his teeth. "So you ripped up a slab of New England coast to get a date?"

My stomach drops to my feet. It takes huge effort not to react. I can't believe what I'm hearing. Seriously? That was what the storm was all about—getting rid of Jason? So Miles could have me all to himself?

No way. Can't be. No one would stoop that low.

Miles shushes him and says something else . . . about Lauren. And then in a stream of sentences that run together, all I can make out is my name. If it were possible, I'd make him take it back. My name shouldn't be a factor in whatever they're discussing. Lauren's either. I'm suddenly super protective of her.

But—what exactly are they talking about?

"Really?"—a hearty laugh—"Ah, so I see. I get it. She's a pretty girl. Remember, though, we need to stay the course."

Miles' turn. Is he using sign language? I can't hear a word he says.

Posh's whisper attempt fails. "If you can work both ends, that's fine. But don't forget our commitment, son. It's not just about me or us, but Aleia, too. We can't let her down. Not after all she's done for us."

My jaw has dropped so much I'm almost drooling. They are talking about Ms. Aleia. *Work both ends? What's that supposed to mean?*

"Sami? Did you fall in?" Miles calls, and I nearly trip into the toilet trying to straighten myself.

I tap my cheeks briskly to snap myself alert. "Just a sec!"

Must work quickly. My mini notebook and pen are out of my tote, and I scribble madly about what I just overheard.

"Missed the mark"
Target = "inland?"
Aleia = partner?

With my notebook safely hidden at the base of my tote under my shorts and panties, I'm out of the bathroom to face a curious couple of Eichens. All Posh's mirth has faded. He stares at me with something close to distrust.

"You okay?" Miles asks.

concerto

Posh turns on his smile and heads to the sand before I can answer. "Let's hit it. I already put out chairs for you."

We gamely follow. It takes a few minutes for my stomach to settle. But the gears in my mind spin all afternoon, thinking about what I'd overheard.

Turns out, it's a good thing Posh is with us today. Romance between me and Miles is not an option. Thank goodness. Even if I don't learn anything beyond my eavesdropping earlier, I'm determined to enjoy the day.

Posh fills every bit of quiet—singing '50s jive, telling jokes . . . mostly talking about the ocean.

"It's nature's medicine, you know. You have a cut or an open wound? Best thing for it is the salt water."

"Well, I don't have any open wounds," I say. "So I think I'm good."

He eyes me in a funny way. "It's part of you, too, you know. Salt. It's inside you, waiting to come out. In your tears, in your sweat."

"In our food." My lame joke doesn't even get a smile. I switch tacks, unable to ignore what's in my heart. "Were there any effects of the hurricane up here?" It takes so much courage to speak the words, my voice sounds different. "The one in Newport last night?"

"Ah, some rain. Waves were huge all through the night." He looks pointedly at Miles, who reclines his beach chair and covers his face with a towel. "It's kind of a miracle today turned out halfway decent, if you want to know the truth."

Yes, I do want to know the truth.

I know I should tread carefully, but part of me wants him to know my suspicions. "Isn't it crazy how a storm so far away has a ripple effect like that?"

"It's really not that far. And it's all connected. You have to be careful. The ocean is like a living, breathing thing. Don't turn your back on it, or it could swallow you whole." His words echo what Miles said last week.

"I know. It can be dangerous," I say, feeling already on dangerous ground. "You have to be careful. Right, Miles?"

Miles mumbles beneath the towel and pretends to sleep.

Posh doesn't say anything for a long while. He looks out to the great expanse of water with an expression similar to how he looks at Miles. It confuses me at first. There's only one word I can think to describe it: pride.

CHAPTER 21

Jason knew I'd gone to the beach with friends. Still, when his text comes through on our way home, guilt dings louder than my notification.

Found them.

Relief fills me. *Thank God. Anyone hurt?*

"Who are you texting?" Miles sounds reproachful.

"Jason." There's no hesitation anymore. "He found his friends."

"Oh, yeah? That's good." He turns away just enough so I can't see his face. What's he thinking?

Another ding: *All okay. Just shaken.*

How r u?

Wish u were here

My heart cries with yearning. There's a good half hour left in the car before we hit Boston. Even if I scrambled to pack, get to the station, and catch a train, it wouldn't get me there until very late. And Gaye and Poppy are waiting for me at the gallery for a download.

My fingers vise-grip my phone. It feels like a cement brick. Jason wants me with him. I can't go. This is what you call SOL. Tears build behind my sunglasses. No text is good

concerto

enough for my feelings right now. All my angst is congealing into an invisible bullet directed at Miles' head.

I turn on him with claws out. "Miles, what song did you play at Showcase last night?"

"What do you mean 'what song'? It's an original. I wrote it myself . . . with Ms. Aleia," he says, indifferent. I want to hate him.

There's got to be more to it. "Wait—so, you never shared it with anyone?"

"Shared it?"

"I mean, did you borrow it? Like, from another piece? Was it inspired by something else? Something famous, maybe?"

"I'm no thief, me lady." He winks, and my stomach goes sour.

"Maybe it's similar to something we listened to growing up?"

Part of me wants this to be true. No magic. No ulterior motive. Whatever vision I had before Showcase, that song a sure warning of what's to come, let it be just a weird coincidence.

"No-ho-ho. Never. We were careful about that."

I bristle at the word "we." Am I jealous?

"That was the idea," he goes on. "To release it on Showcase night." He shifts in his seat. "Why—did it sound familiar?" He twists his face. Borderline panicked.

Backpedal, Sami. "No. . . . No." My voice is cotton-candy light. "I mean, I wish I knew it. I wish I could play it." Now I'm laying it on thick. Too much? "It was powerful," I add softly, the word implying more than I want to let on.

He takes so long to answer, I worry I've blown my

cover. He mouths the word "powerful" to himself in a secretive way.

"That was intentional," he finally says. He gives me his signature smile that now seems cocky.

That didn't go the way I'd hoped. I groan inside.

My watch tells me we have fifteen minutes before we hit Boston—if traffic cooperates. At least. I could be on the train to Rhode Island right now, but no. I'm in the middle of this crazy business with Miles and his music—plucking clues like an amateur sleuth.

Resentment builds. Miles has stolen two Saturdays of my life. Saturdays I should have been spending with Jason. How was he able to lure me away from my boyfriend—the guy I truly love? What's wrong with me that I could be wooed like that—completely swept away, out my senses?

My irritation is so distracting I don't see Miles' hand on my knee before feeling it, warm and firm. Shock and disgust surge as if a tarantula fell on my leg.

"Miles—"

I go to slap his hand away but miss, as my eyes are on Miles—questioning his boldness. He turns, locking his blue eyes onto mine. Something melts inside. Those icky feelings slowly dissolve. He caresses above my kneecap . . . and a sensation travels up my thigh and into my stomach. It takes me off-guard. Paralyzes me. I press my phone between my hands like I'm praying around it.

Miles massages slowly, intensely. Like he's trying to get inside.

I stare at his hand. Those long fingers work my thigh— tan skin against my pale, freshly rosy from the sun. I don't move a muscle. Don't even breathe.

"I missed you today." His voice is soft. Sensual.

concerto

"Miss me? How could you miss me?" My breath gets short. It changes my voice. "I'm right here."

His hand stays there—innocuously caressing near my knee. But a sensation ripples up my thigh to where no one's supposed to go. He doesn't do it, but part of me wants him to go there. Time seems to stand still. It's like I'm outside of myself, watching from above. It's on me to stop him. Swat his hand away or something. But cruel vibrations have all but erased that sadness and frustration I was feeling just a moment ago, missing Jason.

Oh, my gosh . . . Jason!

"Stop!" My outburst shocks both of us, and Miles flinches away.

"I'm sorry," he says. "I didn't realize . . ."

"Miles. You . . . You can't just do that, you know." I'm flustered, fighting against the spell he put me under. I'm stammering to find the right words. "Y-you can't just do whatever you want."

Miles says nothing. His eyes are back on the road. Did he hear me? Is he listening?

I'm still emerging from a dizzy haze, but my words are firm. "You need permission."

He actually laughs. "Can I have your hand at least?" He shows me his palm. "I still miss you."

His attempt at being cute falls flat. "How could you miss me? We were together all day."

"Come on." His palm is still out. He wiggles his fingers, inviting my own. "Give me your hand."

I groan aloud, but part of me can't help but be flattered. I give him a playful high-five. He catches it, though, and entwines our fingers together. I tug my hand away while he tugs it closer, and I feel myself relax—almost against my will. I watch him, agape, as he lifts our conjoined hands to his lips. He kisses all my fingers—one after the other. Even my thumb. His lips are wet, leaving small circles of moisture that catch the breeze and turn cold, sending chills up my arm. He's kissing me. He's *actually kissing* me. Though he's come close in the past, this is the first time.

Those strong hands that can play any instrument are playing me. In a moment, I realize there may be more to his power than controlling the weather. He keeps kissing, going back over my fingers like they're keys on a flute. His lips are shapely and beautiful, more tanned than the rest of him. As they gently kiss, more ripples course through my body. But then something happens to remind me . . . it's me.

My Nevus spilus.

Our hands come to rest on the console, his thumb massaging my birthmark. Does he mean to do it? Does he know what he's touching? Thank goodness his eyes are still on the road because my birthmark is freaking out. All those cruel vibrations that had run through my body seconds ago are concentrated in that one spot. It's like a beacon, a reminder to snap out of his seduction.

My attention is on my birthmark now. It's as if sparks fly from it. It glows softly, pulses from the inside. If he feels it, he doesn't let on. He apparently has something else on his mind.

"I'm glad your mountain man and his friends are safe," he says in an odd, placating tone. "Selfishly, I'm kind of glad it all happened. You know, down in Rhode Island. As awful as that might sound."

My eyes unglue from my birthmark as a buzz of anger rises up. "You're glad it happened?"

"Oh, I didn't mean . . . I meant only that it gave us today.

concerto

It gave me you . . . today."

I'm so miffed by what he's said, I want to scream: *It did not give you me. I was never yours . . . and I never will be.*

But I'm preoccupied with my birthmark. It feels like it's trying to communicate with me and there's a bad connection. It rattles my nerves.

"I can't lie, though," he says. "It's not just today."

Today. What happened today? My mission to uncover Miles' plan and powers took a tempestuous turn. And now my insides feel singed—violated but still on fire. My words are shaky. "What's not 'just today'?"

Miles cradles my hand in his lap. "This. Us. Tell me you don't feel it too."

Exhaustion blankets over the layers of fury and agitation that still fester. I've felt enough for one day. "Miles, I—"

"Don't say anything. I know. I get it. You have someone." He takes his eyes off the road to look into mine—for too long. Or what feels too long. My stomach dips, betraying my conscience. I peel my gaze back to the road. He follows suit, but his attention is all on me.

"Sami, sometimes you can hold onto something too tightly. It's okay to let go a little. Give yourself some space. It's good for you, actually. You know, date other people." He pauses, and it's like the car fills with steam. He goes on, "This is our time. We're too young to have long-distance relationships hold us back. You've got to know this."

My hand is trapped in his. It seems I'll never have it back. It feels like he could swallow me whole. My words are lost, too.

"Just think about it," he says. "I mean, what are the chances we happen to be at the same program here in Boston at the same time? It's not coincidence. It's fate. After all these years, we're thrown back together."

Yes, what are the chances we're here together after all this time? Gears in my mind turn, stirring up more emotions. There's got to be something more to it. It's too convenient. Almost seems planned. A thrill runs through me without my consent.

"We're so good together," he says. "We understand each other. We have the music thing in common, but that's not all. We have history. It's like everything that's happened in our lives have led to this. It just makes sense. We make sense."

There it is. Now I know. It's not about wanting my help. It's not about my musical powers or being Goshenite or Dion. It is about me. He wants me for himself—as his girlfriend. The idea should make me ill, but instead I fight a full-of-helium feeling and try to stamp down what he's said. "Oh, Miles. You really shouldn't—"

"Don't say no. Think about it. Okay?"

Motionless, my mouth gaping like a dope, I'm at a loss. It's too much. There's too much to think about. My body has turned against me, turned inside out with anger and yearning in equal measure. Everything's swirling. And he's still got my hand held captive. It's heated up—from my birthmark or nerves—and is slick with sweat. In a strange dichotomy, my other hand feels bitterly cold.

Soon enough, we're navigating the maze of Boston's convoluted streets, and he needs both hands on the wheel. My birthmark is freed, but it feels sore. Like it's been worked over. I wipe my damp palm down my shorts to get to my tote, which I pull onto my lap. It creates a kind of barrier. I focus on getting my breathing back to normal, quelling those cruel vibrations that still hum at the base of my spine.

concerto

We're here. Not soon enough. He pulls into the alley near my dorm.

"Thanks. It was fun." It sounds ridiculous after all he just did to me. I open the door to go, but he holds my arm. Waits until I meet his eye.

"Promise me you'll think about it?"

"Okay," I tell him, because it's true. Even if I tell him I won't or can't think about it, I still will. I don't want to, but I will. I'll be fretting about it all night.

I slam his car door shut and—*boom*—sounds of the city bring me back to reality. He pulls out, and I blink away his magic spell as thoughts of Jason come to the forefront. My head clears, and truth blooms to the surface.

Miles put Jason in danger. Intentionally. And he did it to win my heart. How dare he? Who does he think he is? And then—he goes and hits on me while I'm trapped in his car? Is he for real? Fury rises up and rattles within my chest. It fuels me.

No, Miles. I won't think about it. It will never happen. I will never be yours. You will never win this way.

CHAPTER 22

When Miles' car is out of sight, I circle back to Boylston and make my way to the gallery. No time to change or freshen up; I'm already running late to meet Gaye and Poppy.

With each step, Miles is put further and further from my mind. What happened in that car? It's shameful how much control he had over me, how my body responded to him against my will. His hands on me like that—disgusting! Never again will he kiss me. How could I let that happen?

He's to blame for the Newport disaster. He's responsible for creating a storm that's killed people—one could have been Jason! He is pure evil.

Gritting my teeth to stop angry tears, my defenses are built up. His plan and powers will be figured out—and overthrown. I am not a feeble little girl. I'm Samantha Frances McGovern. And I'm *Dion*!

My tank top is sticky with sweat by the time I storm into the gallery. The glorious air conditioning is a welcome shock. Gaye sits at the table smack dab in the middle of the large room, which is cleared of art to make room for three sodas. I make a beeline for mine, my thirst propelling me. It's so sweet and cold and good that it gives me a boost. Ice cold root beer. I could swim in a vat of it. Escape from all this madness.

Poppy paces around the gallery as if she's a customer.

concerto

"Tell us everything," Gaye says.

"Miles did it." I nearly spit the words. "He caused the hurricane that hit Newport. Posh confirmed it. He caused that freaking storm. How the heck was he able to do that?"

"Jason's safe, Sam," Gaye says softly.

A streak of sorrow knifes my heart. "But he could've gotten killed."

"I can't think about that. You shouldn't either." Gaye shakes out her hands like she's drying them off. "We need to focus on what's ahead, not what's behind us."

"Do you think he's going to cause another disaster?" Panic rises to my throat. "When? Is Jason in danger? Are we?"

Gaye glances at Poppy. "That's what we're trying to figure out. That's what we need your help with. Tell us what you discovered. Tell us everything."

Taking cues from my mini-notebook scribbles, I retell the one-sided conversation between Miles and his father that I overheard. Poppy takes scrupulous notes on her Mac. She's thorough, asking me to slow down and repeat details. She stops typing, though, when I retell Posh's comment: *You missed the mark. It's supposed to move inland.*

"That's what we were afraid of." Poppy shares a look with Gaye.

"What? What were you afraid of?" I'm out of the loop, and it stings.

"And—what did he say about Aleia?" Gaye presses the table.

"It was something like, 'we can't let her down after all she's done for us.'"

Gaye pinches her chin in thought.

"Does that mean they're partners?" I ask. "They're

working together? Why, though? Why would they want to create storms? And how is it possible?"

The silence from Gaye and Poppy is maddening. They've been swapping information while I'm struggling through a day with Resident Evil, a.k.a. Miles. Not cool.

"Hey! Can I get a clue over here? I'm drowning. Help me out. What the heck is going on?"

"They have special powers," Poppy says. "All three of them."

"Oh, that's a shock. Not. So, what's the deal? You said Miles isn't Goshenite. But he has to be something. How else would he be able to do things with his art?"

Poppy sighs. "Not every Goshenite is magical. Matter of fact, most aren't."

I force a shaky breath. "But what I did with Aquamarine . . ."

Gaye stares me down. "You're Dion, Sami. You're different."

"What?" She just blurted out the Dion thing in front of Poppy, who clearly doesn't share my shock. I pivot to face her, the tips of my ears burning. "You knew? You know about . . . Dion?"

"Gaye filled me in." Poppy flashes a smile at me, her face growing red. "I knew you were someone special when your birthmark went wild in the shop. Still, I didn't realize I was in the company of a celebrity. I read about Dion when I was little but thought it was the stuff of fairy tales. And here you are—all super-powered up—and I was dissing you for not taking notes. Ha! I had no idea you were just waiting to tap into your power."

For some reason, hearing this from Poppy deflates me. "Yeah. A lot of good it's doing me. My boyfriend almost got killed by a magically induced hurricane, and all Dion could

concerto

do was wring her hands in front of the TV."

"Sam, be fair to yourself."

"I am. I've been trying. And even now, when I know that Miles is to blame for these storms, there's nothing I can do about it. How in the world will I be able to fight that kind of power? I mean, Miles must be some sort of Dion, too. How else would he be able to trigger a storm through music?"

"Sami, he's not Dion. Not at all." Poppy almost sounds sad. And then she turns to Gaye in what seems like slow motion. "Tell her what you just told me."

Gaye puts on a stage face, but it lasts only a moment. She takes a long breath, looking me right in the eye. "Sam, how much do you know about Greek gods and goddesses?"

Huh? Flashbacks of Ms. Galvin's class bubble to the surface. *Not the gods again. Why can't they leave me alone?*

"I don't think we have time for a history lesson," I tell Gaye.

"Silly child. There's a reason I'm asking. Now, do I have to start from the beginning, or have you been schooled in Greek mythology?"

My laugh is out of sheer fatigue. "I've been schooled all right."

"Are you being facetious?"

"It's an expression—to get schooled. It's—oh, never mind. The answer is yes, I know more than I'd like about Greek gods and goddesses. Specifically Hermes and—"

"Hephaestus," Poppy chimes in. "Goshenite."

"I didn't want to alarm you," Gaye says. "Or put you off the program, but 'Ms. Aleia' is a dangerous woman."

"Gee, thanks. I gathered as much."

"Do you recognize her name? Does it sound familiar at

all?"

"Aleia? No, why?"

"It's a derivation of Aeolus."

My brain isn't working. It sounds familiar but I can't place it, and it shows in my face. Gaye makes an exasperated noise. "Why don't you use that fancy phone of yours and Goo-goo it."

Her mistake makes me smile, but I don't correct her as I find my browser. "It says 'changeable, or nimble.' What is she—a shape-shifter or something?" My face is scrunched in confusion.

"Oh, useless!" Gaye flicks her hand at my tiny screen. "No, no. What's the next thing?"

"Wait—oh, here it is." The text swirls before I blink it into focus. I read aloud: " 'Aeolus, the divine keeper of the winds.' "

"Aha. There." Gaye nods, a knowing look in her eyes.

"So, what does that mean? Ms. Aleia is somehow connected to Aeolus?"

"She is Aeolus," Poppy says.

It's like I get the wind knocked out of me. "What? She's the freaking god of the winds? No way."

"It's true," says Gaye.

"How do you know?"

"It takes a god to know a god." Gaye leans toward me. Her eyes—I'd never noticed before—are blue and brown and green. Like little Planet Earths. It makes me shiver.

"You?"

"Gaea. God of the Earth."

Time slows to tortoise pace as I take in the room where we sit. The gallery. It's not a normal collection of fine art. My eyes slowly scan the walls, which are covered with

concerto

paintings of landscapes. All different windows to the world, various parts of our planet. Varying seasons and times of day. And—what's this? Carefully, I get up and move in for a closer look.

No way. It's like I've entered a Harry Potter movie. The paintings are not static. They're active. The elements are actually moving. Lakes ripple. Leaves sway with the wind. Mountain ranges welcome a setting sun. Reminds me of Skenesboro, a little. In another, a tropical scene shows a waterfall flowing into a steaming pool. And then, a snow squall obscures a view of the sea. Somewhere north? Or Antarctica? One shows a rainforest. I put my ear closer and hear the call of exotic birds. It nearly brings tears to my eyes. From one to another, I'm seeing every part of Earth.

"They're like secret cameras on the world," I say, sensing power behind the magic paintings.

"How else can I watch over my domain?"

I turn to Gaye and study her anew, realizing she's been here for me all along—the mentor I've been searching for. It dawns on me only now the scope of what we could do together. Together, we could heal the—

OMG! Climate change, global warming—all that stuff I've been worried about, feeling helpless about. Those are real and true issues for Gaye. It's, like, her responsibility. I feel a great surge of tenderness for her.

"Aunt Gaye, the climate. Our precious Earth. How are you—?"

"Sam," Gaye says. "There's a reason you're here. It didn't happen by chance, you know. The Fates brought us together. The Earth—the whole universe—is doomed unless we maintain balance. We need Dion to stop them—"

"From coming inland?"

"Right."

"So . . . if Ms. Aleia is god of the winds, who is Miles?"

Gaye's eyes skitter back and forth, as if checking to make sure he's not here. "His father is god of the sea."

"Posh Eichen."

Gaye nods. "Poseidon."

A hand floats to my gaping mouth. "That means Miles is . . . a demigod? Are you serious?"

"Not Goshenite. Not Dion," Poppy almost mocks. "He's a demigod."

My chest fills with paste. "Okay. You do realize you're talking to a huge Rick Riordan fan," I say. "I've read all his stuff. And you're saying Miles is basically Percy Jackson?"

A bark of a laugh from Gaye. "Sam, that's fiction. It's not real."

"Well, what you're telling me sounds a heck of a lot like fiction."

"I assure you, it's not."

I press my temples. Miles? A demigod? Memories rewind to our shared childhood, our mutual affinity for music, our passion for it. "But, wait. That can't be. I grew up with Miles. I've known him since kindergarten. He's never shown a hint of any kind of powers."

"Well, yes and no." Gaye toggles her hand. "Yes, he's always been a demigod because his father is Poseidon. But he hasn't always had magic."

I blink at her. "So . . . when did that happen?"

"Not sure. Perhaps in the last few years. Maybe with puberty. It sometimes happens then."

Poppy's studying the gallery walls, too. "One thing for sure. His power is growing."

Gaye steeples her fingers. "Yes. To be able to control

concerto

the weather like that is an extraordinary thing. Neither Aleia nor Posh could do that alone. Miles has leveraged his music in order to help his father gain power. There's no question about Posh's goal. He wants more of Earth. It's not enough that he's god of the sea and earthquakes and floods and—of all things, horses! He wants the land. Always wanted to get his trident on my land. He doesn't understand, or care, that he'll upset the equilibrium of the entire planet. He's wanted to control more of the planet for centuries. The mystery is what Miles is supposed to gain from all this."

It's hard to imagine we're talking about the same Miles from my childhood. "Right. It couldn't be as simple as trying to please his father. I mean, he's never been on the outs with his dad. But he's always been—I don't know—independent. Fiercely independent. I can't imagine him doing this just for his dad."

"Then he must have his own reasons," Gaye says.

Poppy adds, "Maybe you could find out."

It all makes my head hurt. "I don't get it. It's always been about music for him. Just—music." Could someone change that much? I question whether I know him at all anymore.

"And now his music is linked to aberrant weather," Gaye says. "Somehow."

"And it's killing our Earth," Poppy says bitterly.

It all clicks. "Oh, god. Aunt Gaye, the rising waters. The ocean's footprint. It's growing. Miles is responsible for that?"

"Oh, let's not give him all the credit for climate change. He's just ramped it up a notch." Gaye's shoulders fall. I see such despair in her eyes, I want to hug her. "They are winning. But it's not too late. We can stop them." She pauses, and a flicker of terror crosses her face. "We have to."

Bone tired suddenly, I drink more root beer, and then Poppy's gentle touch on my birthmark startles me. "What happened?"

I slap my other hand over it. "What do you mean? You can tell it was . . . active?"

"I think it still is."

She's right. My birthmark is still aglow, trying to communicate.

"You didn't even need henna."

Gaye stands, smacking the table. "Sam, you need to get to the piano. Now."

She's right. As tired as I might be, I have to play. The first step in stopping them is knowing what their next move will be. It's up to me to find out.

CHAPTER 23

It's not just my birthmark nudging me. I feel it in my whole body. It's crucial I play piano. Now. The run-walk back to campus is a blur, with an urgency that's all-consuming.

There's a waiting list for the piano studio. I robotically write my name on the third line from the top. Waiting out the thirty-minute slots ahead of me, I have almost an hour to kill. With my back to the wall, I slump onto the floor. Right there in the hall outside the studio. Hopelessness presses down on me. I should probably go to my dorm and change. Grab a shower. Sunscreen and sand stink on me. Smells that were once paired with freedom and anticipation now prompt different feelings altogether. Sharp and angry, bordering on hate.

My birthmark doesn't glow, but it pulses like a throbbing headache in my hand. A hum of pain crawls up my arm. I had thought henna was a necessary trigger, but now the thought of having henna anywhere near my birthmark makes me cringe. It would be unbearably painful.

Lights are dim in the hallway. Closing my eyes, I try to sort out what Gaye and Poppy told me. Miles' motives are unclear. And it just now occurs to me to question why Ms. Aleia would want this. Why would she partner with Posh to cause these storms? Why would the god of winds want to help him "move inland"? Is it power?

concerto

From that gods and goddesses project with Ms. Galvin freshman year, I remember that Zeus is the mack daddy god of Olympus. His symbol is the lightning bolt. So, doesn't he control the weather? Or is it Aeolus? Reaching for my phone, I open a browser to check, when the studio door suddenly flies open, making me jump.

"Oh, sorry." It's that petite Asian girl who's in my Psychology of Music class. Shareen, I think her name is. Shareen Fang. She's wearing a Red Sox T-shirt and baseball cap. She talks so fast, her words run together: "Did you want studio time? I signed up for this slot but I have to go. My boyfriend's waiting for me at Fenway. They're playing the Yankees tonight, you know. Have you been to a game yet?"

I squint at her. I've hit my max capacity for new information, and she's really throwing me for a loop with this baseball stuff.

"Huh?"

Her laugh is over in a blink. "Sami, right? You can go in. Use my slot. There's still almost twenty minutes left." She gestures to the piano in a fluid arc, as if directing traffic. I haul myself off the floor and stare at her, not quite grasping my good luck.

"Go." Shareen actually pushes me into the studio. "Quick! Before someone notices you're squatting." She gives me another super-fast laugh and disappears before I can thank her.

The studio door closes with a profound thud, and the room goes still. I'm as struck by the eager silence as I'd been during my first visit. It's like the walls are on pins and needles, waiting for me to play. I shake out my hands before positioning them at middle C and wait.

Nothing happens.

Maybe I'm too nervous? Maybe there's too much on my mind? I take a few deep breaths, ignoring the beachy smells on my skin.

Clear your head, Sami. No thoughts. Nothing. Empty your mind.

I force my fingers to do scales, and the room fills with the simple, comforting sound. Over and over, deconstructing chords into arpeggios spanning more than one octave. The familiar climb of notes is meditative. A balm for my soul. I'm like a brand-new student, starting fresh. My eyes close again, and I relax into the utilitarian sound. Each note is distinct, almost harsh, with no melody to carry it. It's oddly refreshing, as if establishing order to what is usually chaotic, albeit beautiful, improvisation.

A song trickles in, forming from my scales and arpeggios as a natural progression. It filters in softly from the background. A ballad, soft and soothing. I must be sleeping now because a dream appears. My dream is of home. I'm in Skenesboro again.

Jason and I are on one of our after-dinner walks like we used to in our early dating days. Our steps are innocent, tentative. We're just getting acquainted, but we are perfectly matched. We laugh together. I want to hold his hand but stop myself. The excitement of new love buoys me. The sweet scent of happiness fills the air. We're floating with it.

The song that had been playing in the background now takes center stage. My hands are moving, my fingers are busy at the keys. Sweeping, dramatic melodies fill the studio. Big energy. But outside of myself. My dream continues . . .

As Jason and I head toward the canal, Skene Manor watches over us from its perch on the mountain. As it had when I'd first moved there, its imposing presence chills me.

concerto

Ignoring it, I zone in on our synchronized footsteps—Jason's and mine.

As we turn near Saunders Bridge, we're forced to stop. The canal water is higher than normal. And it's rising rapidly. Then, in seconds, clouds shut out the sunlight and blanket us in gloom. Rain begins. Drops mark the sidewalk in perfect tiny circles. They quickly fill in, darkening the ground beneath our feet. The whole world becomes gray.

Jason shuffles back, grasping my hand urgently, and suddenly we're a couple with a two-year history. The exciting newness is replaced by a secure, deep love for each other, which can be felt through his touch. The rain pelts us, matting our hair to our foreheads. The water in the canal creeps to street level. We watch, shocked and horrified. We're helpless.

"The lock must not be working. Lake Champlain must be flowing through." Jason tugs my elbow to follow. We run along the canal toward Lock 12 before thinking things through. We don't have a plan. What can the two of us do if the lock is truly broken?

We run until we are out of breath, and then we keep running. We run as the canal overflows onto the street beneath our feet, soaking our shoes. We slip through the slosh, running without pause, having faith our treads will find the pavement. Our legs get soaked in seconds. Droplets splash up onto our faces, obscuring our vision. There's so much water. Is it raining upwards? It's an upside-down world. And then we see it—

The lock isn't broken. It's irrelevant.

Beyond it, Lake Champlain has become a monster. "A living, breathing thing"—as the Eichens describe the ocean.

Waves surge, tides erupt like a turbulent ocean. And it's taking over our little mountain town.

My music takes on a familiar tune. Similar to what I'd played over two years ago up on Skene Mountain—a tune I've avoided playing, afraid my magic might destroy something important. Now, though, it feels right. It's my own, and I lean into the music, feeling energy with every chord. I'm so deep into my dream, I can't pull myself out of it. Even if I could, I don't want it to end. It hasn't finished talking to me yet.

In that strange way dreams do, everything shifts, and I'm alone. No Jason. Just me. I climb up to the incline near the lock, away from the rush of water, tó get above it all—a bird's eye view. From this vantage point, Lake Champlain looks as endless as the sea.

In the sky over the water is a cloud-like apparition. It has Miles' likeness. He's hovering over the water, circling his hands like conductor. He's controlling the chaotic movement of the water.

Something in my heart lurches, like I'm hooked up to a defibrillator. Heat gathers at my chest. I unzip my jacket for relief. When I do, blue light flashes over the water. Miles blinks and shields his eyes, as if the light blinds him.

My magic is here. It's always been within me.

At my song's climax, I throw my arms back, lift my chest to the sky Supergirl-style. Blue laser light—my magic—washes over the roaring waters, shushing it. Calming it to stillness. The wind quiets. It's even stopped raining. The cloud-like figure that resembled Miles dissipates, as if taken away by the breeze.

In the fresh calm, my music descends into its denouement. A safe feeling falls over the entire town of

concerto

Skenesboro. Sun peeks through the gloom as the storm clouds disperse. Everything lights up into color again. Overwhelming relief brings me to my knees. My gratitude is a silent prayer to the distant mountains. Still deep in my dream, I grasp the pendant at my chest and kiss it lightly. To my shock, it's a ragged gemstone, uncut and fresh from its mineral rock: Aquamarine.

My magic is here. It's always been within me.

CHAPTER 24

BoomBoomBoom!

Eyes open, I slowly come to. It's like I've broken a fever. Sweat runs down my temples. The tops of my hands are slick with it. My heart thumps against my ribcage.

BoomBoomBoom!

That's not my pounding heart; it's the door. How long have they been knocking? How long have I been in the studio? My hands flinch off the keys, and I press my birthmark with the pad of my thumb. It's quiet but hot to the touch, as if it's just shut down.

"Just a sec!" I scramble to pull myself together, still processing what I'd seen. I wasn't even playing that rigorously—was I?—but the vision was very clear. More like a nightmare. It's got me rattled.

It hits me: Miles is targeting Skenesboro.

But, why Skenesboro? That would be crazy. It's in the middle of nowhere. Why would he care about an itty-bitty section of upstate New York?

And what about the pendant I wore? Was that really an Aquamarine gem that projected all that blue healing light? I mean, *Aquamarine* Aquamarine? The stuff I blew up two years ago?

BoomBoomBoom!

That's not Aquamarine exploding; it's the knocking.

"Coming!" I grab my tote and throw open the door,

concerto

ready to bolt to my room—but—"Ahh!" Someone's blocking me.

Miles fills the doorway. My mouth falls open. Any words I have for him get sucked away. Dread travels up my spine, flaring the hair at the nape of my neck.

"Sorry." He folds his arms calmly. "Didn't mean to scare you." He's still wearing beach clothes. Why hasn't he changed? A weird tingling itches my brain, wondering what he's been up to since dropping me off. He didn't follow me to Gaye's gallery, did he? He wouldn't spy on me.

"Are you waiting for the studio?" I squeak. "I didn't see your name on the signup sheet." My hand is stuck to my chest, stamping down my thundering heart. Inexplicably, my fingers fiddle around my neckline, searching for the Aquamarine pendant that of course isn't there.

"No. I'm not here for the studio." He studies me evenly. It's unnerving.

"Oh, that's right. You're too good to practice." It's meant to be flirty but comes out bitter, almost angry.

Miles doesn't answer. Just keeps staring at me. He's so calm it's maddening.

"What are you doing here, then?"

His arms fall to his sides. His face softens. "I'm here for you, Sami."

"But—how did you know I was in here?" I flick my hand at the signup sheet. "My name isn't listed here, see? I took Shareen Fang's slot. Well, she gave it to me." For no good reason, I expect to see Shareen there in the hallway, coming to my defense. She's not here. No one is. The place has gone X-Files. Where are the other musicians, the others on the signup after Shareen?

"Sami." Miles' voice is soft and intense. He steps closer

172

to me. The air pulses with his pheromones. His eyes are pools of yearning. I steel myself for his persistent request: dump Jason for me. And—this moment? Finding ourselves in the same place at the same time will be chalked up to serendipity. It's meant to be. His mewling voice grates my memory: Music fills our lives. It just makes sense.

But, no. He's not here to woo me. He slits his eyes. "What were you just playing?"

That gives me pause. "What was I playing?"

His lips curve in a dangerous smile. "Yes. What were you just playing?"

His face is an inch from my own. I step back into the darkness. "You can't hear anything out here." My mouth is desert-dry. "It's a sound-proof studio."

He cups my shoulders beyond the edge of my tank top, touching my bare skin with his long hands. It gives me a jolt. His fingers are ice cold. His eyes consume me.

"I didn't hear it as much as feel it." His forehead accordions like he's concerned. His tongue circles his lips, searching. He's unsure. Something's thrown him off, and it's decidedly unattractive.

It must show in my face, because his changes in an instant. He smooths his brow, clamps his jaw, and narrows his eyes again. One sharp squeeze on my shoulders and he brusquely shifts me to his side, tucking me under his arm. He leads us out of the studio. We move as a single unit out the door into the harsh light of the hallway. His arm encircles me, holding so tightly it feels wrong. Like he's taking me captive. He walks; we walk. It's a clumsy dance. The more I struggle, the firmer his grip on me grows.

"Miles? What are you doing?"

"Come on. There's someone I want you to see."

concerto

Through the corridors, we pass dark, empty classrooms. That's right; it's Saturday night. This place is a ghost town. If it were a weekday, these halls would be buzzing with activity. The eerie quiet jars me.

Miles nearly cracks my clavicle, folding me in half by the shoulders. My gait is rushed to keep up with his, making me trip over my own feet.

My phone dings inside my tote. It's torture not being able to check it. Even though Gaye or Poppy have more reason to ping me right now, I know it's Jason. I can feel it. My longing for him is so strong it makes me want to weep. Oh, Jason, what have I done? I've fallen into a trap. A deceptively beautiful trap called Miles Eichen. Shame creeps up my throat as acid reflux.

Miles still smells like the ocean, which is now rancid to my senses. How could I have been charmed by it? Or by Miles? He's a freaking demigod. He is powerful and he is dangerous. And he's leading me around campus like a prisoner.

With every awkward step we take, I'm more repulsed. Who cares if I blow my cover? I never signed up for this. Gaye and Poppy can get the information another way. Get me away from this guy.

"Miles, if this has to do with what you asked me earlier, I want you to know: it's not going to happen."

"What's that?" He's distracted.

Make it right, Sami. "You and me. Us. We're not going to happen. I have a boyfriend. His name is Jason Hill. And he's the best guy in the world. I'm not breaking up with him."

Miles' flat silence surprises me. He's expressionless.

"Miles? Did you hear me? We're not a thing, and we

never will be. I don't want to go out with you. We can be. . . friends . . . but that's all." The word makes me gag—in this case, truly an F-word. Would friends do this to each other? Take them forcibly across campus to an unknown destination?

But Miles doesn't react to the F-word. Or anything.

If I could stamp my foot, I would. "Miles, where are we going?"

Down the long hallway, a rectangle of light shines from an open door. A professor's office.

Panic time. My sharp intake of breath gets stuck in my clogged throat. No. I'm not taking another step. I dig my heels to the floor, and it's like they make tracks in the tiles as Miles drags me along. Toward the menacing light. No. I don't want to go. It's not even her office hours, but I'm certain Ms. Aleia will be there.

CHAPTER 25

"There you are," Ms. Aleia says, clearly expecting us. "Please, sit."

Miles deposits me in a hard-backed chair and stands behind it as if steering a wheelchair. Once freed from his grip, my first instinct should be to run. But curiosity keeps me here.

"What's all this about?" My voice is edgy.

"Oh, dear." Ms. Aleia frowns, feigning concern. "It seems we've upset you. My apologies. How about a cold drink?" She slides a Styrofoam cup across her desk. "Pink lemonade. For you."

Her smug smile tells me not to trust her.

"No, thanks. I'm not thirsty." I actually am, but after the Aquamarine fiasco, I don't dare consume anything from a questionable source. Especially one that reminds me of Coach Payne.

She lifts her slight shoulder in a miniscule shrug. "Suit yourself." As she sips, I watch the pink liquid climb the straw. My salivary glands pop.

"What do you want, Ms. Aleia?"

"Not what I want. It's what you want." She up-tilts her chin. "Miles, sit down. You're making the girl nervous."

As Miles lowers himself into the other chair, his knee slides against mine. Goose bumps surface, spreading to other parts of my body. I shift away and tug at my shorts, wishing

concerto

Miles would just go away.

"What do you mean, 'it's what I want'?" She might be referring to Miles. Huh. Does she think she's Cupid, too? "I have a serious boyfriend, you know."

Ms. Aleia's eyes go wide before she bursts into an ugly cackle, exposing her yellow teeth. Maybe Gaye has it wrong. Ms. Aleia can't be a god. She's a witch.

"Do you think I'm playing matchmaker here? That's funny." She shoots Miles a look and opens her planner. She sighs loudly, as if dealing with us is tedious work. Her words sound practiced. "I've been thinking, Samantha, about your desire to practice music therapy. I think I've come up with some ideas."

What? Music therapy? That throws me off. My once "lofty goals" now make me want to roll my eyes. So much has happened since I'd asked Ms. Aleia about practicing rather than theorizing music therapy, it feels irrelevant. Or, for me, abandoned.

"Oh, well, I'm not sure—"

"Yes," she interrupts. "I'm confident now is the time to get started. That way, by the end of the program, you could conceivably be a practitioner. Just think what it would do for your resume. You'd be a shoo-in for acceptance here at Berklee, I can assure you that."

A blanket of despair falls over me. Do I tell her the truth? That I never wanted to practice traditional music therapy but, instead, wanted to heal the Earth with music? Staring at Ms. Aleia, knowing what she's been up to with Miles and Posh, I realize my goal would have been a clear threat to their cause. Talk about motivation. She doesn't even realize the boost she's just given me.

My turn to bring on the charm. "Thank you, Ms. Aleia."

Maybe I could glean information to help Gaye. My words are careful. "What did you have in mind? Do you have a connection at one of the . . . hospitals in the area?"

"Hospitals?" As if she'd never heard of them. "No, no, silly girl." She sounds so much like Payne, I bristle. "First we have to assess your music. I'm not talking about talent. You wouldn't be in this program if you weren't already exceptionally talented. I'm talking about its . . ."—she bats the air—"energy."

"Its energy?" My ears are perked. *Like, magic?*

"Yes. Energy. We need to assess your music's energy. Only then can we see what it's capable of."

She couldn't possibly be referring to Dion. Could she? "Let me get this straight. You want to get a sense of my music's energy—like healing energy—to see whether it could help . . . the sick?"

A slow, devious smile fills her face. "The sick. Right. Yes. That's it."

She's definitely not referring to the sick. She wants me to use my music to help her summon her windstorms and natural disasters and crap. Does she think I'm that naïve?

A flutter of anger fills my chest but dissipates with the promise of opportunity. Yes, she does think I'm that naïve. And if she thinks I'll go along with her twisted plan to effectively take over Gaye's domain, it might give me the leverage to save it.

But why would she need me? She's a god, working with another god and a demigod. I have to think Dion's powers are Romper Room in comparison, regardless of what Gaye told me.

I make my eyes go doughy, my voice airy. "Really? You think I could do it?"

concerto

"Oh, yes." Her eyelids flutter. "But we have to rehearse. Together. I was thinking—"

"Sorry, but I just had a thought—I mean, Miles isn't in our music therapy class." I want to ask: *what's he got to do with this?* It's too big an elephant for this tiny room. "Is he studying it, too?"

Ms. Aleia is flustered. "Right you are. No, he's not in our class. Couldn't fit it into the schedule, I guess. But I've been tutoring him. He's very much interested in music therapy. Aren't you, Miles?"

"Most definitely." He sits up. "Ms. Aleia, aren't you going to tell Sami the most important part?"

Ms. Aleia warns him with her eyes. "Which part is that?"

"Well, as we discussed"—it's obvious they hadn't—"if Sami and I work together. If we . . . " —he does air quotes—"collaborate. If we blend our music together, it will be more effective." The last word he says with such relish, it's almost comical. He rubs his palms together like a stereotypical villain.

"Oh!" Ms. Aleia leaps from her chair. "Of course! How could I forget that? Yes, Samantha. Think of it as a team effort. You and Miles together. Perfect."

Together? Huh. They want to combine a demigod's and Dion's powers—for what? What kind of magic would that create?

I hide my birthmark in my lap. "I didn't know music therapy had to be a group effort."

Ms. Aleia clamps her lips in an impatient grin. "There are lots of things you don't know, Samantha." She runs a finger down her planner. "Now, let's get something scheduled. Time is of the essence. How about tomorrow, Sunday?

Samantha, are you free around noon?"

CHAPTER 26

I agree to rehearse with Miles—if only to discover why they are interested in my powers. My one saving grace is that I'll have all morning to prepare. After they let me go, I head back to the dorms and take a long-overdue shower to finally wash away the beach that's coated my skin all day. Hot tears mix with the water flow. How could Miles force me into that situation? And Ms. Aleia? She's got to be in violation of some professor's code of conduct. She should be reported to the dean. Terminated—never allowed to teach again!

It reminds me, shamefully, of when I went to Skenesboro High's principal to report the abuse of Aquamarine in the athletic department. He didn't want to hear it, was happy to be ignorant. As if poison could justify a school's championship record. What if Berklee Administration has a similar reaction? What if they protect their staff at all costs, or if they're in collusion with her on a secret mission? Besides, my reporting her could mar my academic record and possibly prevent my acceptance here. I don't want to risk that.

Back in my room, I dry off quickly, throw on my PJs, and turn the fan on high. Time to take control. I arrange a meeting for tomorrow morning with Gaye and Poppy at the henna shop. There's got to be a way to solve this through my music. Hopefully, they can help me brainstorm how.

With that done, I stand in the middle of my room, unsure

what to do next. The whir of the fan should be comforting, but it feels stuffy and confining in here. My bedding is damp from the humidity. I'm too antsy for sleep, anyway.

Something's tugging my heartstrings: Jason. Finding myself at my desk, I take up a pen. Forget texting. I'm going to write him a letter. A real, bona fide letter to be sent in the mail. The blank page grows the longer it waits for me to write. But once the pen starts moving, words come like I've turned on a faucet.

> *Dear Jason,*
>
> *I knew being apart was going to be hard, but I had no idea how hard. I feel so far away from you. Sometimes I wonder if the distance is taking you from me—for good. It's not just that you're in another state. We haven't talked. Too much time between calls. Confusing stuff keeps happening. I miss you. Jason, I need you.*
>
> *Miles is here. Miles Eichen, the boy I thought I loved in New York City. The one I told you about when I first moved to Skenesboro. I should've told you sooner. I swear I didn't know he was here until I saw him at Orientation. And then, well, we've been hanging out. As friends.*
>
> *He took me up to the beach on the North Shore. His father lives there, right on the ocean. Anyway, I thought it was as friends, but now I know he wants more. I might have led him on a little. I didn't mean to. I know it's nothing I want. He's nothing I want. I*

think of you constantly and miss you so much.

Gosh, that sounds lame. My pen dances a little before it writes:

> *I'm so sorry.*
> *Love you,*
> *Sami*

That doesn't help much. But it'll have to do. I'll put it in the mail tomorrow on my way to Poppy's shop.

Writing that took everything out of me. I fall into a dreamless sleep. Morning comes in seconds.

Boston's streets are sleepy and kind of empty as I make my way from my dorm to Newbury Street. Summer rain makes the air thick. Maybe this is why I have trouble taking a full breath on my way to the shop. It has nothing to do with the bullying I experienced last night—being ganged up on by Miles and Ms. Aleia.

Or Jason's letter that never found a stamp or a mailbox this morning.

It still sits on my desk in my room. Now, in the light of day, I'm not sure if I'll send it to him at all. I mean, he just survived a freaking hurricane. He rescued his friends from a near-death situation. It would be too self-serving to throw this at him now. Right? Besides, it's better to talk face-to-face. Even if I don't have plans to see him anytime soon. That, in itself, is enough to tear my heart.

By the time I get to the shop, my insides are tangled with worry and grief and yearning. Inside, the now-familiar smell of incense and cloves brings me an iota of comfort. The shop

concerto

is chock-full of newly delivered inventory. Seeing Gaye and Poppy is like getting oxygen. I can finally take a decent breath. We sit on overstuffed tuffets. Poppy brings us spicy licorice tea.

And, begin.

I tell them everything: my vision at the piano, being kidnapped by Miles, and Ms. Aleia's suspicious plan for my music. Poppy's taut expression tells me she's concerned. Gaye doesn't react but keeps a smooth composure that's oddly off-putting. What is she thinking? When my story's out, a weight is lifted. It's like I've handed it over.

Beneath her glasses, Gaye rubs her eyes. "Skenesboro must be a target. My guess is that they're moving inland to the lakes region. Making their way to the Great Lakes. Lake Champlain is accessible enough. The Champlain Canal links to the Hudson River, which drains into the Atlantic Ocean—which they already control."

"But why Skenesboro?"

"Coincidence?" Gaye suggests.

Poppy speaks quietly, "Um, newsflash? It might have to do with you, Sami."

"What? With me?" My first impulse is to deny, but then . . .

Puzzle pieces start to fit. Miles attacked Newport, where Jason was. Not only did he nearly destroy Jason and his friends, but he made it impossible for him to come up here to visit me. Now he plans to devastate my hometown—conceivably when Jason and I are there. Is he mad that I'm rejecting him? Is he really trying to kill off the competition? Oh, this will certainly win me over. What a twisted, sickening courtship.

But no. This is bigger than puppy love. This is about Poseidon and Aeolus gaining power. Miles is their minion.

186

So why does it feel so personal?

"You look like you've seen a ghost, Sami." Poppy refills my mug. It warms my hands and has a spicy aroma.

"It's not about me," I say, wanting it to be true.

Gaye scrunches her forehead. "No, of course it's not about you. For Posh. It may be slightly about you for Ms. Aleia. She suspects you have powers to help her. She's going to try and get your music to work to her advantage. That seems obvious. Miles, on the other hand, is a spoiled child. Who knows what his personal motives are?" She taps her lips, eyes on the ceiling.

"What do you mean? Do you think he might be doing this for other reasons? Maybe going against his father?"

Gaye shrugs, and it seems to drain her energy. "I think he's playing with the powers he only recently discovered he possesses. Seeing what they're capable of. Spreading his wings, so to speak. Typical teenager, really."

"But Posh—"

"Who knows what goes on in the minds of teenage boys? Teenage girls, either, for that matter. Posh assumedly has no idea what's in his son's head, although he should. Hormones affect even demigods."

"Oh, geez," Poppy says. "Are we really talking about the birds and the bees?"

"I said hormones, not sex," Gaye says matter-of-factly.

Poppy blushes vibrantly. I hide behind my mug of tea, feeling my face do the same.

"But Gaye, why do they need me? I mean, they're all-powerful gods. Why would they need my powers?"

"Gods are not all-powerful, Sam. As you know, each god has his or her specialty. It's not like they can do whatever they like."

concerto

"So, they want me to collaborate with Miles because my magic can reach where theirs can't?"

"Think about what you've been able to do. You've restored balance by destroying a toxic natural mineral. They must need a more intimate source to the Earth."

"And I thought Aquamarine was a thing of the past. What about the pendant . . . the one I wore in the dream? There's got to be something to that."

Gaye paces in the shop's limited free space. "Minerals have powers. That's no secret to you. You experienced that with your Aquamarine up in Skenesboro . . . ?" She ends this like a question, her thought unfinished. I wait, but she doesn't continue.

I fiddle with the neckline on my shirt. "I know. The whole Aquamarine thing in my vision threw me off. Isn't that a done deal?"

Gaye almost laughs. "Oh, Sam. Do you really think you destroyed the entire Earth's reserves of Aquamarine?"

"No, I mean, of course not. But, in my vision, it was Skenesboro . . . and I had that pendant. And it seemed to give me magical powers. I wasn't even playing the piano."

"In your vision, you weren't. But the vision came to you while playing."

"Right."

"Maybe it wasn't Aquamarine," Poppy says. "There are other blue gemstones. Topaz, sapphire . . . maybe it was one of those."

"I don't think so," Gaye says. "Ironically, Sami's magic is linked with the very substance she was destined to destroy. It's definitely Aquamarine."

Gaye certainly knows her stuff. Where was she two years ago when I got mixed up with the volleyball team? No matter, now. This is bigger than Fasha or Dion. I know it, Poppy knows it, and Gaye knows it. Her anxiety is palpable. I have to help her fix this. It's the only thing that keeps me from all-out crying right now. If there's anything I can do to prevent Posh and gang from stealing her domain, I'll do it. But how?

"I'll have to go back up the mountain and see if there's any left," I say dejectedly. Gloom weighs down on me. "I doubt there is. Last time I was up there, it looked like a combat zone."

"Who says it has to be from there?" Poppy jumps from her quilted tuffet. "Wait a minute. I think I have something."

As Poppy leaves for the front room, I survey the shop. It's a lesson in archaeology: hippie clothes that look like burlap, chimes and drums from exotic cultures, dresses made from tapestry, colorful woven blankets, pipes, and vases and vessels of stained glass. My tea sits on a worn wooden table. No wonder Poppy spends so much time here. It's like escaping to another world.

The sound of a cabinet opening and closing, and Poppy's back. Her grin is unusually wide, and she holds a small square box in her henna-covered hands.

She gives it to me without a word. Gaye nods for me to go ahead. I open it. And I can't believe what's inside.

An Aquamarine pendant. An exact match to the one in my dream.

CHAPTER 27

The pendant from Poppy's shop is nothing I'd choose from a jewelry store. It's something yogis would wear. Of course, this has nothing to do with fashion. About two inches long, it hangs vertically from a silver ornamental setting on a black leather cord. It doesn't look like much, but I sense its power. I dangle the cord at arm's length, marveling at how the gemstone catches the light.

Gaye studies it over her glasses. "Is it authentic? Looks like it."

"It is," Poppy says. "And it's raw—well, uncut anyway."

"It's worth a shot."

I put it back in the box, wanting distance from it. "What's the plan, then? Should I wear it today at rehearsal? They might notice . . . something different."

Gaye pushes her glasses back. "No, don't wear it yet. Let's get a sense of how they're planning to use your talents. But keep it with you." She taps her watch. "Oh my, time flies."

Poppy checks the clock near a big statue of Buddha. "Shoot. I was supposed to open the shop ten minutes ago." She hurries to unlock the front door.

"I need to get back to my gallery. My windows on the world," Gaye says with a small, sad smile. "Gallery opens at noon on Sunday. Stays open 'til five. If you want to come

concerto

after your meeting today."

"Thanks," I say, not taking my eyes off the pendant. It stays in the box, which I hold away from me like it's on fire.

To my surprise, Gaye embraces me. "We'll figure this out, Sam. Try not to worry. It's not all on you. You're not alone in this."

Her determined tone lifts my spirits. Her courage is inspiring. "You aren't either. I promise, I'll do whatever—"

"Hush now." She pulls on her cape. "Go. Meet them. Play with Miles. See what you can learn. They won't hurt you. That much, I know for sure."

"How are you so sure?"

"Because, child, they need you." She's out the door before I can respond.

On Newbury Street, she holds her head high, as if the rain doesn't bother her at all. Two ladies come into the store shaking the water out of their hair. Something strikes me as odd. "Poppy, isn't all this rain unusual for summer?"

Big, fat raindrops pelt the storefront window. "Maybe. Weather in the Northeast is always cray cray. I wouldn't cry wolf, blaming Miles just yet."

"You're right. I'm getting paranoid."

"No. You're getting in tune."

The two lady customers are giggling about all the hemp clothing. After they've gone to the other room, I say, "Poppy. Tell me your story."

"What story?"

"What's your talent? When did you find out you were Goshenite?"

Her smile is glowing and prideful as she brings out what looks like a comic book from beneath the counter. She lets the art speak for her.

"Cartoons?"

She deflates. "Cartoons? Seriously? Don't you know anime when you see it? It's Japanese."

"You're not Japanese." It's a stupid thing to say.

"No, dork. Not me. The style of art. Actually, anime is animation, which I like to do as well. In comic form, it's called manga."

I take a closer look. "You did this whole book? It's amazing. The detail is—wow. I've never seen anything like it."

"I've always been able to draw. But story creation was always my challenge."

"So, do you work with someone on that, then?"

"Not exactly. Henna is my secret weapon, too."

I want to talk to her more about it, but we're interrupted by the hemp-loving ladies who've come to check out a bright-colored tapestry. They start peppering Poppy with questions. Time for my exit.

The thought of going outside in the deluge right now is too much, though, and I have forty-five minutes before the rehearsal with Ms. Aleia and Miles. Thoughts of Jason pull at me. While Poppy's busy with her customers, I sneak into the back hallway to find some privacy. I sit on a box in the jam-packed storage area in the back of the shop and dial Jason.

"Please pick up," I chant as it rings.

"Hey." His voice is like butter on warm bread.

Tears prick, startling me. "Jason." I don't know what to say. No words seem appropriate, after what he's been through. "How are you?"

"How am I? I don't know. I guess okay."

"I mean, how are things?"

concerto

"Things are weird. RISD was lucky and had no flooding. So, they've restarted classes, and on the surface, everything's back to normal, but nothing feels normal. Far from it."

"I bet." My voice wavers. "I miss you."

A long pause. Is he yawning? "I know. I miss you, too." His words are quick. "Let's talk about you. What's going on up there, anyway?"

"What do you mean?"

"I don't know. Aunt Gaye called me last night. Kept me on the phone for a good while."

"What about?"

"Well, first she wanted to make sure I was okay and all my friends were okay. Then, she told me you guys were working on something together. Like, a project."

"She told you . . . about our project?"

"Yeah, but she was all secretive about it. Just told me you might be distracted and not to take it personally."

"She said that?" I'm grinning through tears now. Leave it to Gaye to make everything better.

"Yeah, which is funny since I'm the one who's been distracted . . . with the storm and all."

"Yeah."

"Yeah."

Guilt tugs at me, thinking of my last car ride with Miles. Here, Jason's in survival mode, and I'm falling into temptation. Still, Gaye has given me a gift, and while it may have bought me a little time, it's on me to do the right thing. I need to tell Jason the truth.

"Gaye and I are working on something together. And when the time is right, I'll tell you everything. But there's something else, too."

My words get stuck. I wish I had the letter in front of me to give me a script. Heat rises up my spine. Is it too late to backtrack?

"What's that?" There's not an ounce of suspicion in his voice. Makes me feel worse.

How do I tell him without crushing him—or crushing us? I feel myself pull back. I can't help it. "Well, it's nothing really. Just that an old friend from New York is in the program. I don't know why I didn't tell you before. You might remember the name—"

"Oh, wow. Really? Is Lauren there?"

Lauren.

It's like a bucket of cold water pours over me, my brain ringing loudly with what I should've thought of days ago. Of course—Lauren! Why haven't I reached out to Lauren yet? She knows Miles better than anyone.

My words are quick. "Um, no. I wish Lauren were here." It becomes urgent to get off with Jason and call Lauren—like, now. "You know what? You just reminded me. I owe her a phone call. Gosh, I really should call her now. Can I call you back? I could—"

"Sure. No prob. Love you."

Click.

That was kind of sudden. *Why was he so quick to hang up?* I shake off the hollow feeling that just swooped into my gut. Give the kid a break; he just survived a hurricane. And I've got work to do.

My pulse races as I work my contacts to find Lauren's name—right next to Miles, of course. But then, I'm at a loss. After all this time, what's the protocol here? No communication save a brief email exchange in the past three years and now a random phone call? Yikes.

concerto

I throw her a text.

Can u talk?

Woop. Delivered.
Okay. Good.

Staring at my phone until my vision goes wonky, I summon those swirling dots that tell me she's writing back. But—nothing.

Screw it. I'm calling. My foot taps rapidly against the box in front of me as I wait out the ringing. It seems endless.

"Sami?" she says with joyful surprise, as if she'd been hoping I'd call for years.

"Oh, Lauren. You answered." A laugh. "How are you?"

"Good. Good. How are you? It's been a long time."

"I know. Too long. And I'm so glad you're . . . good. Really glad. And I can't wait to hear all about everything. But there's a reason I'm calling—"

My words are stuck again. Ugh, why didn't I plan this out a bit better? It's like I've forgotten how to talk, for crying out loud.

"Oh? Is everything all right?" She sounds concerned.

"Yes. Well, I think so. It's just that . . ." It comes to me. "Hey, did you know I'm in Boston? I'm doing the summer program at Berklee School of Music?"

"Oh! Really?" Loaded pause. "Ahh, I think I know why you're calling." She sounds disappointed.

"You do?"

"Miles Eichen. He's there, too."

"Yes, he is." This is unexpected. She's making it easy for me.

"Sami, I know it's been a long time. It would take hours

for me to fill you in. You know, Miles and I dated for quite a while."

"I know."

"It ended kinda ugly."

"It did?" Second thoughts swirl. Do I really want to know those details?

"Sami, he's not the kid we knew and loved growing up. He's . . . different."

"I'm getting that sense."

Her voice sounds strained. "Are you guys . . . ?"

"No! No. We're not dating. I have a boyfriend from back home. But, Miles and I . . . we're kind of hanging out. Just, you know. Like, friends. But things have gotten a little bizarre."

Dead quiet on the other end. Lauren doesn't even sound like she's breathing.

I go on, nerves making me ramble. "I mean, I think I might know what you're talking about—Miles being different." For some reason, I can't form the word "demigod" in reference to Miles without choking. Or laughing. I try another tack. "He took me up to his father's beach house. The past two Saturdays, we've been at the beach up there. Spending time near the ocean. And with his dad."

"Oh." The word weighs a ton.

"And music. Well, you know as well as I do how much he loves music. But it means more now. It seems to have a certain power now. Does that sound nuts?"

"No, Sami. I know exactly what you mean."

"So, I wanted to see if you could tell me anything about Miles I should know? I know you were in a pretty serious relationship and your breakup was probably hard and you must still have feelings—"

concerto

"No, that's not it." She nearly spits at me. Big sigh. "The only feeling I have for him is—well, it's complicated. There are many feelings. None are good."

How to follow this? "I'm sorry for that."

"Well, it's certainly nothing for you to be sorry for. But Sami, you will be sorry if—" She catches herself. "Listen, I'm not sure if this is why you called. And I don't know how to say this without just coming out and saying it, so . . ."

"Go ahead. Say it."

"You really need to stay away from him. Miles, I mean. He's not a good person."

Like, causing natural disasters aimed at killing your boyfriend? I need to hear her say it. "Like, how do you mean?"

"Let me put it this way. He will make you do things you don't want to do."

He'll make *me* do things I don't want to do? That takes me aback. At first, I want to correct her. No way would I let that happen. But then, Miles had taken me forcibly to Aleia's office yesterday. And, earlier, he put his hands on me in the car. He kissed my fingers, one after another, making my body feel things that betrayed my heart. Lauren's right. He has made me do things I don't want to do. But, is she referring to something more serious? A recent article in the student news talked about the prevalence of date rape on college campuses. Something tells me Lauren isn't talking about sex, though. "Like, what kind of things?"

"It's going to sound weird."

"Trust me." I chuckle. "It's not going to sound weird."

"I really don't like talking about it. Especially by phone. And it's been so long since I've seen you. It's like you're a stranger."

"Lauren, please. I wouldn't be calling you if it weren't important. I'm meeting with him today, and I'm not sure what he's planning."

"Are you going to be . . . making music?"

"Yeah. Think so."

She makes a noise, almost a cry, and doesn't say anything for a while. I wait, my foot tapping that stupid box incessantly.

"Listen to me very carefully." Her voice is uncharacteristically firm. "Under no circumstances should you play music with him. Period."

"But, he's expecting me in, like, twenty minutes. We have a rehearsal planned. I can't just not show up."

"Don't play music, then."

"Lauren, what the heck? That's kind of the point of the whole meeting."

Long pause. I can't tell whether she's crying, but her voice is clearly distraught. "Tell you what," she says finally. "If you have to play, then play. But make sure you stay alert. And keep track of time. Can you do that?"

I temper my confusion. "Yeah, sure. I can do that."

"Then you should be fine." Her voice has narrowed, thin as a needle. I almost don't recognize it. "I need to go. Sorry."

Click.

CHAPTER 28

Racing through the rain to get to the studio in time for our dreaded rehearsal, knowing Miles will be there, brings up so many emotions. Mostly resentment. And disbelief. How could I have been so taken by him? Lauren's words roll through my mind.

He's not a good person.

He will make you do things you don't want to do.

I fight a sick feeling as I splash through the soggy streets. It's early enough on Sunday that most students aren't back from their weekends away, so the campus is still pretty deserted. Ms. Aleia and Miles are probably there at the studio waiting for me.

The studio: the scene of yesterday's kidnapping, Miles taking me against my will. Does it matter that it was to a place as innocuous as Ms. Aleia's office? It never felt innocuous to me. It never felt safe. I didn't want to go there. So, yeah, it was kidnapping. Thoughts of Miles are curdling by the moment.

I push open the studio door and hear an abrupt needle-off-the-record halt to music.

Miles is seated at the piano and looks as if he'd been going at it for a while. His temples glisten with sweat, while rivulets of rain run down mine. It hits me; this is his rain. He did this, didn't he? He's got a worked-over look to him. He cracks his knuckles, and our eyes meet. Sourness roils in my

concerto

stomach. This is not going to be easy.

Why did I agree to this?

Clutching my tote that holds the still-boxed Aquamarine pendant, I step tentatively into the dimly-lit, soundproof room. The door closes behind me automatically, its hinge on a spring, making me jump. The intended convenience feels like an affront. It's like the building itself is conspiring against me.

"Hi," I manage.

"There you are," Ms. Aleia says matter-of-factly. "Right on time. And you're all wet."

They both stare at me. Waiting.

"I was . . . outside." Unsure what to do next, I wait for instructions.

Miles' voice is edgy. "Well?"

"Go ahead, Samantha." Ms. Aleia gestures to the piano bench. "Have a seat."

When I hesitate, Miles shifts to make room on the bench.

I'm supposed to sit with him? "We're going to play together?" A duet? How quaint.

"Yes. Sit." Now Ms. Aleia sounds irked.

"But, what are we supposed to play?"

"Oh, for the love of—! Just sit down and see what happens." She gulps the air as if to take the words back. Her hands flutter near her ears. "I mean, improvise."

"Yeah, improvise." Miles snickers. "Like jazz."

I make my way to the bench like it's the freaking guillotine. My rain-soaked skin begins to frost in the temperature-controlled studio. Goosebumps blanket me, and I fight against a full-body tremor. It distracts me so much, I hardly feel my bag being lifted from my shoulder.

Ms. Aleia, holding my tote in the air, gives me the once-over. "Making space for you to work is all," she says, depositing my bag in the corner.

The pendant—is it hidden enough? My phone—is it silenced? It feels wrong to have my stuff so far out of reach. I nearly wrench my neck keeping my eyes on it.

Ms. Aleia rolls her wrist, urging me to the piano.

I float onto the bench. The piano looks foreign suddenly—a treacherous friend. Ms. Aleia hovers like a predator. It's all at once claustrophobic in here. It's hard to breathe. I'm sweating now. Did the AC shut down? I don't hear its whirr. My eyes discreetly pan the room, eager for an exit strategy.

Ugh. I'm already drowsy. Is there any air in here? There aren't windows. The large digital clock near the bulletin board has been shut off, frozen at 8:15 a.m. I replay my morning. When did it start to rain? Has Miles been playing since then? It should be noon by now. Is it? Wait—how am I supposed to—?

Panic strikes. Lauren's voice rings loud in my head: *Keep track of time. And stay alert.*

I'm hyper-aware of Miles sitting next to me. His body heat comes off in waves, violating my personal space. His usual beachy smell is mixed with sweat and the plasticky odor of the room's foamy insulation. He nudges my elbow, businesslike, without a hint of flirtation.

My hands take position on the keys. He grins crookedly and begins to play.

I play, too.

After a standard warm-up of scales, my shoulders relax a bit. My body reacts to the familiar dance—hands on the keys. My senses react to the comforting sound of the piano.

concerto

This is my talent. This is my destiny. What's there to be scared of?

More at ease, I close my eyes, expecting a vision to appear. But nothing does. It's dark behind my lids.

Our chords are in sync, miraculously harmonizing into a pleasant tune. It's a slow ballad we're playing—the kind that used to make me feel antsy. Now, it has an unexpected calming effect on me.

Then—a loud *swish* covers the music like a tarp. Our melody is muffled beneath it. I zone in, that tingly feeling in my body telling me it's coming: a vision. Odd that my birthmark is quiet, though. Deadened. Music fades; it's like I'm falling into a dream.

—and my mind goes still.

"Great session. Very productive. Good work, Samantha." Ms. Aleia's words reach me as if from a dream.

"Thanks." My voice is hoarse. Thirst has filled my throat with sand.

I blink a few times, letting my eyes adjust from complete darkness to the dim light of the studio. My hands ache. When I lift them from the keys, my wrists crack. My fingers are so stiff I have a hard time gripping the strap of my tote, which Ms. Aleia hands me without a word. My movements are slow, as my body feels rigid from inactivity. I make my way to the door, wanting more than anything to get out of here and away from these people.

One push sends a streak of light, like a bolt of lightning, into the studio. With one hand on the door, primed to leave, I look back and am met with Ms. Aleia's strange grimace.

She stares, wide-eyed and unmoving, like she's possessed by Hades himself. Miles doesn't look up. His eyes seem to be closed, in fact. He's slouched over the keys—maybe sleeping? I look from one to the other, confusion rooting me in place. My mind races to process what happened here. It doesn't make sense, but I know it's true . . .

I've been playing. For a while. It seemed like only a moment, but my body tells me I've been playing for quite a long time.

I don't remember a thing.

Miles looks up, recalling I'm here, and mirrors Ms. Aleia's creepy grin. She clasps her hands below her waist, forcing patience. Preoccupied, she's eager for me to leave. Miles shifts on the bench to face me, his lips poised to speak. It jolts me into action.

The weight of the studio door is heavy. It's a relief when I step away, allowing it to close. The door's spring-hinge nudges me all the way out, and I stumble into the hallway. Leaning against the wall, I take a breath. Blink a few times. Feeling dazed.

That was odd. They let me go without planning another session or talking next steps. Not even a goodbye.

Whatever!

Like a zombie, I toddle my way to my dorm room. A good nap is in order. Just thinking of my bed, my soft pillow makes me drowsy on my feet. As I pass the big bay window near the study lounge, I automatically look outside and—

What's this?

It's getting dark. The sun is setting. Wait—what time is it? How long was I in the studio? We met there at noon. How could it be—?

My phone has so many notifications on its face, my

concerto

thumb can't scroll fast enough to get to the end. But that's not what makes my breath stop.

My phone tells me it's almost seven p.m.

CHAPTER 29

An about-face and I'm racing downstairs toward the exit with only one thought on my mind: *I've got to get to Gaye*. It's irrational, though. Her gallery closed at five. I have no idea where I would find her. Our meeting this morning was ages ago. I've been playing piano with Miles for over six hours.

I sprint toward the exit, yet when I get closer to the glass, I halt in my tracks.

It's still raining. Not just any kind of rain. A fat, furious rain.

Slowly, I push open the door and—ignoring the burst of cold air—I step outside. At once, chilled to the bone. It's not the only shock to my system. I can't believe what I'm seeing.

There's an inch of ice on the ground. Covering everything. The sidewalks, the streets have a thick glaze to them as if the whole city had been dipped in shellac. The rain is freezing on contact. How is this possible? An ice storm in Boston . . . in *July*? Just yesterday, it was hot and sunny. Bathing suit weather. Beach weather.

Not anymore.

It's like I've been transported to Antarctica. My sweaty T-shirt ices my skin in seconds. I scramble back inside, feeling my toes already numb. Through the glass, I watch in horror as a lone car attempts to cross Mass Ave and slides sideways into a telephone pole, its tires useless. The driver gets

concerto

out and instantly falls, his feet kicking out from under him. He tries to stand once more but falls so hard, he ends up crawling his way into the shop on the corner—probably to call AAA.

Ice. Everywhere. Ice.

My hand is covering my gaping mouth. I'm trembling all over. Not just from the cold. I haven't taken a full breath since before the studio.

The studio!

Am I so distracted by what's going on outside—this insane ice—that I've forgotten what happened in the studio? It hits me: whatever went down in the studio is connected to what's happening outside. This weather is beyond unusual. And it stinks of magic. Evil demigod magic. I know it's true with everything in me: Miles created this storm.

Gulp. That would also mean I helped create this storm.

OMG—Miles and I created this storm!

If I can't get to Gaye, I at least have to get in touch with her.

Suddenly, I'm acutely aware of being out in the open. Here I am, inside the dorms near the exit. This building is attached to the hallway leading to the studio, which is attached to the long corridor leading to Ms. Aleia's office. I'm trapped in this maze of evil demigod magic. The only safe place is my room.

Racing back upstairs toward the dorms, I chant a prayer under my breath that Miles won't find me, that I won't run into him . . . or Ms. Aleia.

Luck is with me. Next thing I know, I'm in the safety of my room, my back pressed against the door, panting like an Alaskan sled dog. Several minutes pass before I feel it's safe to move deeper into my room. Even then, I close my blinds before turning on the light.

It's like a light bulb goes off in me, too.

Hurrying now, I reach into my tote for my phone, but somehow the box with the Aquamarine pendant is what comes out. It gives me pause. The small box feels strange. When Poppy first handed it to me, it almost felt alive. It was like holding a box of electricity. Now, it feels empty. My hand shakes as it opens the lid. Beneath the tissue is what used to be the Aquamarine pendant.

It's still a pendant. But is it still Aquamarine?

A stone is still lodged in a silver setting—but the gemstone is no longer that bright blue, signature of Aquamarine. It's cloudy, mostly white, with a slightly greenish hue. That's not the only change, either. It's cracked in several places. Wiggling the stone in its setting, it would be easy to dislodge it from the silver. Like it's weakened. Unrecognizable.

Not only did we create an ice storm, but we destroyed this rare Aquamarine stone.

I've got to get in touch with Gaye.

Phone in my hand, I scroll through my notifications quickly. Poppy and Gaye both have tried me. Jason, too. My heart cries to reach out to him.

Stay focused, Sami.

Gaye's phone goes right to voicemail. Or it tries to go to voicemail. I get the robot chick telling me "the caller you're trying to reach does not have an active voice mailbox."

Seriously? I squeeze my phone as if I could get juice from it and suppress a scream that could shake the building. I toss my phone onto my crumpled comforter, giving up, and a wave of exhaustion hits me.

concerto

I slump onto the bed. My attempt at a much-needed deep breath erupts into a sob. Who knows how long I cry for? After, it's like my tears have covered my body with a warm blanket. Leaning back on my pillow, I survey my room.

Desk, lamp, bookshelf, bed. Hardly any personal items. A single picture of me and Jason on the corkboard, the eco-friendly water bottle I got from Poppy's shop, a box of hot pink paperclips Mom thought was a must for this program—whatever—and a small glass box etched in gold. It's got three tiny shells in it. A start to my collection . . .

The memory of Miles giving me that box comes rushing back. How flattered I'd been. How self-conscious I'd been—naked underneath my bathrobe, alone with him in my room. I hadn't ever done that with Jason, even. It's like Miles had skipped over courtship right to sheer intimacy. And then, the romantic gift—so feminine and elegant. How dizzy with gratitude I'd been, mistaking it for something close to love.

Love? With Miles? Agh-ick!

How could I let that happen? It enrages me now, the power he's had on me. What he's done to me. Making me feel that way. He probably put a love spell on me or cast some other kind of evil demigod magic to make my heart flutter. Why not? I have no idea what he's capable of.

In a burst of anger, I throw the little glass box against the far wall, hoping to break the sucker. It makes a miniscule dent in the plaster and stays intact. Maddening! It fuels my fury. I hit my goose-feather pillow—such unsatisfying resistance! Hopeless. I fall onto it to muffle a scream-cry and keep my face buried there until sleep takes me.

≀

I'm awakened by knocking. How long have I been out? What time is it? It must've been a deep sleep. It takes a while for me to come to. The knocking keeps up methodically and reminds me of a pendulum swinging. Hypnotic. It could put me to sleep again . . .

It gets louder. More urgent. I pull myself out from under the covers, rubbing my eyes. Power's out and with it, my alarm clock. It must be the middle of the night. Using the flashlight on my phone, I check behind my closed blinds to see what's happening in the sky, if anything. It's completely dark. Even the buildings are black as pitch—only a wink here and there of exit signs and emergency lights.

A full moon illuminates the longest skating rink ever, as ice covers every visible surface as far as the eye can see. Mass Ave is cluttered with tree branches. A downed power line makes Boylston Street impassable. And it's not just that one street; it seems the entire city is shut down. It's not raining anymore, though. That's a small comfort, I guess. Still, the air is sticky with an incongruous, clammy humidity. I make my way to the door, my flashlight making my creature comforts look like something out of a horror flick. And it slowly comes back.

The studio. The ice storm. The Aquamarine.

My door is open before I can think things through. Before I ask who is there. Before it's too late.

It's Miles.

CHAPTER 30

"Well, hello, sleeping beauty." His voice is predatory and full of slime. He charges into my room without invitation, as if it's his space to own.

"What are you doing here?" My voice is grainy from sleep.

He hands me my eco-friendly water bottle from my desk. "Here. Drink."

It's safe. It's my water. I have no reason to hesitate.

It hardly matters; I'm so parched, I'd drink anything. It's room temperature and slightly sweet. I glug the whole thing down. Miles replaces the empty bottle on my desk. His movements are deliberate. He's playing doctor, and I'm his patient, helpless and weak.

No, thank you. He's not welcome here. I force myself awake enough to tell him this with my eyes.

"How are you?" He reaches for me while taking a seat at the foot of my bed. Next thing I know, his arms are around me, and I'm curled in his lap, trapped in his embrace. He's warm and smells of salt air.

"Why are you here?" I ask, telling myself to get the heck up. Though somehow, I can't seem to move.

"I came to check on you. See how you're doing." His voice is like a balm.

His arms make a pod of safety, as ironic as that seems.

concerto

Irresistible. My mind screams—*don't trust him!*—but Lauren's warnings seem a distant memory. What was it she told me again? Why did I feel so scared?

Oh, so sleepy. My eyes close on their own. A strong tug of sleep pulls at me. There's no fighting it. I begin to drift . . .

"Tired," I say.

"I know." He shushes me, rocking me like a baby.

"What time is it?"

"It's late. Shhh. It's okay. You can go back to sleep. I'll be here when you wake up."

No. No. *No!* I bite my lip to shock myself awake. Lauren's voice screams inside my head: *Stay alert! He's not a good person!*

Wrenching away from Miles, I fall onto the floor in a clumsy mess. My closed blinds filter light in from the moon, illuminating his face. It's a mask of composure. I scramble, finding myself in a crab position, clawing backwards toward the door, gasping for oxygen to help me fully awaken.

A silent, mocking snicker. "What are you doing?" he asks with an eerie calm.

He'll make you do things you don't want to do!

My head slams against the door—and the notion of sleep is gone. I shoot up. Standing, I tower over Miles, who is still seated at the foot of my bed. My hands are fists at my sides. My insides are boiling over with rage.

"I know what you've done. I know it was you. I know who you are." My quivering voice belies my conviction. "I know everything, Miles." The last bit sounds unconvincing, even to me.

"Right," he says slowly.

Is he mocking me? "I'm telling you . . . if you don't stop. If you don't . . . I'm warning you . . ." My ridiculously empty words trail off. What the heck am I doing, threatening Miles—a demigod? Still, they've chosen me for a reason. I'm Dion. Magic is within me. But if the extent of Miles' power is a mystery, so is mine. "I'm not helping you," I say, tears building.

Don't you dare cry, Sami!

"Sami." His tone is placating, sticky sweet. "Come here. Let's stop this nonsense." He holds his arms out for a hug. Or to trap me in his manipulative safety-pod or whatever that was that almost put me out a few minutes ago. No way. Not happening.

I dig my heels in, keep my tears at bay. "I know who your father is. I know who Ms. Aleia is. I know what you're up to, all of you."

Miles has a bemused look on his face. Almost smug.

I've caught a talking virus. Even if I should keep my mouth shut, I can't. Like a boulder rolling downhill, it's a cruel inertia. "You created that hurricane that hit Newport. You made this ice storm. All this ice in the middle of summer. You did it."

A pause. He sweeps sand or something off his shorts. The absent, casual gesture totally infuriates me. Is he even listening?

"It wasn't only me that made the ice storm, Sami," he says finally, in a whisper. "You've got to know that."

My fist finds the wall. I want so badly to be strong, but my voice reveals my weakness. "What was that, anyway? What did you guys do to me? What the hell happened in that studio?"

Miles, on his feet, towers over me easily. "Asks the girl who claims to know 'everything.' " He grins coyly. The flirt is back.

concerto

"Why?" I ask, and a sob escapes. "Why are you doing this?"

I hate that I'm crying. Tears stream down my face. I refuse to wipe them away. I ignore them. I hate them. Miles looks down on me with contempt.

"Answer me," I say through gritted teeth.

"Sheesh, you're demanding tonight." He cups my shoulder. I shove him away. He softens all over. "Can we calm down and talk about this like normal people? Like friends?"

I smack tears away and cross my arms. "Normal people? Friends? Some friend you are."

"Sami, please." His eyes are sincere now. There's suffering there. "Don't do that. I can't lose you, too." He's showing me a side to him I haven't seen before. Vulnerable. It has an effect on me I didn't expect. My arms drop to my sides in slow motion. The fight has left me temporarily.

"Tell me, Miles. Tell me what's going on."

He makes his way back to the foot of my bed and he folds into himself. He talks into prayer hands which hide his trembling chin. "I didn't ask for any of this."

His jaw clenches, suppressing any tears. "I haven't always been this way. When we were little, Sami? You remember, don't you? Our lives were filled with music. Innocent music. Do you remember listening with my dad's huge headphones, staring at the ceiling—"

"Conductors to an invisible orchestra." I smile at the memory.

"Yes. It was perfect, wasn't it? I miss those days. When everything was simple. When no one expected anything of me. When I wasn't . . . before I became a, a—"

Pause. Swallow. "A demigod?"

Miles flinches as if I smacked him. His eyes flick to mine in a flash of bitterness. "I hate that word." His tone is beseeching. "Please don't think of me that way, Sami. I'm not this mysterious creature. I'm me. I'm Miles. I'm the Miles you grew up with."

My head is shaking no before he finishes his spiel. Lauren's words roar back: *He's not the kid we knew and loved growing up.*

"No, Miles. You're not the same. It's not the same. Nothing is." The sadness in my voice surprises me.

He turns away, toward the tiny dent in the wall where I threw the glass box. If he notices it there on the floor, he doesn't mention it.

"I guess you're right. In ways you could never guess." A bitter laugh. "But music is still the most important thing. Music has always been my life. Even as a kid, I was able to play . . . anything, really. But then, when I was, like, fourteen or fifteen, it started to change."

My antenna goes up at that. Gaye had said his powers might have come to light during puberty. I sit beside him but resist taking his hand despite the sudden bloom of tenderness for him.

He wipes his eyes even though they're dry. "It was like, as my voice changed and other . . . changes to my body,"— he actually blushes at this—"it was like . . . I couldn't play anymore."

"What do you mean, you 'couldn't play anymore'?"

"I couldn't freaking play! Not violin. Not piano. Not drums. Not anything. My technique was erased—zapped out of my body and mind"—he snaps his fingers—"like that."

"But you can obviously play now. What happened? It must have been a temporary thing."

concerto

"That's the confusing stuff. One day, something happened. I'll never forget it. It was early December. Two and a half years ago. A cold, brisk day. Dry, though. Nothing in the forecast for snow or anything. I was determined to play, but it felt like I was wrestling my violin. It kept fighting me. I would apply more rosin and retune the strings. Over and over. But it didn't make any difference. Finally, I hugged the thing like a baby . . . and cried." He swallows hard. "And that's when it happened."

"What happened?"

"There was a rumbling inside me. Like, an earthquake in my body. At first, I thought I might puke or something, but then it changed. There was a surge of energy. Like—an awakening. My violin was calling to me, glowing in my arms. It was screaming for me to play it." His face opens, joyful. "I did. Oh, boy did I ever. It was—oh, gosh—it was perfection. I mean, I'd never played that well in my entire life."

"Wow." I'm pinned to his every word. "Go on."

"Of course, I was happy about it. Over the moon, to say the least."

"I bet."

"But then, I realized the result of it. I saw what I'd done." He stops. He fidgets, his mouth moving, searching for the right words.

"What do you mean? What did you see?"

"It was snowing. Like, a blizzard. A sudden, crazy snowstorm."

Even though I blame him for Newport and the ice storm here in Boston, I have doubts about his story. "It could've been a coincidence. I mean, how can you know that you made it happen?"

He gives me a sly, knowing look. "I knew it was me, Sami."

"You can't just know."

"No, I knew. I knew it was me. The way you know when you're hungry and need to eat. Everything in me told me." He pauses. "Not only that. It was thundersnow."

"What's thundersnow? I've never heard of that."

"I know. It's very rare. It's basically like a regular thunder and lightning storm, but instead of rain, there's snow. Sounds kind of simple but when you see it live, it's—unbelievable. It's like fireworks in ice."

A prickling sensation falls over me as his description triggers a sort of déjà vu. I stare at my hands, my birthmark barely visible in the dim light, and try to recall the significance. The only time I experienced a storm anything like what he just described was on Skene Mountain, when a sudden blizzard hit in the middle of my neutralizing Aquamarine. The snow was so abrupt and extreme, we were all stunned. Someone—Brenna's mom?—actually said aloud: *What made it snow like this?*

No one expected an answer. No one pointed any blame my way. But I knew it in my bones as sure as I knew what I had done to Aquamarine. I remember that moment vividly, staring into the fire roaring in Brenna's front parlor, magenta flames eerily reminiscent of the explosion of light from the cave. I knew what made it snow that day.

My music, I'd answered.

I knew it then.

And now, this.

Miles' thundersnow.

The timing matches up. Two and a half years ago. Early December. That's when I destroyed the Aquamarine at the

concerto

cave on Skene Mountain. Exactly then.

But it was just a snowstorm, right? It wasn't thundersnow. It was me that made lightning, of sorts. Tiny explosions to destroy the rock mineral. Explosions that burst with light—like fireworks. It was me who did all that. It was my music.

Could it be?

Lightning strikes my inner pores as a burst of recognition flashes through me. My instincts are on high alert, making me light-headed. My vision goes blurry as my mind crawls into the truth.

That thundersnow wasn't only Miles. It was me. It was my music.

CHAPTER 31

It can't be a coincidence. There has to be a connection. When I fulfilled my Dion responsibilities at Skene Mountain, using my piano to destroy magical Aquamarine, did I trigger thundersnow? Or—if Miles' violin caused the thundersnow on that December day, are our powers somehow linked?

Here, I've pinned Miles as the bad guy. But if my music does as much destruction as his, I'm equally guilty. It's like the floor drops out from under me. The world is colored anew. Have I been unintentionally helping Posh and Ms. Aleia? Have I been hurting Aunt Gaye? My stomach twists as an old fear creeps into my consciousness: my music caused destruction—not just on Skene Mountain, but across our great planet. Climate change, melting ice caps . . . *What if I'm to blame?*

Miles is still talking—a hum of words which blend together beneath my questions and guilt and insecurity. But then I hear a name that snaps me back and turns on my ears.

Lauren.

"What about Lauren?"

Miles is slightly taken aback by my interruption. He frowns, visibly uncomfortable. "Lauren was there. She and I—we were a couple, but we were also competitors. We'd been fighting for the All-State solo for a few months before the thundersnow. We practiced together. We pushed each

concerto

other to be better. But when my music became something else—when it caused something else—everything changed. Not just between the two of us, either. She was different, too. Sometimes she seemed like a totally different person. I felt like I didn't know her at all. Everything was screwed up. And I was freaking out."

His voice cracks and—I can't believe it—a tear glints in his eye. "Of course I went to my dad because I was completely unhinged. That's when I learned who I was." He throws a fist into his palm. "I can't help it that every time I play—when I play something *inspired*—crazy weather happens in the world. I don't mean for it to; it just does. But what am I supposed to do? Stop playing? It's not like I can hang it up, Sami. Would you be able to?"

"I . . . I don't know."

"Of course you wouldn't. You can't stop doing the one thing that makes you happiest in the entire world."

"If it were hurting people, yeah, I think I'd be able to refrain."

"I never wanted to hurt anyone." He pinches the bridge of his nose. "I can't take responsibility for that. It's too far removed from my music. Too many things would have to line up just right to affect an individual."

My jaw drops. I'm at a loss for words. Is he kidding me? Doesn't he know how deadly these storms can be?

He goes on, stoop-shouldered and doe-eyed. Totally in denial. "My music can't be entirely to blame."

I want to fire back—*Okay, Miles, how about taking 99.9% of the blame?*—but the word sticks. Blame. Panic ripples through me. *Am I to blame, too?*

I have to find a solution—not just for Miles but for me as well. "There's got to be some way to control it. There's got to be a way for the music to stand alone."

My conversation with Jason comes to mind. I'd been so determined to find meaning and purpose in my music. Never did I think I'd be faced with this. Now I wish I could be free to play for any reason or no reason at all. Just play. Beneath my words to Miles is hope for me. "Maybe you could find a way to strip away the magic part so you can just play. You know, for fun."

Miles is already shaking his head.

"I don't think that's possible. To make it worse, it seems the—disasters—feed my talent. Like, it works both ways. My music fuels the storms, and the storms fuel my music." He waits, studying me.

Mom says my emotions show in my face, and the last thing I want is for Miles to see what I'm feeling. Pursing my lips to appear thoughtful, I casually go to collect the little glass box from the floor and the three tiny shells that have escaped. In Miles' line of vision, I tenderly place it on my desk, replace the shells, and latch it closed. A peace offering, of sorts. I'm more akin to Miles than I'd thought. It feels wrong to cast all the blame on him.

Miles doesn't react to the gesture. "Sami, say something. Please."

What the heck am I supposed to say? *Don't worry, Miles, it's okay? Hey, I think I'm destroying the world, too? Let's be evil twin powers!*

Stalling for time, I open the blinds. A hint of rosy light tells me it's pre-dawn—a promise for a new beginning. As much as it pains me to admit, Miles and I are on equal footing here. And I need his help to navigate this unexpected revelation about my magic. My music.

Why is this happening?

concerto

How can I control it?

But to ask Miles these questions would be to admit to having these powers. Though Miles believes I helped him create last night's ice storm, he doesn't know—he can't know—about what I did to Aquamarine on that fateful December day. He doesn't suspect I have anything to do with the thundersnow he blames on his violin session of two years ago.

I don't trust him enough to tell him. What would he and Aleia do with that knowledge?

Miles rubs his eyes, which are ringed with dark circles. I hadn't noticed how tired he looks until now.

"I should go," he says sadly. He needed something from me I'm not able to give.

"Okay." My fingers are locked together, picking at cuticles. Rattled, I'm trapped between wanting him here to figure this out and wanting him gone so I can be rid of him.

Lauren. Maybe I'll get in touch with her again. Ask her more questions. Get more specific—

I'm still reeling when he takes my cheek in his hand and leans in close. My body goes rigid. *Is he going to kiss me?*

"I didn't ask for these powers, Sami." He puts his cheek up to mine. His lips tickle my ear. "You've got to believe I never wanted to hurt anyone." His soft voice pours into my ear and travels through my body like liquid. "I'm a victim in this," he whispers. "Can't you see that?"

CHAPTER 32

Miles wouldn't leave until I promised to perform at Showcase with him before the program is over. *Sure, Miles. Whatever.* What a girl will do to be left alone.

After he leaves, I fall into bed. Only then do I remember I wanted to contact Lauren again. She had warned me against playing music with him but never told me why. And although I now know the danger, I'm sure there's more to it from Lauren's point of view. When it comes to dealing with Miles, she's the expert. My phone's sitting all the way over on my desk, though, and I'm too tired to grab it. Later. I'll text her later.

Most of my Monday is surrendered to sleep. Missing classes seems a mild offense compared to causing an ice storm in the middle of a hot Boston summer.

It takes most of the day for the ice to thaw. And thaw it does, miraculously, Boston's notorious summer humidity staying true to its reputation. Though a state of emergency is called, the city comes to life a little by sunset. Or at least it seems that way from what I can see out my window.

The local news station reports most of the serious damage hit closer to the South Shore, and many suburbs are still in the dark. It's amazing how quickly the heart of the city bounces back. However, passing people on the street, it's clear that the extreme, bizarre weather affected more than traffic and the electrical grid. It shows on their faces: people

concerto

are scared.

Poppy is at the gallery already, sketching in her journal at the center table. Gaye emerges from the back room looking as if she aged five years since I last saw her. The whole gallery has a droopy feel to it, like it's taken a hit. And the lighting is different.

"Aunt Gaye, did you lose power?"

"The lights flickered is all." She sounds tired. "We're fine."

Perusing the gallery, though, it doesn't seem fine. Something's off. Studying the magical, moving landscapes, I find New England. Boston, specifically. It's as if a dark cloud covers the city, making the skyscrapers opaque, the city lights muted. Not destroyed, but tainted.

That's me. That's my doing. It's enough to make me want to cry. Pivoting to the center table where Gaye has joined Poppy, I start my teary confession.

I tell them everything: My duet with Miles at the studio—our marathon song fogged over by amnesia, which cracked and clouded the Aquamarine pendant. My terrifying discovery of the ice storm that was triggered by our music—mine and Miles'. I share what I learned from Miles when he came to my room later, and finally—my hunch that our powers are similar . . . if not intertwined.

"It's all my fault." Sobs overtake me as I sink into a chair.

At first I think it's Gaye who's rubbing my back, comforting me, but it's Poppy. Straightening, I try to refocus. Gaye sits across the table, bobbing her foot, a serious look on her face. Makes me want to take back my tears.

"Sorry," I blurt, wiping my cheeks dry.

Gaye shushes me with a flick of her hand. Then, she taps

the table with Poppy's drawing pen. Waiting for her response is excruciating. "I was wrong," she says calmly. "You should've worn the pendant."

I can't hide my shock. She's not going to yell at me? Just the opposite, she's taking some responsibility for what happened. "You think I should've worn the pendant? Why? What would that have done?"

"It would have offset Miles' power and redirected your own." Gaye stares at the Boston landscape painting, which is gradually brightening.

Poppy opens her journal to an intricate design in the shape of a giant raindrop. "What about the henna?"

Gaye's eyes widen. "Ah, yes. The henna. That could've been useful for Sam, too. Next time, we'll have to—"

"It can't be near my birthmark." I cover my Nevus spilus protectively. "It hurts too much."

Poppy shakes her head. "Sami, don't you realize that the henna activated your birthmark? And if your birthmark is like a portal to your magic, it would make sense that henna is a trigger."

"That's exactly right," Gaye chimes in. "And it's also why Ms. Aleia reprimanded you for doing henna. Henna is known to unlock dormant Goshenite magic. Aleia might not know about the Dion part, but she definitely knows henna can interfere with her . . . agenda."

Poppy's on her feet now, too. "The henna could be more important than the Aquamarine. I mean, if Sami wore henna last night, it would've prevented her from blacking out at the piano with Miles. It would've kept her alert, at least. Even if it hurt a little."

"Did you know henna was going to have that effect on me? The real magic happens with Dion. How did you know

concerto

henna was magical?"

Gaye sounds like a teacher. "Henna is a plant, child. Its botanical name is *Lawsonia inermis*. And it's my business to know what grows from my planet, isn't it? I've always known henna was magical, but its effects are usually so mild that it doesn't attract much intrigue."

"The designs on the skin are technically called Mehndi," Poppy says. "It originated in India."

I gingerly circle my birthmark with my thumb. I'm not a fan of how that henna made me feel. I mean, who wants to sign up for pain like that? "I don't know."

"Well, we aren't sure what will work," Gaye says firmly. "But we should leave no stone unturned. The next time Sam is asked to play alongside Miles, she'll have all her weapons. She will have the henna and the Aquamarine. We cannot afford another error. Who knows what would happen? If the scale tips too far in their favor, getting it back will be impossible." She pinches her lips with worry and then turns to me.

"You really think henna and Aquamarine will help me? The pendant from Poppy's shop was destroyed."

"Right. Aquamarine has unique magic, and you are the one person who has been able to control it. You, Sam. Dion. And it was too far away from you. If you'd been wearing it, I think there would have been a different outcome. But a lot of that depends on you." Gaye gets up from the table and paces the room. The pitch of her voice rises.

"As we've discussed before, there is so much of your magic to unlock. We haven't seen the half of it. It's time to tap into it—to be proactive. No more waiting for it to come to you. Henna and Aquamarine are tools you can use for your own purposes. And, as always, it's your birthmark that

228

will lead you."

My shoulders go rigid with fear and panic as I'm overwhelmed with doubt. I stare at my left hand, a sudden hatred for the mark bubbling up. *It's time.* Gaye didn't have to say it; I feel the urgency, too. Danger is all around us. The Earth is on precarious ground. People's lives are at stake. What if I can't do it? What if Gaye's wrong and my magic is weak and limited? What if I try . . . and fail—and people die as a result?

"Aunt Gaye, I'm scared."

Gaye meets my eye, her face blank.

"And it's not just me." My voice quakes. "People are scared."

"I know."

"It seems like, I don't know. There was no reason for it. I mean, it didn't help Posh expand his domain. It just scared people."

"Maybe that's part of his goal," says Poppy.

"To scare people?"

"Poppy might be on to something," Gaye says. "Posh's strategy might be to trigger an evacuation in order to take control of the shorelines and even the inland waters. Instilling fear in people must be part of the plan. He's got to control people. It's the dictator model. Scare them to death so that they need you."

"But why would he want that? Just for evacuations?"

Gaye palms the sky. "Maybe he's power hungry. Maybe it's not enough to have dominion over the Earth; he wants dominion over the people who live on it, too."

"I don't know. He doesn't seem to care about people at all."

"Ruling people and caring for them don't always go

concerto

hand in hand."

Memories of the Mr. Eichen of my childhood don't match up with the powerful god-of-sea Posh Eichen known to me now. He'd traveled a lot, and he often whisked his family away on cruise vacations, but when he was home, he always made things fun. He liked to sing and dance, always had a joke on hand. His smile was big and effervescent, and he laughed with his whole body. That, of course, was when he was still married.

Miles' home was filled with love, the aroma of home cooking ever present. Miles' mother puttered in the kitchen, stirring salty soups and sauces, pulling sweet breads from the oven. Was the divorce his undoing? Miles had played it down when he told me about his parents splitting up, but it's never an easy thing.

Darkness clouds thoughts of my own father—abandoning my mother before he even knew me. I could never forgive him for that. But at least I didn't have to live through a bitter divorce and custody battle.

For the Eichens, it had to be a turning point. After all these years, seeing Posh at the beach, he was a shadow of the man I knew. His laughter less flowing, the jokes more strained, although his reverence for the sea was unrelenting.

Drumming my fingers on the table, I stare at the knots in the dark wood, trying to reconcile my memories with the new Posh—but thoughts of demigod Miles keep getting in the way. What he'd said last night, how he never asked for his powers. All he wants is to make music, to be a great musician. *I'm a victim in this.* It makes me wonder: is his father forcing him to create these storms? If so, it might make our job a bit easier.

With that idea, a renewed energy fills me. "If what he

told me is true and his heart isn't truly in it, I should be able to talk him out of it."

Gaye lifts an eyebrow.

Poppy smirks. "And what exactly will you say? You do realize you're talking about going up against the power of Poseidon here. Miles can't just decide not to play along with his father's plan."

"Well, maybe I won't play, then."

Gaye leans on the table. "If you don't play, they'll still create a storm. There will still be a disaster. The only hope we have to stop them is through your music. You're Dion, Sam. Have faith in your powers."

Poppy grips her journal, white knuckled. "It's the only way to gain control."

That terrifying doubt creeps in again. "What if I can't get to that level of power Gaye's talking about? What if all I can do is have these visions and be a puppet for Aleia and Miles?"

Gaye swats the air. "Nonsense. It's time to be strong, Sam. It's time to act like Dion. When are you expected to play with Miles again? Have they asked you?"

I swallow what feels like a brick in my throat. "Miles made me promise to perform at Showcase with him before the program is over. But nothing's officially scheduled."

Gaye's grin is mischievous. "Well, you won't be performing at Showcase this Friday, because we'll be on our way to Skenesboro."

"We will?" Poppy and I ask in unison.

"Why are we going to Skenesboro?" I add.

Gaye throws up her hands. "For Aquamarine. Skene Aquamarine."

Poppy waves toward Newbury Street. "I have other

concerto

Aquamarine pendants at the shop, I could just—"

"No, no, no," Gaye says. "We're not taking any chances here. We're not risking another mishap with another pendant from your shop. No offense, Poppy. My gut tells me it has to be from the cave on Skene Mountain, so that's where we're going." She gives her belly a pat. "My gut is quite reliable."

"I'm not sure what's left of that cave, Aunt Gaye," I say. Images of that early December day come flooding back: exploding rocks, a laser blue light show, blinding fireworks. And then—ash and debris everywhere. "I can't say there's any Aquamarine left up there."

"Oh, no. There is." Gaye chuckles. "But it might not be easy to find. We'll need all hands on deck. Poppy, you can get next weekend off, I assume. And I'll tell Jason he's needed there, too."

Oh! Jason! My heart leaps at that.

"And who's that pretty girl with the scars?" Gaye strokes her neck.

"Brenna? She's at Tisch right now, in the summer program."

"She's got the weekend off, doesn't she? Let's get her there, too. Something tells me we'll need her."

My grin could fill the room. *I'm going home. And all my best friends will be there.* The thought warms me from the inside out. Relief and gratitude well up. "Oh, Aunt Gaye. You're not mad at me, then?"

Gaye does a double take. "Why on earth would I be mad at you?" She winks. "Why on this god's green earth would I ever be mad at you, Sam? You're going to help me save it."

CHAPTER 33

When I first laid eyes on Poppy, with her badass tattoos—well, henna tattoos—and piercings and pseudo-noir vibe, the thought never crossed my mind that she would ever be my bodyguard. However, ever since our gallery meeting when we decided to go to Skenesboro, she has not left my side. Night and day. Through my classes and study breaks and three meals a day, she is there. It's easy to avoid Miles with a menacing sidekick. He acts like he's a little afraid of her. He mopes when he walks, hunching his shoulders. Whenever we've passed in the hall, he gives me these sad puppy dog eyes. Ms. Aleia has been more neutral, all business, teacher to student. Until today.

She catches me after class as Poppy and I are about to leave. "Samantha, can I have a word?"

Why not? I pivot back, feeling untouchable, knowing Poppy is there.

Ms. Aleia looks past me, shooting daggers at Poppy. "Privately?"

Tension thickens the air. Poppy gradually eases back to wait in the doorway, keeping me in view.

Ms. Aleia's smile is strained. "I was impressed with your piano playing last weekend. I understand you and Miles spoke about performing in this week's Showcase? How about a rehearsal this evening to prepare?"

Before I can say anything, Miles appears next to

concerto

Aleia—her menacing sidekick. Now I'm surrounded. My invincible feeling disappears. One look at Poppy tells me she feels it, too, the shift in power. She starts toward us, but then backs off. Ms. Aleia and Miles both tower over me, shrinking any shred of confidence I had.

"Um . . ."

To my surprise, Miles saves me. Kind of. "Maybe a rehearsal isn't necessary," he says, giving me a gift of procrastination. His eyes on me are intense. "It's no secret we make great music together. It's, like, a natural chemistry. I don't think we need to practice. Do you, Sami?"

"Um, no." Gosh, I sound like a weenie. *Say something smart, Sami!*

Miles squares his shoulders with a sideways smile. "I think if we meet a little early for Showcase, that would be fine." He closes the space between us. His briny body heat steams off his skin, oppressive. "Maybe we should talk about what to wear. It would be cool to coordinate."

There's so much I want to say. My mind screams: *Don't look at me like that. We are not a thing. We are not a team.*

But what comes out is: "I don't do ruffles."

My unintentional joke is a rollicking success. Miles and Ms. Aleia both crack up. I steal a glance at Poppy, whose confusion is painted all over her face. She mouths: *What's going on?* She scoops the air impatiently. *Let's get out of here!*

"Okay, no ruffles," Ms. Aleia says, beaming. "You two can figure out your wardrobe another time. Let's plan to meet at five in my office on Friday."

"Good." Miles puffs his chest.

Now or never, Sami. I can't have them thinking I'm actually going through with Showcase this Friday. Not without

Skene Aquamarine. I find my voice: "Actually, sorry." Why is it hard to say? "I'm not really going to be here for Showcase."

Miles' grin drops. He eyes me through slits. "What do you mean? You're not 'really' going to be here? Either you're here or you're not. Where are you going to be?"

Do I tell them? Is it supposed to be a secret? A desperate look at Poppy doesn't give me an answer. *Say something!* I'm so flustered, all necessary caution is out the window.

"I'm going home," I say, relieved that it's out. "For the weekend . . . had it planned."

Now I know why they call it a pregnant pause. The whole room bloats with it.

"Oh, really?" Miles says. "You didn't mention this the other day when we talked about Showcase."

"I—I didn't think, um. I thought you meant any Showcase, not necessarily this week's. You said before the program is over, right? There's still time. Can't we plan on next Friday?" That way I can have all my reinforcements in place . . . and my nerve.

Ms. Aleia doesn't try to hide her disappointment. Her glare cuts through me. "I suppose. That will be the last Showcase of the program." She turns to Miles. "And our last chance. It better happen." She tosses folders into her hobo bag and storms out of the room.

Miles looks me up and down like he's checking for visible secrets. "Going to Skenesboro, then?" His question is loaded.

Poppy is here, back at my side. "What makes you think she's going to Skenesboro?" Poppy eyes me askance.

Miles gives Poppy a cursory look. "What—are you two bosom buddies now?"

concerto

Poppy drapes a stiff arm around me. It's awkward. Weighs me down.

"Yup," she says.

"Sami just told us she was going home." Miles' attention is solely on me.

"Oh, well. I think we're going to Skenesboro. We might go to . . . New York City. Or somewhere." My cheeks are burning.

"You just said you had this planned for a while," Miles says. "Is your mountain man going to be there?"

That nasty moniker used to bristle me, but it has no effect on me anymore. Jason is my guy, period. Miles can try to diminish him in any childish way he wants, but I am staying true blue. And—I get to see him Friday. Finally! Jason's as thrilled as I am we get to see each other on home ground.

Ahhh, Jason.

Despite Miles looming in front of me with those wolfish eyes, my thoughts go straight to Jason and our phone date last night. Our conversation wasn't awkward; it was easy. Normal. Comfortable. He was so sweet. We reminisced about the things we used to do together back in Skenesboro, how we made nothing-doing somehow fun. He told me he missed me—and he didn't just say it. He told me specifically what he missed: my lips, my smell, how my hair tickles his face when we wrestle in his living room, how my body feels pressed up against his when we snuggle on his couch. When we got off the phone, I felt as if we had had a date. A real date. It more than reinforced my love for him. It nurtured my heart.

"You're right," I say, thoughts of Jason lifting me up. "I'm not going to New York City. I'm going home to Skenesboro. And yes, my boyfriend is meeting me there. His name is not mountain man, it's Jason. He's an amazing artist and an amazing guy. And he loves me."

Miles' eyebrows hit the ceiling. Before he can make a snarky comeback, I pull away, tugging Poppy's arm. I lead her down the hallway, hoping he doesn't follow.

"So, you agreed to play at Showcase with him? Next Friday?"

"Yeah. Bought us some time. We'll have all my secret weapons by then. Skene Aquamarine, your henna . . ."

"I wonder if there's something else we're not thinking of. Something that would make you a sure thing."

That makes me stop. "Hold on." I duck into an empty classroom and pull out my phone. My insides churn a little remembering what Lauren told me. *Under no circumstances should you play music with him.*

I open Messages to text her. My fingertips go cold, hovering over the keypad.

Showcase performance w Miles next Fri.

Writer's block. What exactly do I want to say here?

Thought u shd know

SEND

Now it's Poppy who tugs on my arm. "We shouldn't linger anywhere we might get cornered. Come on."

Putting my phone away, I follow her to the hallway. No sign of Ms. Aleia or Miles anywhere. "It's okay," I tell Poppy. "I think I successfully put them off for a while."

"Yeah, but why would you tell Miles where you're going this weekend?"

"Why not? I have nothing to hide."

concerto

"Yeah, but what if he goes all stalker on you and follows us up there?"

"Follows us?"

"I don't know. I'd be careful, considering that vision you had."

Oh, no. My insides begin to squirm. Poppy's so right. My vision about Skenesboro!

Images surge back: the Champlain Canal flooding over, the giant rogue wave out of the normally placid Lake Champlain. Jason plodding through waters by my side as we make our way to the lock. And then, the Aquamarine pendant like a star glowing forth from my heart, quelling it. Was it just a vision, or will it come true?

What did I just do—invite Miles to destroy my home? Oh, if I could take back the words.

CHAPTER 34

En route to Skenesboro, Gaye drives and Poppy rides shotgun while I sprawl out in the back. It's weird going home. It feels like I've been gone for years with all that's happened. Gaye plays soft music as she drives, her hands dependably at ten and two, and doesn't talk much. Poppy's spiky hair is pressed against the passenger window. A cute purring snore tells me she's dozing.

We drive up New Hampshire and through Vermont, and although I've done this ride before, I'm riveted by the landscape we pass. The rolling hills of New Hampshire feel like giant hugs. Then, off the highway, as we travel the winding roads of Vermont through the countryside, the hills are punctuated by farmlands and bright red barns, and the towns surround white chapels with steeples that pierce the sky. I'm struck by the majesty of Gaye's domain. And this is just a tiny speck. Diverse and mysterious, what a beautiful world. It's the best distraction, temporarily taking me away from the whole Miles fiasco. The farther we drive, the more distance grows between us, and it's easy to let him slip from my mind altogether.

If only I could.

We're on a mission, I'm reluctant to remind myself. Tomorrow, we're venturing up Skene Mountain to find the elusive Aquamarine mineral that will hopefully help me overpower Miles' music with my own. And stop the next disaster

concerto

from striking, in whatever form that may be.

Welcome to New York! announces the blue roadside billboard. Next stop, Skenesboro.

"Right to your house, then, Sam?" Gaye asks.

Jason won't be here until late tonight, he'd said. How I wish I could see him right away.

"Yeah, I guess. We should go right to my house."

Gaye turns off Route 4, and Skene Manor comes into view. Emotions flood me. As much as I thought I wouldn't miss this nowhere place, the familiar sights are a welcome comfort. I miss Jason. And I miss Mom.

As we pull into my driveway, a whole different meaning of home comes into play. Jason is there on my front porch, his arms open and ready for me to run into them.

He's here!

"Oh, oh, oh! Let me out. Let me out!" I'm out of the car before Gaye puts it into park.

"Jason!" I jump onto him like a monkey, laughing and crying happy tears. He twirls me around and plants a whopping kiss on my cheek.

"I missed you," he whispers into my hair. "God, I missed you."

I melt into him. "I missed you, too."

This makes it all worth it. This is better than any crystal. This is worth gold.

The next morning, we meet on the grounds of Skene Manor—me, Mom, Brenna, Aunt Gaye, Poppy, and Jason.

Behind the manor, we find the infamous trail. Two and a half years ago, I trekked up with the goal of neutralizing toxic Aquamarine. Then, a few days before I left for Berklee, I'd wanted to see the clearing, the cave, in hopes of summoning inspiration. I wanted to make amends for what I'd done—all that destruction.

Four weeks ago, every step was a trial. My legs were like lead, weighed down by guilt and uncertainty. And yet, I hadn't known about the thundersnow. I had no idea what Miles was doing with his violin in an entirely different part of the state. Or how his music and his magic had triggered that strange, violent storm.

Today, though, in the middle of July, it's hot. It's like we have to swim through the humidity. Not halfway up and we're all chugging water. Sweat soaks our T-shirts. Rather than feel guilt and uncertainty, I'm determined. And with my posse surrounding me, I'm lifted by the energy. Aunt Gaye has given me direction when I felt lost. As confusing as my visions have been, she and Poppy have been there to help me figure it all out. We're doing the right thing. I have to believe that.

Jason syncs his steps with mine, asking softly, "Do you think about what happened to Coach Payne?"

A shiver runs through me despite the heat. "Of course I do. But it's been a long time."

"Right. I'm not superstitious or anything, but it kind of seems like we don't want to disrupt the cave. Like, we could resurrect her or something." Jason's laugh masks his fear.

"Oh, Jason. Don't even say that." Images from my last visit to this place rush back—when Brenna led me into the shadows to see the tower of rubble that used to be the cave.

My steps slow as my confidence is shaken, that nightmarish feeling taking hold once again: a chill surrounds me, a ghost's embrace . . . It's her. Her aura emotes. It's frantic.

concerto

Despair, a clinging hope. Unyielding wrath. *Coach Payne is here—*

It wasn't her; it was my mind playing tricks.

By the time we reach the clearing, I'm weary. My water bottle is empty, and my energy is drained. Surveying the gutted, ash-filled space, I fight a pang of despair. To get to where the cave used to be, we have to clear out the brush, dismantle the nest of dead trees. Beyond that, we'll come up against the tower of rubble. It will be a Herculean effort to get through it all. And what if it's for nothing? How could there be anything of value in this chaos? It's hard to believe we'll find a trace of Aquamarine, no less an intact crystal.

Poppy pans the clearing in less than a second. "Is this it? I thought you said it was a cave?"

I see it through her eyes—and hope sags. "It is. Or was. It's beyond those dead trees there." Only Brenna and I know the treasure map. I should take the lead, but something roots me in place. "Aunt Gaye, are you sure there's still Aquamarine up here?"

Mom's pacing near the tree line, worry painted across her brow. "There can't be." I hadn't thought it might be traumatic for her, this journey. Of course it must be. As a mother, to revisit the site where your daughter basically vaporized her volleyball coach, your old classmate. Regret strikes a mighty chord. She pleads to be excused. "Why don't I go help Brenna's mom with lunch?"

She's gone before anyone can answer, and I deflate even more.

"Maybe there's another place?" Poppy tries to sound encouraging. "Maybe farther up the hill? I mean, this looks like someone took a giant machete and sliced out part of the mountain, tossing trees around like Pick-up sticks in the process."

Gaye seems undaunted. "This is the place. Sam, would you care to show us the rock?"

Brenna gives me an encouraging nod. "Go ahead, Sami."

Deep breath. Pushing fear aside, I step beneath the tree cover. "We'll have to clear this brush." As I say it, I push aside a large branch with more ease than I thought possible. Without a word, Jason's beside me, moving the larger pieces. Gaye and Poppy work together to roll away an exposed root and stump. Quickly, we untangle the murky nest of trees and light shines through.

I catch my breath. "There it is."

The tower of rubble had seemed to glow within the dense tree canopy—and called to me. Now, exposed to daylight, it's muted and stubbornly unreceptive. And huge.

Poppy's laugh echoes in the clearing. "I hate to tell you this, bonehead, but this is no cave."

My steps are shaky as I clamber over the rubble and debris. My voice is shaky, too. "We have to move the rocks."

Poppy doesn't follow right away. "Move the rocks? Oh, like, no biggie? Are you looking at the same pile of boulders I am? We need some major machinery to do that."

Jason lifts a rock the size of his chest, tosses it to the side like it's a beach ball. "No, we don't. Come on."

"Holy Magoo, Sami, you didn't tell me your boyfriend's the Hulk."

Poppy's eyes pop wider when Gaye moves an even larger rock.

"A fringe benefit of Sami's magic, it seems, was the shift in composition of these rocks. Once dense and loaded

concerto

with gemstone, now they are porous and light—similar to pumice." Gaye passes her a watermelon-sized boulder, which Poppy handles with ease. "Pumice is a lava froth, which means it's formed as a result of explosions. Usually volcano. When Sami neutralized Aquamarine on this mountain, she affected this massive wall of granite in the same way with her explosions. And thank goodness. We have to get through this to find the good stuff."

Jason's already made a huge dent in the pile of rubble. Watching him work alongside his aunt, it's a wonder that Jason is spared from the antics of the gods. Or is he? When I first met Jason, seeing his extraordinary paintings, I'd assumed he was Goshenite. Then, after being together for over two years, he proved himself to be a normal, albeit super-talented, guy. But if his aunt is Gaea, wouldn't that make him some sort of demigod? It's in his blood. He's the nephew of the god of the Earth. What does that make him? Rick Riordan didn't go into that. Neither did Bullfinch's Mythology.

Curiosity gets the best of me. "So, Aunt Gaye, are you sisters with Jason's mom or his dad?"

Aunt Gaye gives me a curious look. "Neither."

Now I'm confused. "Wait . . . how—?"

Jason laughs. "She's not really my aunt. Not by blood, I mean. She and my mom were best friends back in the day. I've always known her as Aunt Gaye."

"Oh." Why am I disappointed? I should be glad Jason's a regular guy. I mean, Miles turned out to be a demigod, and look how well that's doing for his love life.

Jason handles most of the awkwardly sized boulders. Brenna and Poppy use shovels for the smaller pieces. With the larger rocks and boulders cleared, we're faced with a giant ash heap. Gaye brandishes her broom. "Work carefully. We are searching for a treasure here."

We're all tired. We've been at it for hours now. Still, we follow Gaye's lead and start sifting through the ash.

Her broom choice made me pause back at the manor. Most of us had chosen shovels, except Jason, who brought a pickaxe. It's clear, though, as she sweeps away a large clump of ash, that Aunt Gaye's instincts are spot on.

It's like that book from my fifth-grade class about dinosaur excavation—how carefully scientists needed to dig for fear of damaging precious bone or fossils.

Jason gently taps the pickaxe to find that sweet spot where the ash ends and rock begins. Poppy sweeps with the flat back of a shovel, studying the ground intently. Brenna uses her hands, clutching the solidified debris and removing large congealed ash chunks.

But everyone comes up short. The ash seems endless. It's like searching for a diamond in the sand. Impossible.

For a moment, I'm suspended—questioning whether being here at all is the right move. My eyes go to the tops of the trees. Two years ago, I could see bare branches alongside the tall pines, dark black against a backdrop of gray. At the time, they showed themselves as musical notes in my mind—floating off sheet music, free in the skies. Now, the birches and aspens are pushing their way through. The sky is almost obscured as the forest has leafed out, lush with so much green. I sigh without meaning to. Aunt Gaye glares in my direction.

"We're not quite there yet, Sam. Are you planning to help?"

concerto

My answer is action, whether it's fruitful or not. Kneeling, I scoop ash with my forearms and hands, staying low to avoid eye contact. Soon, my jeans look like they've been dipped in confectioner's sugar.

"Here's something." Jason holds up a rock the size of a baseball.

Gaye examines it for less than a second and tosses it aside. "Nope. Not Aquamarine."

"How can you tell?" Jason asks.

"It's my business to know my planet, Jason. You know that."

Jason pauses his pickaxe to smile at me in that sweet way he does, and I'm reminded how lucky I am to have him. And how I almost screwed it up beyond repair. A twinge infects my gut, knowing we still need to have the Miles talk. I blow him a kiss anyway, feeling more determined by the ash-scoop.

We come upon a hard surface where the cliff wall used to be. Brenna throws down her shovel and works her hands over the face of the rock, coughing away the powdery ash that covers it. "It was right around here."

Gaye follows Brenna's lead, feeling around the surface for a give or an opening. Or—

"What exactly are you looking for?" My voice is meek. Do they really think they'll find—

"The cave," Brenna says matter-of-factly. Just then, she grips an edge out of nowhere. "Here," she says to Gaye. As if they had this planned all along, Gaye works a few feet from where Brenna stands. I should help them, but I'm frozen in place. It's not a layer of stone I'm looking at; it's solidified ash. They gently pry at the edges until it loosens, and the chunk of dead gray earth crumbles with an empty *thud* and falls into darkness.

"Aha!" Gaye exclaims, clapping dust off her hands.

It takes me a moment to process what I'm seeing. Queasy, I lean forward, staving off another visit from Payne's ghost.

The cave . . . is still here.

It is, but it isn't. It's changed. It no longer stands vertically but slopes to the ground—as if we could fall right into it. Like, a miniature sinkhole. It's less than two feet around and pitch black. Looking in, nothing is visible. It's like a black hole at the center of a galaxy. A dead void. Nothingness.

Until Gaye turns her flashlight into it.

And the sparkle almost blinds us. Brenna gasps, clutching my arm. I cry aloud in awe and relief.

"There she is," Gaye says triumphantly.

Deep inside the hole, about fifteen feet down, a lone blue crystal shatters the blackness. The shard of Aquamarine matches the size of Poppy's pendant. That's the only similarity, though, as I blink into the chasm in disbelief. The bright blue crystal illuminates the rocky sides of the tunnel, shifting with the slight motion of the flashlight like a disco ball. It takes my breath. To the naked eye, it appears that Gaye's light gave it life.

CHAPTER 35

"Hot tamale!" Poppy claps her hands. "Now I get why we had to drive all the way the heck up to Nowheresville. And I thought a pendant from the shop would do it. Ha!"

"How are we going to get it?" Brenna asks. "It's so far down."

"If only there was a way we could fish it out." Jason squats close to the opening. "But we'd need something to snatch it up."

"Yeah, like one of those crane game grabber things you see at arcades." Poppy is the only one who laughs. "At least I'm trying," she adds, looking pointedly at me.

Moving away from the light, I gather myself. "Sorry, I . . . it's just kind of a shock to see it." So many memories, so many images course through my mind of that day when light—this light—took Coach Payne.

"What should we do?" Brenna sounds worried. She's got good reason. Even though we've found it, all is for nothing if we can't physically get it. Gaye has been quiet, thoughtful; this is her problem to solve.

Giving myself space away from the chasm, I realize how dark it's become. Glancing up beyond the tops of the tall trees, the sky has darkened.

"Is it supposed to rain?" I squeak, unable to talk about weather in any normal cadence anymore.

"Sam." Gaye turns the flashlight on me, and my eyes

concerto

burn from the intensity of the light. Her plan isn't going to be one I like. "Sam, it has to be you. I don't want to risk anyone else infecting the mineral. It has to be Dion. You have to go down there and fetch it."

"What?" That's crazy talk. No way am I tunneling down into a chasm for a piece of Aquamarine. "You're kidding, right?"

She turns off the flashlight, and for a moment, everything is awash in gray stain. Damp and muggy. A sharp yearning for that intense blue light we just discovered—that light I'd thought was gone forever—astonishes me. I tug at my T-shirt, which sticks to my skin like plaster.

Aunt Gaye is watching me. She doesn't say anything. She doesn't need to.

"You don't have to, Sami." Jason touches my arm. "If you don't feel comfortable, I'll go down there."

"No." Gaye shakes her head once. "It has to be Sam."

Brenna knows enough not to ask why. "We'll be here, Sami. We'll be able to pull you out. You're not going to do this alone."

Alone. That word is rich.

That first time, my magic required complete solitude. And I was brave enough to know it and own it and insist on it. What a weakling I've turned into. I'd be terrified if I were here alone now. It ticks me off to think I've changed so much—for the worse.

Jason's beside me, his whole aura bent with worry. "It's okay," I say to him before turning back to Gaye. "I'll do it."

Rock climbing is a sport I haven't ever practiced, which

becomes apparent as I clumsily scale down the narrow crevice toward the crystal. My pulse races as sweat streaks into my eyes. When I try to wipe it away, I lose my footing.

Whaa!

I slip into a free fall, pinballing against the harsh rock down the chasm. A hollow fear scatters my senses. Terrifying—it's like I'm falling down a well.

Bam!

I land hard, in a tangle of limbs. All my joints get knocked out of place.

"Aaghh!"

My scream echoes up through the pit.

"You okay, Sami?" Jason calls.

Gritting through tears, I check myself over. It's a miracle I didn't break any bones. Or the crystal. The skin on my knees and elbows is raw and red and stinging with fresh scrapes. I catch my breath.

"Yeah, I'm okay."

Gaye's flashlight has become my spotlight.

"Do you see it?" Her voice is tinged with concern.

"Yeah, yeah. It's right here. No problem."

"Well, come on," Gaye says urgently. "Grab it and let's go. The rain's started."

"Okay. Just a sec."

My height is not my friend. Bending down in the narrow passage proves impossible. I hadn't thought I was claustrophobic, but it seems I am. Panic churns as I squat, knees grating rock, deeper into the fissure. I blindly sweep my hand near my feet for the crystal—the stone cold and rough. The awkward way I'm forced to bend, my neck tips back. Facing the opening, Gaye's spotlight stings.

"Can you turn that thing off for a sec?" I call to her. "It's

concerto

not helping."

Gaye complies, and I'm left in darkness and an eerie silence, trying to find our prize.

You're not alone, Sami, Brenna had said. But it feels awfully lonely.

A sharp edge catches my elbow, drawing blood. The air is thinning. My chin knocks against the rock wall. I hear myself whimper and almost ask to be saved. But then—

Aha!

Euphoria replaces panic, and a squealing laugh escapes me. It feels like glass—smoother than I expected—as if it's been cut and polished. I wrap it in my fist and call up, "Got it!"

As I carefully unfold myself from my cramped position, it happens—

Like an explosion.

I drown in light.

𝄋

Blinded by the sudden burst of light, I hold tight to the crystal and bat the air that has grown thick and particle-y with a sudden damp heat. My coughs echo as if I'm in an endless tunnel.

What happened?

My eyes slowly adjust. The base of the chasm has bloomed into a wide cave. My arms can move freely without hitting rock-lined walls. The way up and out isn't visible.

"Aunt Gaye? Jason?"

The names echo. Then fizzle.

No answer. Terror grips me.

Am I trapped?

252

"Gaye! Jason!" I call, frantic.

They can't hear me. I'm truly alone down here.

Stay calm, Sami.

I try to get my head around it. If I were trapped, it would be total darkness. Right?

But light pokes through. I blink into it as my vision adjusts. I survey the cave, sure that the light must guide me to the surface. But it doesn't make sense.

The light has color—like fire. And its source is not overhead, from the sky, but from underneath, seeping from a far corner of the cave floor, as if I'd broken through to another layer of earth. A volcanic layer?

Fog fills the space, making tiny prisms of the air particles. Colors flicker from reds to purples, like a kaleidoscope.

A stark recognition snaps me alert. My gasp is loud in the echo-y chamber. This is familiar. The colors, the light—it's just like that day. Exactly the same. My panic shifts to an altogether different kind of horror. This is my doing.

Could it be?

It's as if, down here, time stopped at that day in December. Penetrating fear pins me to one place. My breath has caught.

No. This can't be happening. This isn't possible.

She's here.

I feel her presence before she becomes visible. She's an apparition made of mist. The mosaic of light is behind her, shadowing her features. Yet, I recognize her easily.

It can't be.

My body wracks with tremors. My wide eyes prick with petrified tears. My lips part to speak—*How? Why?*—or to beg for mercy. All I choke out is: "Coach."

Payne swirls like the Ghost of Christmas Past, coming

concerto

near but not touching. She carries an unspoken wisdom about her: secret, valuable knowledge. "You found me," she says, her breathy voice not unkind.

I clasp the crystal to my chest. "I didn't . . . I wasn't . . ."

"I know. You didn't think you were looking for me. But you found me all the same."

Words shudder out: "How are you . . . here?"

"You don't remember?" she singsongs. "How could you forget? You were there, Sami. You made me this way."

My mouth is clogged. It's like I'm swallowing stones. "Coach, I didn't mean to . . . I never dreamed that would happen."

She twists around me again, angling her face to the light. I steal a glance at her and regret it instantly.

She's gaunt and bug-eyed, her cheeks sunken craters, her eyes glowing marbles. She's a shell of herself, as if partially decomposed.

"I never meant to hurt you," I say, averting my eyes.

"Did it hurt?" she asks, breathy. "I can't remember."

Tears trundle down my cheeks. "I can't tell you how sorry I am."

"Oh." She unfurls her fingers from a swath of light, splashing sparks into the air like paint. "This was always my fate, Sami. It was only a matter of time."

The crystal nearly slips from my sweat-slicked hands. Fumbling with it, I tuck into myself. "I came for—we needed the . . ." The word Aquamarine is impossible to say. "Something's happened," I manage.

"Yes." She draws out the S like a snake. "I know. You need my last shred of Aquamarine to save the world." Her skeletal jaw opens in a haunting grin. Is she mocking me? "But first, Skenesboro. Then, the rest."

254

I straighten, searching for an escape. But the fog is too thick. "Coach, this is bigger than the high school rivalry. This is real." *How do I get out of here? How do I get away from her?* "I need to go."

Her figure suspends in midair, and her wispy gossamer-like costume churns fluidly by the chasm's floor. As creepy as she is in motion, she's much more terrifying standing still. Her laser-like eyes bore into mine.

"Silly girl. I'm not talking about how you decimated the Fasha—and any hope for another Skenesboro athletic championship. Ever." She loops around, and the mosaic of light blinks alive. "Not that I'm bitter."

I cower, hearing that. "It had to happen, Coach." My tone is pleading. "You know it had to happen." My eyes squint closed, shutting out the light. Shutting out the tears. Shutting out Payne's horrifying image. "I'm sorry for what happened to you. But I'm not sorry for what I did—what I had to do—to Aquamarine."

She zooms in close. Her cool presence grazes my cheek like a kiss of wind. "Ah, yes. But now you need it, don't you?" Her voice scratches my inner ear. "You have a greater mission. How lucky you are that you failed to destroy all the Aquamarine."

"We're not sure. We're trying—"

"Hush, now," she snaps. "Listen to me."

She moves in front of me. It takes all my courage to meet her eyes.

"Trust Gaea," she says. "Her instincts are made from this world. The mineral you hold in your hand is part of that world and part of Gaea. It will give you the power you need because she makes it so. Believe in it."

concerto

What's this? Payne is helping me? And—she under-stands what's going on. How much does she know?

I look down at the crystal and get another shock. Before my eyes, my birthmark flashes and dims to a glow. I've been so distracted I didn't feel its angry pulse.

Payne follows my gaze. It was my birthmark—my Ne-vus spilus—that tipped her off I was Dion. It prompted her to get me on the volleyball team so she could control me with liquid Aquamarine. It had been my downfall but also my uprising. Does she know its power now?

I circle it with my free hand. "I-I used henna. Mehndi. And I had these visions."

She swirls away from my birthmark, as if it pains her. "Yes. Henna. It's what bridges the magic."

"What do you mean 'bridges the magic'?"

"Haven't you noticed? Your music has power again. Power that had been dormant for quite some time. Believe in your music."

"Why are you helping me?"

"It's Gaea I'm helping, silly girl." She clicks her jaw together—bone on bone. It chills me. "Did you foresee the Champlain Canal overflowing?"

"Yes," I say, barely audible. *How could she know that?*

"I'll be damned if my home gets wiped out by some overzealous weather lovers. You and I agree on that, if noth-ing else." She lifts her translucent arms overhead and raises her voice. "First, Skenesboro, I said. Then, the rest." Her lifeless arms drop, and her entire figure seems to dissolve, leaving only her glowing eyes.

Her voice reaches me in a looping echo: "Our beloved hometown is in trouble. Waters are rising at this very mo-ment. Go. Now."

Poof—she's gone.
I'm in complete darkness.

CHAPTER 36

Real fear didn't show itself until now, as shadows completely envelop me. Holy crap—I'm buried alive. There's no air. I'll die in this dark, dank cave. Alone.

No!

"Aunt Gaye! Jason!" I scream the names. My eyes are clenched shut; tears seep from the corners.

No answer. Complete silence.

"Gaye! Jason!" I screech so loud my throat is scraped raw. And again, "Gaye! Jason!" I crane my neck to the sky or where the sky is supposed to be. It's disorienting. Which way is up?

"Brenna! Poppy!" Oh, my god—I'm hyperventilating. I squeeze the crystal as if it can propel me out of this mess. The next thing out of my mouth is primal: "Mom!" A sob escapes as I collapse, pitching into a ball, folding the crystal into my body.

My knees and elbows are scraped to a pulp on the way down.

Wait—something's changed. My knees hit rock . . .

I sober in an instant. That spacious cave has narrowed. I feel around, eyes wide, wishing for a glimmer of sight. Still, I can feel it. The rock walls are tight around me. I'm at the bottom of the crevasse. The same chasm I'd dropped down moments ago to find the crystal.

Relief floods through me like oxygen. My way out is

concerto

up.

I can do this. I can get out of here.

I tuck the crystal into my bra and grip an edge—any edge I can find. And I begin to climb. Up. My way out is up.

"Gaye?" I whimper, my energy sapped from climbing. I need to save my breath.

Up. And up.

It's farther than I'd fallen. Payne brought me deeper into the well. My climb is never ending. *Will I ever reach the top?*

My piano-playing fingers clutch the coarse mineral surface—and it dawns on me how strong they are. They lift me. I'm able to scale the wall like Spiderman. A surge of energy hits. It's now boundless with my will to survive.

And survive I will. At my next heave upwards, I see daylight. Gaye and Jason peer down at me from the opening, astonishment on their faces. I'm so flooded with relief I almost fall back.

Don't stop, Sami. Keep going.

As I get closer to the top, rain pelts me, nearly pushing me back down. It soaks me in seconds, compromising my grip. I cry out as my footing slips. My heart goes to my throat. I'm falling again—

"I got you." Jason is there. He's hooked his arms under mine. "I won't let you go."

Tears spurt from my eyes. My heart swells.

With Jason's help, I scramble out, kicking rock and mud on the way. It's messy and chaotic and not graceful at all. But I'm out. Jason hugs me hard as we tumble to the ground, and I weep-laugh, overcome with relief and gratitude.

"Sam." Gaye's voice is firm. "Tell me you were successful. Tell me you have the crystal."

Still in my bra, it pokes my breast. I welcome the pain. "Yes." The word's a breath.

My fatigued, useless arms loop around Jason as I give in to his embrace, letting myself be held. I could stay in his arms until the end of time. Just like this. At this moment, nothing else matters. I don't notice that everyone besides Gaye and Jason have left, probably gone back to the manor. I hardly notice the ferocious rain that drums down on us. At this moment, I don't really care.

"Sami!" Brenna's panicked voice reaches us from the woods. "Sami!" She bursts into the clearing, her hair plastered to her forehead, her clothes matted to her body, mud splattered across her jeans. Her face is a picture of fright. Drained and breathless, she sinks to her knees—and puts any remaining energy into one single word, shouting to us across the clearing: "FLOOD!"

I'm running toward Brenna when I spot Poppy on the trail behind her. "The canal!" She palms her heaving chest. "It's overflowing! Just like you saw, Sami. Quick!"

Jason stays by my side. We run together down the trail, leaping over roots and rocks like gazelles. Branches lining the trail slice my fresh scrapes; blood mixes with rainwater and oozes down my limbs. I hardly feel it.

I must be in shock. Even though Brenna and Poppy's warnings still echo in my mind, I can't believe the canal's overflowing. Just like my vision? Just as Payne predicted? It hasn't been raining that hard or that long, has it? A flood couldn't develop in a matter of minutes. How long was I down in the chasm? I still haven't processed that Payne reappeared—and here I am running to the next crisis. My

concerto

mind's spinning.

Thank God Jason's by my side. Our steps are synchronized—Jason's and mine—as if we were the same person. I squeeze his hand, a silent promise to never let go. When things calm down, I will make this—I'll make everything—right.

Skene Manor comes into view, and just like that, we're on grassy land again. We scurry to the front of the house for a glimpse of the canal. Mom and Mrs. Potter are there in the gazebo, their hands knotted with worry. Looking past them, taking in a bird's eye view of the village, I immediately recognize the horrific scene. It's the same from my vision.

The canal has overflowed. Its surrounding streets are covered with water, as if the canal forked and made tributaries around the buildings. A few people at street level slosh through, rippling the flood waters, giving me a sense of how deep it really is. Their feet are covered. It's at least a few inches high already. It's rising by the second, as if the entire village is trapped within the lock.

My mind almost can't handle any more. I stay rooted where I stand, the rain like rubber bullets on my skull, trying to noodle it out. It's happening too fast. I wasn't prepared for this. *What am I supposed to do?*

My fists clench. Miles did this. I know it. My bones rattle with fury in my body. *Miles!* His name thrums against my conscience. How could he do this—now? Who cares if Posh is desperate to take over the inland waters? This is my home! And with Miles' callous methods, he's endangered not only me, my family, and my best friends, but everyone else in my hometown. Is he trying to intimidate me? Is he trying to get rid of Jason?

Not a chance will that ever happen.

"The lock must not be working," Jason shouts over the roar of the storm. "Lake Champlain must be flowing through."

His words echo my vision; he'd said the same thing then. Something clicks. With the crystal still safely tucked near my chest, I turn to him. "We have to go to the lock."

He shakes his head, spraying water. "We can't. We'd be at risk."

He's right. It would be reckless to go down there. Maybe there's another way.

In my vision, I was above the water level—on the elevation near the lock. Miles was a cloud-like apparition hovering over Lake Champlain, conducting the motion of the water. The crystal flashed over the water—blue lightning, calming the waters and evaporating the cloud-like figure in the sky.

I was up high.

Aha. Jason's right. We don't have to go to the lock. I'm already at the highest point of Skenesboro Village. I can do it from here.

I run to the edge of the Potter property, craning beyond the copse of trees to see the lock. It's too far to the right. Out of sight. Will it still work?

Rubbing the crystal to my sternum, I try to activate it somehow. But it's cool against my chest. There's zero energy from it. This isn't how it's supposed to go.

"Come on!" I say aloud. "Work!"

The downpour intensifies. The air has turned to water. The village is no longer visible, no less the canal or the lock. The deluge is too much; it's like trying to see through a waterfall. The rush is deafening. I block my ears and squeeze shut my eyes, despair winning.

concerto

Jason tugs on my elbow, and I hear someone shouting my name. Looking where he's pointing, I make Poppy out from the rush of water coming from the sky. She's jumping up and down, yelling, pointing wildly at Skene Manor.

She wants me to go inside?

She makes a bullhorn with her hands, and I make out another single, powerful word: "PIANO!"

CHAPTER 37

Mom hands me a towel as I rush to the front parlor, home of the Potter family's antique piano. To my surprise, everyone's there, sitting around like I'm about to put on a recital: Mrs. Potter, Gaye, Jason, Brenna, and Poppy. This won't work at all.

"Everyone out." Manners take a backseat in a crisis. No time to say please.

"You can do this." Gaye holds my shoulders a moment, and I feel a transfer of confidence. She is the true leader, not me. Only when she leaves does everyone follow.

Jason hesitates at the doorway. "You sure?" he asks, like he had two years ago before leaving me to neutralize Aquamarine at the cave. I'm torn between wanting him to stay and needing him gone.

"Stay close," I tell him and turn to the piano.

It's as if I'm greeting an old friend. This family heirloom must be one of the first pianos ever built. Running my fingers along the discolored, uneven keys, it occurs to me it may very well be unplayable. Or completely out of tune. Will it still work?

It has to work.

Rain continues to pound against the glass. It's loud, but I can't let it distract me. I breathe to calm my nerves. Deep inhale. Slow exhale.

Since the moment I began climbing out of the chasm,

concerto

the Aquamarine crystal has remained close to my heart. Closing my eyes, I focus on it, trying to absorb its energy into my veins.

I position my hands and wait for the magic to reveal itself.

Clear your head, Sami. No thoughts. Empty your mind.

I do scales, ignoring the tinny pitch of the vintage piano. After a few measures, I'm used to the unusual sound, even comforted by it. I repeat scales, relaxing into it.

Eventually, without meaning to, the scales transpose into a melody. A ballad, the same I'd played at the studio back in Berklee. At the very moment when my vision began . . .

And so it begins again.

It's a recurring dream—so familiar, yet tinged with foreboding.

Walking with Jason, our steps tentative but perfectly matched. We laugh. It feels like we're flying.

The song intensifies into a sweeping, dramatic melody. My hands are moving, my fingers are busy at the keys. Big energy. But outside of myself. The dream continues . . .

Rain. More rain. Copious amounts of rain. The canal is rising, creeping to street level. Jason and I run without pause, water sloshing over our feet. There's so much water. Too much. It's raining upwards. An upside-down world. Then we see it—

Beyond the lock, Lake Champlain has become a monster. A living, breathing thing. Waves surge, tides erupt. It's like the ocean, and it's taking over our little mountain town.

My music takes on a familiar theme, similar to what I'd played two years ago last December. I lean into the music, feeling energy with every chord . . .

In that strange way dreams do, everything shifts and I'm

alone, standing near Skene Manor, looking down upon the drowning village.

Wait—this is different. I can't see the lock from here. Or Lake Champlain. I need to see it in order to—

Whoosh!

Miles appears before me, ghost-like, his dark hair curling at his shoulders, clad in linen clothes with a messenger bag strung across his shoulder. Memories of our recent reunion play out, scene by scene. It's like I'm watching a silent movie. The movie of us. Our first hug in the student center, going to the first Showcase and our burrito dinner later that night, our pseudo-date at the beach, waves crashing me against him, his strong arms sure around me, his glass box gift, the near kisses . . . My senses are going loopy; briny smells of sand and salt air invade my olfactories—and it brings all those confusing feelings back. Against my better judgment, I'm drawn to him. My heart lurches. Even though I fight against it, I'm attracted to him. I like him. I can't help it.

No. This isn't right. What's going on? Is my mind playing tricks on me?

The image of Miles shifts, his visage enormous and disembodied, hovering in midair over the village. Looking straight at me, that irresistible movie-star grin on his lips. His stunning good looks take up all my vision, and his next words are my air—filling me, tickling my insides:

I didn't ask for these powers, Sami.

I never wanted to hurt anyone.

I'm a victim in this. Can't you see that?

My body goes limp. I'm not sure how, but I'm still playing—the antique piano tinkling in the background. It's intoxicating, the dream. I have an irrational urge to jump into

concerto

it, surrender to it, come what may. It's like a drug. Its pull is stronger than a riptide.

Whoosh!

The image changes, and it's a slap to my senses. Miles is gone, blinked out like a bad connection. In his place—I can hardly believe it—is Payne.

Coach Payne!

Exactly how I left her in the chasm, her figure is composed of mist and colored light. She is gaunt and skeletal, and her glowing marble eyes glare at me. Her fury emanates off her being like sparks. "You're giving your magic away! Don't you see what he's doing? He's leeching your magic—taking it and abusing it. He and his father think the Earth is their own personal snow globe they can shake up at their will. He needs your magic to accomplish his goals. Don't let him have it! Be strong! Don't fall into this trap. Our beloved hometown is in trouble. First, Skenesboro! Focus, Sami. Skenesboro needs you!"

Her words jolt me. At my sternum, the crystal buzzes, zapping me with electricity. Righting my posture, I regain control over my hands and the vintage keys at my fingertips. My birthmark pulses hot as I tackle one of the hardest pieces I've ever tried to play—what pianists all over the world deem unplayable: De Schlözer's Etude in A-flat.

I zone in. Only the music now. My hands go wild—a blur. Sweat soaks my hairline. My fingers scream in agony, pain shooting up my forearms. Tears escape as I blink the vintage keys into focus. It's messy. This antique instrument does not do the piece justice. Neither do I. Venturing from the composition, I make it my own, improvising on the spot.

Like jazz, Miles had said, that cocky twist to his lips.

Screw him. I'll show him.

I push on, pounding the ancient keys, hoping they don't crack from the impact. It's angry and beautiful and fills not just the parlor, but all of Skene Manor. I remember my vision.

Lifting my heart skyward, throwing light across the water, calming the rapids. Stopping the rain like turning off a faucet. In the calm, Miles' cloud-like figure dissipates, as if taken by the wind.

Whoosh!

A blast of light forces me to shield my eyes. Before I decide to stop playing, my hands are still.

Peeking from my closed lids, I see the room awash in a bluish light—light that originates from the crystal tucked at my chest, glowing inside my T-shirt. The light holds an energy of safety and calm.

Did I do it? Did it work?

Holding my breath, I slowly do a 180 on the bench to look out the window. My breath comes back in an exultant sigh.

The rain has stopped.

CHAPTER 38

Gaye finds me with my palm flat against the window glass, my head resting against the cool surface. She stands beside me in silence, her gaze out the window. My arms feel like they're made of jelly, and they drop to my sides.

"It stopped," I whisper.

Gaye's profile shows me tears. It's the first time since meeting her, since learning that her domain is under attack, that I've seen her cry.

"This is just the beginning," she says quietly.

I know what she says is true, but I don't respond.

"This may have been a ruse to distract us," she says after a while. "Flexing their muscles, maybe. They're planning something bigger. I know it."

"I didn't see anything—nothing about the future."

"You don't have to. Not for this one. We have to get back to Boston and back to my gallery. My paintings often give me clues as to what will happen."

I want to assure her it will be okay. A promise to do whatever I can to stop them. I tip away from the window and realize it had been holding me up. I reach for her, and my vision goes blurry. I'm so lightheaded, it feels like I'm floating.

"Sami," Jason calls from behind. His arms encircle me as I fall. And everything goes dark.

concerto

𝄽

It takes all night and Sunday morning for the village to dry out. I prove to be utterly useless, sleeping most of that time. Poppy is the one who wakes me gently, rolling my shoulder back and forth on the mattress.

I'd slept hard, dreamless and unmoving. Rubbing crust from my eyes, it takes a few moments to register what's happened. Hiking to the clearing, spelunking down the chasm, the dream-like meeting with Payne, the rain, the canal flooding, the antique piano, my music . . .

"You can sleep in the car, Sami, but we've got to go. Gaye needs to get back to the gallery."

Propping on an elbow, I fight sleep's determined pull.

"Here," Poppy says, looping something around my neck. She tugs my hair through it, pinching my scalp on the way. "Now you don't have to keep it in your bra." She laughs, and it's, like, the best medicine. For a moment, all my worries are gone, erased by my friend's laughter. It's not her only gift; she's given me a necklace. She fashioned the crystal into a pendant similar to the one from her shop. It serves as a reminder of our work ahead.

"Okay, now." She slaps the mattress. "Up and at 'em."

I massage my temples, trying to get my thought-juices going. Sleep has made me lethargic. From Brenna's bed, I blink her digital clock into focus. I've been asleep for almost fifteen hours. The last thing I remember was fainting in her front parlor when Jason caught me.

Jason!

"Is Jason here?" My voice is groggy.

"Yes. He's here now, but he's got to get back to Rhode

Island." She lowers her voice. "He's been doing some digging while you were asleep."

"Digging?" I'm wide awake now.

"Asking questions, bonehead. After seeing you stop a major flood with your music, you think he's just going to shrug and say, 'Yep, that's my girl'?"

A flicker of panic shakes me. I need to make this right. Now. "Can you send him in here? Please?"

By the time Jason comes into Brenna's room less than a minute later, the bed is made, and I've even changed out of my sleep-wrinkled shirt.

"Hey there, sleepy head." As we hug, Miles' creepy version of a similar greeting replays: *Well, hello, sleeping beauty*. Guilt pings, but it's Jason who pulls away.

"You've been out for a while." He leans against Brenna's desk, studying me. He's as far away from me as possible in this small room. "So I've had some time to corner Aunt Gaye about what the heck's been going on." He pauses, and the room fills with tension. "Crazy day yesterday."

I can't read his tone. It has a bitter edge. "Yeah."

He clucks his tongue. "I guess you don't have to worry about finding your magic anymore. We got that box checked."

I look at him askance. Is he angry? Annoyed? "What did Aunt Gaye tell you?"

"Well, turns out that secret project you're working on involves some pretty heavy hitters in the god world." He coughs out a laugh. "Yesterday's rain was their doing, she said. Un-freaking-believable."

"I know. Jason, I—"

"And you went up against something—someone, I should say. But Gaye wouldn't tell me who. I asked Poppy

concerto

and she, like, turned beet red. So, would you like to fill me in?"

"It's a team, actually. There are three—" I stop, hyperaware that I'm avoiding the Miles talk. I take a deep breath. *Back up, Sami.* "Okay. Jason, remember when I told you that my old friend from New York was in the program?"

"Yeah. Not Lauren."

"Not Lauren."

Realization falls over his features. "Miles."

Jason knows the history. He knows about my first soul-consuming crush that felt like love. He knows about my heart-wrenching jealousy when Miles chose Lauren over me. He knows about the heartbreak that followed me to Skenesboro. It's all there in that one word: Miles.

I scramble to fill him in on what's important. "Miles. He's the force I'm working against. At least, he's one of them." Details elude me. I'm distracted by Jason's unreadable expression.

"So, let me get this straight." His voice is laced with sarcasm. "Your heartthrob from junior high is now an evil wizard?"

"This isn't funny. This is serious."

"I know it's serious. So serious you failed to mention it to your boyfriend all this time. Why haven't you ever mentioned he was there?"

"Are you kidding? What the heck, Jason? You left me on an iceberg."

Eyes wide, his face opens in shock. "So, you found someone close by. You couldn't handle the distance so you—"

"I can't handle the distance? I came to Rhode Island, and you totally ignored me!"

274

"That's bull. I did not."

"I came to see you, and you treated me like . . . nothing—no one special—dragging me on a bunch of stupid group dates."

He shakes his head. "You didn't want to be there, and you know it."

"What?" I can't even legitimize that statement. "What about Sydney?"

"What about Miles?"

OMG—Did he just prove my hunch? "What the heck, Jason!"

"What? Syd is our friend. End of story. There's nothing going on."

"It didn't seem that way. You two seemed very cozy. At the concert. At breakfast. She was, like, a permanent fixture—on *my* visit!"

He screws up his mouth like he smells something rancid. "Seriously? Syd? She's like—one of the guys. I'm not even going to talk about that, it's so ridiculous."

"Really, why have you been ghosting me ever since you left?"

"I haven't been ghosting you."

"Really? Let me show you my phone. Or you show me yours. How many missed calls from me? How many texts? If that's not ghosting, I don't know what is."

"Whatever. You're just avoiding your own stuff. Tell me what's going on with you and Miles."

I'm too angry to confess anything close to being tempted. "Nothing."

"You're lying."

Steam shoots from my ears. And I thought I was mad before. "You know what? I'll tell you everything. I'm going

概# concerto

to be brutally honest. And then, I want you to be honest with me."

"Good. Go. I'm listening."

He's not listening, though. He's tightly wound, arms folded and teeth clenched. Whatever, I'm letting him have it.

"Yes, Miles is in the program. Yes, he did try to make a move. But—"

"I knew it!" Jason grinds his fists. "If I ever see that guy . . ."

"Nothing happened," I blurt, deadpan. "Truth." That's something I can say with pride. Nothing happened, despite him aggressively trying. Despite him taking me to the beach and making a pass at me in his car, I stayed true. Despite him crawling into my psyche and messing with my emotions, I stayed true.

Jason doesn't say anything. He's suddenly far away. The way his neck gets flushed and jaw pulses, I know he's fantasizing about beating Miles to a pulp.

"Jason, listen to me." I take his hand, which is so different from Miles'—rough and calloused, the knuckles stained with paint. I love this hand . . . and the guy it belongs to. "I love you. There's no one else. I see Miles' true colors. Whatever feelings I may have had for him in the past are long gone." Another truth. Even if I thought they were resurfacing, those feelings have vaporized.

He finally looks at me, but he's not really seeing me. I squeeze his hand three times—*I love you*—our secret message to each other. "And you don't have to fight for my honor. I'm a big girl. No, actually. Scratch that. I'm *Dion*. And Miles is the enemy. He has no idea what he's in for. I don't need you to swoop in and save me. I'm going to take care of it."

He huffs a laugh, and I see a little of the anger leave him.

I go on, eager to finish the job with Jason by my side. "Come to Boston next weekend. Friday night. I'm going to be performing. With Miles. And it's something I need you to see."

He squints a little. "You just told me he was the enemy. Why would you be on stage with him?"

"Trust me. What you saw yesterday? That was just a preview." I lean in close so our lips almost touch. "Next Showcase, I'm going to blow him out of the water."

CHAPTER 39

Jason pulls away. "You and Miles on stage? Performing together? Why would I want to see that?"

"Trust me. This isn't going to be a polite duet. And, like yesterday, I need all the support I can get."

The anger has left him, but he now looks pained. "I don't know, Sami. I don't know if I can give that to you. I have to think about stuff. I think we both should think about stuff."

About us? I'm too wary to ask. "Please come Friday. You haven't been up yet and this . . . you've got to see this."

"I don't know. I'll think about it." He moves toward the door. "I have to go."

He leaves me. Alone in Brenna's room. His sudden absence floods my veins, like poison colonizing.

Wait—what just happened?

The door is ajar, and I hear Jason say goodbye to everyone downstairs, his voice aloof, belying our argument. Resentment strikes; he didn't even tell me goodbye.

I stare out Brenna's window, trying to assure myself that we're okay. Jason and I—this is just a little blip. *Give him space.*

My breath fogs the glass. Past that is the trail to the chasm, as is the infamous scar on the hill. It's charged with meaning now, that scar. It had been a reminder of the destruction I'd done. Now it's a call to action. There's more

concerto

work to be done.

The muted light tells me it's late afternoon. Time to leave. I close my eyes and tell myself to breathe. I'll have to put this fight with Jason out of my mind. I have to believe it will all be okay. I can't imagine sitting in a car for four hours without reassurance, though. I can't imagine sitting through classes all next week, wondering if Jason will come to Showcase. Or if, God forbid, he wants to break up.

I won't survive. I'm sure of it.

But somehow, I do.

Poppy's here to pick me up for class, having reclaimed her bodyguard role to protect me from Ms. Aleia and Miles. Her silhouette is framed in my doorway, the tips of her spiky hair glowing like they're on fire.

"What's going on in here, anyway? It's all dark and gloomy."

She charges to the window and opens the blinds. I wince from the brightness as if it scalds me.

"You know, we humans need light," Poppy says. "This room is depressing as anything. And there's no air in here. How can you even breathe?" She clicks on my fan.

I sink back into bed. "I don't think I'll go to class today."

She swivels to me, fists on hips. "Oh, no, missy. You are going to class."

"It's too bright in here," I murmur, pulling the covers over my head. I stare at the fibers of my bedding.

Poppy takes a slow breath. My mattress dips with her weight. She touches my shoulder through the covers. "Have you heard from Jason?"

"No." I sound more angry than sad. "He's totally ghost-ing me. Again."

"Have you tried to get in touch with him?"

"Only every day. He's never ignored me like this be-fore. It feels like a breakup."

"Don't lose hope." Poppy sighs. "He just needs time."

She's trying to be kind, but her words prick fear into my heart. Scary things can happen in time. Give something time, and it changes. Like, in time, he will forget about me. In time, he'll move on. In time, he'll fall for someone else.

She palm-slaps the mattress. "In the meantime, this isn't doing you any good. You can't hide from Miles anymore. The kid knows what's up."

That jolts me awake. I throw back the covers. "What? What do you mean? Miles knows something?"

"I overheard him talking to Ms. Aleia." She pauses, an expectant look in her eyes.

"Poppy! Tell me what you heard."

"I didn't hear everything. But he said something about upstate and things stopping before they really started."

"He's talking about Skenesboro. Did . . . Miles say an-ything about me?"

"I didn't hear your name. He would be brainless to say it aloud. Anyway, they mentioned taking a different ap-proach."

"What approach? What did they say?"

"They didn't say. Just that they needed a different one."

I'm out of bed in a flash. I need out of here. Suddenly, this room is toxic. "Come on." I throw on yesterday's clothes. "Don't worry. It'll be fine. Let's get to class."

"You're telling me not to worry? Really? Sami, you're,

concerto

like, shriveled. I've tried to give you some space but—
geez—could you buck up a little?"

"Okay, okay."

The dorm wing is quiet, telling me classes are already
in session—which means we're late. I hook my arm into
Poppy's and pick up my pace.

She nudges my ribs. "Are you going to be ready for Friday? It's Tuesday. Showcase is only a few days away."

OMG—Showcase is only a few days away. Why ha-
ven't I heard from Lauren? It's been almost a week. A weird
panicky feeling strikes. "Hold on."

My phone's in my hand as I duck into an empty classroom. I can't bring myself to text her again. I'm calling her.

As it rings, Poppy gives me an impatient look and stands
watch by the doorway.

Voicemail.

"Hey Lauren. It's Sami. Not sure if you got my text last
week? But I wanted to let you know that I'm performing
with Miles this coming Friday here at Berklee. I know you
warned me about it before, but . . . well, I guess I wanted to
see if there was anything else you wanted to tell me before I
play music with him again. So, call me back. Thanks."

I tap red and face Poppy's wrath. "We are so late. So
much for lying low. Let's go!"

Poppy's right. I need to clear my mind of Lauren and
Jason and anything else that could distract me from the task
at hand. The flood in Skenesboro was no joke. The danger is
real. And I know that if I'm not wholly committed to my
music, no magic will come from it.

I haven't touched a keyboard since Brenna's vintage piano in Skenesboro three days ago.

As if Poppy reads my thoughts, she gives me a hushed

pep talk, chanting in time with our steps. "Eye on the prize, Sami. We have to win this for Gaye. You're coming to her gallery tonight, right?"

I'd almost forgotten we'd scheduled this meeting. "Yeah, yeah. Of course, I'll be there."

We round the corner and stop just short of Ms. Aleia's classroom. The door is open. It's true that we're late; class is in session. But she's not lecturing. Small groups have formed into some kind of workshop. I'm surveying the room, strategizing how we could sneak into one of the groups, when Poppy nudges me, bringing my focus to the front of the room.

And the needle scratches off the record.

Miles is there, standing beside Ms. Aleia, his messenger bag slung over his shoulder as if he's any other student. But he's not just a student. He's a demigod. And he's here to strategize with Aleia on how to wreak havoc on Gaye's domain.

Seeing him now, knowing all he's responsible for—not only the storms but also the upset with Jason—I have a visceral reaction. I want to puke. His eyes are hungry on me, that slight smile twisting his lips. The smile once irresistible now seems slimy and duplicitous. It dawns on me what a feat it's been I haven't run into him since returning from Skenesboro.

Good work, Poppy.

She tugs my arm, mumbles something. But I stay put, too angry to back off. I'm ready to fight. All that gloom I'd felt moments before has shifted to rage. Who does he think he is? He will be stopped. No matter what he's planning to do. Hopefully, my magic will be enough.

"There she is," Miles says.

concerto

"There you are," Ms. Aleia says.

They're both talking directly to me, yet with such veiled aggression, I bristle.

"What's up?" I approach them with courage I didn't know I had.

Ms. Aleia is all business. "Showcase is in three days. When are we rehearsing?"

I look from one to the other, my insides recoiling. Miles' grin has turned almost lewd, while Ms. Aleia seems to have grown talons from her eyeballs. They want to rehearse. Our last rehearsal rendered me helpless, vulnerable to their whim. I need to know what they're planning for Showcase so I can be prepared. But how? A rehearsal might clue me in; it might trigger a vision. Should I meet with them?

No. A rehearsal might also knock me out cold . . . again.

"I thought a rehearsal wasn't necessary." I mimic Miles. "Right, Miles? We have what you called 'natural chemistry.' What was it you said? That we didn't need to practice as long as we meet early that night?"

Miles chuckles. "Right. And wear ruffles."

"Very funny."

Ms. Aleia goes even paler than her norm. "I don't think that's wise. Do you, Miles? The best performances require practice. Even if we only meet for a half hour, it would—"

"I can't," I interrupt. "Sorry."

As I turn away, Miles blocks my path. "How about coffee, then?" His smile is less sure.

"Sorry. I really can't."

He grips my sleeve, lowers his voice. "Why, Sami? What's going on? I haven't seen you since—forever. Why won't you just get a cup of coffee with me? I want to—talk to you. We need to talk." He's pleading with me. It's all I can do not to scream *I know what you did to Skenesboro! How could you?*

Miles must read something on my face. His hardens in a moment. "How was your visit home?"

"Good." *Aloof, Sami. Play it cool.*

"I heard you got some crazy rain up there."

"You heard?"

He stares me down. "But no thundersnow. That's a relief."

OMG. He's taunting me. Over his shoulder, Poppy and I meet eyes. Hers tell me to tread carefully.

"Why . . . would there be thundersnow?"

"You're right." Miles gets in my face. "Better question would be: how was it that the rain stopped just like that?" He snaps his fingers right near my ear, catching and yanking a wisp of my hair. A sliver of pain shoots into my temple, and it's like he's accessing my inner thoughts. I feel him clomping around in there, messing with my mind.

Ironically, it's Ms. Aleia who saves me. "All right, kids. Enough. Miles, we spoke about being a gentleman, especially with Samantha." She flicks my birthmark with her fingernail, and I feel a sting shoot up my arm. "Now, when can we rehearse?"

Poppy pulls at my elbow. "Sami and I have stuff going on. We're working on a project for my . . . boss. And she really doesn't have time to rehearse the next few days."

Ms. Aleia ignores Poppy completely, sharpening her glare on me instead.

"Let's meet at five then, before Showcase." Miles glides the back of his hand down my arm. The skin-on-skin contact chills me.

concerto

"Okay." I rub where he touched my arm. *Fine. Leave me alone.*

"And don't get any funny ideas."

Ms. Aleia snaps, "Enough, Miles. You have only one job. I'm not feeling so confident that you're going to get things under control here." Her eyes rove toward me before locking on him again. "I trust you won't let us down?"

I'm so shocked to hear Ms. Aleia speak so openly about their partnership, I'm stuck in place. Miles chuckles, fanning away the redness in his face.

"It's time you got to class." Ms. Aleia leaves us, skulking toward the groups gathered in the back of the classroom.

Miles turns to me, a look of impatient disgust on his face. "Wear red." It's not a request; it's an order. His unfamiliar tone is rancid to my ear.

He turns to leave, his rigid gait altered from tension.

"Why red?" I call. Anxiety creeps into my tone. *Just tell me now so we can prepare.*

He doesn't answer. Not with words anyway. He turns slowly, and I rear back. He gives me this look that cuts to my core. In that look, he holds all the power. And he knows it.

CHAPTER 40

At the gallery later that day, Gaye looks like she hasn't slept since the Skenesboro flood. The worry lines around her eyes have become permanent wrinkles. My ears burn with shame. I've been holing up in my room, dodging Miles, and whining about my fight with Jason, while Gaye's entire domain is at risk. How self-absorbed can I be?

In the dimly lit gallery, the landscape paintings are abuzz with an unusual energy. They seem to be screaming for help. They remind me of those Discovery Channel documentaries about the effects of global warming, except these are real-time. It makes me feel even more helpless.

"Can I see Skenesboro?" I ask meekly.

Gaye is somber as she leads me to her back office, where she has a painting reminiscent of Jason's landscape, showing the village of Skenesboro with Skene Manor in the background.

"It's dry," I say, though I'm hardly relieved.

"Mostly. The lock is still not functional. And buildings surrounding the canal are pretty much destroyed from water damage." She clasps her hands prayer-like. "But it could've been so much worse. I'm not sure I thanked you properly." I start to protest, but she stops me with a gentle touch on my shoulder. "Thank you, Sam." She gives me a sad smile.

"I just wish it never happened."

"Me, too."

concerto

Gaye stares into the Skenesboro painting. I can see the gears turning in her mind. If I could only see things through her eyes. God of the Earth—how does she do it? I couldn't imagine bearing that kind of burden.

"Aunt Gaye, I want you to know, I'm ready for Friday—for whatever happens. I won't let you down."

Gaye nods. "I know you won't. I trust you've been using the past couple days to get prepared." She waits for affirmation, but I frown at my hands, unsure. How could I prepare when I don't know what they're planning?

As if on cue, Gaye gets down to business. "Poppy's at her shop working on your design, so she won't be joining us tonight. But you need to go there Friday afternoon, before Showcase, to get the henna."

"Yes, I'm planning on it." Worry creeps in. "Do you think it will be enough? My magic, I mean? We don't know what their plan is."

"Well, I've been doing some sleuthing. Come with me." She leads me to the front room conference table, which is covered with large sheets of paper. Maps. She smooths out a large, antique map of what looks like—

"Is that Boston?"

"Yes. In the 1640s."

"It hardly looks familiar."

"That's because the footprint has completely changed since then."

My brow wrinkles. "How do you mean?"

"Did you know Boston is mostly man-made?"

"Oh, I did hear that. Didn't they dredge the Charles River to expand it?"

"Yes." Gaye looks pleased. "They manipulated that river quite a bit over time, installing dams and such. But

288

that's not all they did." She unrolls another map of current-day Boston, places the antique onionskin map over it. The effect is astonishing; it's clear how much Boston land has grown since the 1640s.

"Wow. Look. Faneuil Hall wasn't even there. I didn't realize they had built it up like that. How were they able to do that?"

"Actually, much of the land was taken from other areas. Bunker Hill was carved out and brought in to extend the shoreline. And huge, glacial hills in Needham were taken to fill in Back Bay."

"Okay. That's crazy. So, they made the city bigger. They made it the Boston we know and love." I remember exploring the city on one of my first days here. The cobblestone streets of Beacon Hill absolutely charmed me. The vitality of Faneuil Hall Marketplace was infectious. The Freedom Trail made me feel like I'd entered a time warp. I gingerly trace the old 1640s border, realizing none of those landmarks would be here if it weren't for the expansion. "It's a good thing, right? They did the right thing to expand the borders."

"For people, yes. For the gods, it's much more complicated."

"Oh, no. What are you thinking?"

"I've been poring over these maps, trying to predict what Posh might be planning." Gaye pauses, her expression growing serious. "Boston is especially vulnerable because its foundation is unstable." She waits, letting it sink in.

Staring at the maps, I try to see it how Posh would see it. I study the space between the borders. Boston had been so much smaller. Before the 1640s, there was more water. More ocean. More of Posh's domain.

concerto

My legs feel rubbery all of a sudden. I slump into a chair, Gaye's theory crystalizing in my mind.

From Posh's perspective, humans have infringed on his waters—building up land from the shorelines, messing with the Charles River, moving glacial hills from inland. Taking what is rightfully his.

My defenses go up. And my fist pounds the table.

"You can't be saying that Posh would want to go back to the way it was in the 1600s. That would be insane. This is a thriving, established city. Thousands of people would be affected. Homes would be lost. Businesses, too. They finally finished the Big Dig after all those years to make the water-front what it is today. All those city parks. Why would he want to—"

"Sam. I've had these same thoughts. You're absolutely right. It would be catastrophic."

She turns to the east wall to study the landscape of Boston. The light has not fully come back in the painting. It looks muted, clouded by shadows. Foreboding. If Gaye is right and Posh wants to reclaim his waters, most of this painting would drown. It would decimate the city.

"That's what he wants," I say aloud. "He wants it to be catastrophic."

"I believe so."

"But why? What's his goal?"

Disgust is written all over her face. "He's been ticked off about Boston's land growth for centuries, ever since they started expanding it."

"Why would he want to change it now, though?"

Gaye hums a sigh. "It's quite an undertaking. I suppose he couldn't do it alone."

"He needed Miles."

"And Aleia. And you."

Me. I shudder. "Why me?"

Payne's image floats into my subconscious, her words from my last vision ringing loud and clear. *He's leeching your magic—using it to accomplish his goals. Don't let him have it!* "They need my magic. But why?"

"For the same reason Posh couldn't have done this without his son. You're the direct link to humans. You and Miles. Your involvement assures their control. In order for their plan to work, they need to control the people first."

"They need my magic because I'm human?"

"That—and they need Dion's magic. Your control over a certain Earthly mineral links you to their cause in a very literal way."

Realization cracks open like an egg. "Oh, no. They know what I did with Aquamarine. They want me to blow up more Earthly minerals? That's not going to happen. That was a specific thing. I had to destroy—"

Gaye pats the air to calm me. "Hold on. They're not planning to blow anything up. Not yet, anyway. Not for a coastal mission such as this. No. Friday will be all about amplifying Miles' power, I'm sure of it."

My nerves hit hyper drive. "What are they planning? How do they want to reclaim the borders? We're not talking about a flood here, are we?"

"Well, there will be a storm, of course. He'll probably do something drastic to trigger panic, which would lead to an evacuation. Control the people. Get them out of the way. Then, he'll have a go at the land."

Awful images come to mind. "It seems so drastic and unnecessary."

"To you, it does. To him, it's principle."

concerto

"But it's not your doing," I say. "You're not at fault for this. You shouldn't be punished."

"No, you're right. I personally did not add new land to Boston's original borders. But in Posh's eyes, more land means less water, which ultimately means less of his domain." She gazes at the landscape painting. "It's such a beautiful city."

"Yes, it is." My fists clench at my sides. "And it's not going anywhere."

CHAPTER 41

Tonight is Showcase. No classes for me today. I can't risk running into Miles or Ms. Aleia before our agreed-upon meeting time. Hiding out in my room, I try not to die from wait-time anxiety. I listen to my favorite music. I write in my journal a bit. I troll Jason's Instagram, and learn that he went to the Lippitt House Museum yesterday. With who, I wonder? Sydney? My texts to him have gone unanswered all week, but today I need a reply. After pacing my room, biding my time, I break down and call him.

Voicemail.

"Jason here. Not. You know the deal." *Beep.*

I click off. Why does voicemail even exist anymore? It's officially annoying. The last thing I want to do is annoy Jason. But my heart tells me Showcase will be the last straw. If he doesn't come to Showcase, then I'll know we're done.

I'll text him instead. Again.

Showcase tonite. Pls b there.

I can't bear for Jason to ghost me again. Not today. I go to shut my phone down when it dings. A text. From Miles.

Where r u?

Crap. He's probably with Ms. Aleia. They might think if I'm not in class, I may not do Showcase. How much I'd like to ice him out. But I have to play the game. All they

concerto

need to know is that I'll be there—

C u @ 5

That's it. Notifications: OFF.

Poppy expects me soon. After a long shower and some primping, I'm on my way to Henna on Newbury.

The shop feels more and more like a second home. The musky smells and colorful clutter bring me comfort as she works on my hand. In just a few hours, I'll be on stage with Miles, my music against his. My magic against his.

Poppy's artistry is masterful. Her concentration face is a slight pucker. The design is strange and beautiful—not the typical Mehndi. Down my forearm, she inks flowing arcs that resemble ocean waves. They overlap and grow larger closer to my wrist. Menacing. It almost looks like a creature is clawing at my birthmark.

"Do you know what you're going to play?" Poppy asks.

"It doesn't really work like that." Miles' words echo in my mind: *We'll improvise. Like jazz.*

Around my birthmark, Poppy blends the claw-like wave into a swirl design reminiscent of a whirlpool. Her work is impressive and exact.

"Do you know how you're going to stay conscious?" she asks.

"Isn't that what the pendant and the henna are for?" I say, irritated.

Poppy pauses, still holding my hand. Her voice is grim. "I don't know, Sami. There's no playbook. No one's ever done this before."

Her question has merit. The last time Miles and I re-hearsed, I apparently lost consciousness for over six hours, only to find that we'd created an ice storm with our music. This is what Miles and Ms. Aleia are banking on—the same type of collaboration. Our music working together to summon a storm or another weather-related disaster.

What makes me more anxious is that Lauren still hasn't gotten back to me. What if there's something I'm missing?

"Can we stop with the interrogation? It's making me nervous."

Poppy gives me a wary look. She's quiet for a while, focused on her art.

My insides tense as my birthmark heats up. My leg starts jiggling. I need to get up and walk around.

"Stop moving."

"What if it doesn't work? What if I zone out and accidentally create an earthquake or something?"

She snickers. "That sounds so weird. 'Accidentally create an earthquake.' I'd laugh if I didn't know it could actually happen."

"Or what if the opposite is true and my magic does nothing? Miles is a strong musician. What if my music doesn't overpower his?"

She looks at me, serious. "It has to." She bends closer to my hand, adding fine detail that will only be noticed up close. "I had an idea. Not sure if it has any bearing on what you're going to do, but . . ."

"Tell me. Please. I'm open to ideas."

"Have you been to Jake Ivory's over on Lansdowne Street?"

"No. Why? What is it?"

"It's a bar that puts on a kind of show. Darci, my boss, knows the manager there. She took me with her to drop off an order of essential oils. It was early. Hadn't opened yet.

concerto

And they were warming up."

"Warming up? Oh, for a performance. I get it. Jake Ivory's—as in, piano?"

"Right. They have these two pianos on stage facing each other. And they, like, duel."

"They compete. Like a contest?"

"It's more like a conversation. A duet, kind of. You know, it's a show for the bar crowd. Not anything serious. Darci says sometimes it's so loud in there you can't even hear the piano."

"Sounds frustrating—for the musician, I mean. So, what's your idea?"

"I just thought, if we set up the stage the same way and gave you that kind of distance from Miles, it might help keep you awake, for one. Also, it might help combat his magic."

"Like, I'd have my own piano on the other side of the stage? Two pianos? That's a tall order. I'm not sure if we could logistically make that happen."

"I can. I know the tech guy. He does lights and back-stage for the Showcases. I'll have him set it all up for you."

"Really? You'd do that?"

I visualize dueling pianos for Showcase. It makes sense. I sat right next to Miles on the bench the last time we played, connected to him like an organ grinder's monkey. Our thighs touched. Our fingers flirted with each other's. It must have been easy for him to gain control.

Poppy's almost finished with the design on my hand. The effect is incredible. It looks so exotic. A sharp pulse pricks beneath the skin of my birthmark, which is hot to the touch. I don't mind the pain anymore. As Poppy said, it will help me stay alert. A faint blue glow is visible through the ink. Not enough to draw attention to it, but it reassures me my magic is there.

The more I think about Poppy's idea about the dueling pianos, the more I like it.

"I think you're right. I can't be sitting right next to Miles like before. There are a whole host of problems that might come up aside from the magic. Not to mention if Jason happens to show. He wouldn't want to see me sitting right next to Miles."

"Is he coming?"

"I don't know. He hasn't responded."

Poppy winces in sympathy. "So, what about Miles. Still kinda into him?"

"What? No!"

"Easy, now. Geez," she says, palms up.

"I never liked him," I insist loudly.

Poppy narrows her eyes at me. "Right."

"It's true."

"You can be real with me, Sami. I know you were into him before, and if you're not anymore, that's fine. Actually, it'll work better tonight if you don't have feelings for him. Even more distance."

I hate that she could tell I liked him. "I didn't want to like him."

"I know. But he's a charmer."

"He charmed you, too?"

Poppy puts away her henna instruments. "I don't go that way," she says, grinning mysteriously.

"What do you mean?"

"I like girls. Didn't you know that?"

My eyes go wide. I never gave a thought to Poppy's sexual orientation. Yet she's accurately perceived my attraction to Miles. And she knows exactly how I feel about Jason.

concerto

She knows all about me, and I know practically nothing about her.

How one-sided has this friendship been?

"I'm sorry."

"Why sorry? No reason to be sorry." She grabs the Swiffer and dusts the corner shelf. "Don't worry. You're not my type."

It feels good to laugh. "Oh, good. My love life is complicated enough without you getting involved."

We're both laughing. I love it when Poppy laughs. It's like she doesn't want to but it bursts out like a growl. Make me laugh harder. I'm doubled over, a hand on my stomach, when a customer comes through the door, its bell jangling loudly against the glass.

Poppy's laughter cuts out before mine. "Sami," she hisses.

Looking up from my doubled-over position, I'm shocked to see Miles standing there in the shop, staring at me, a bemused look on his face.

"What's so funny?" he asks.

My hand is hidden at my midsection, thank goodness. My instincts tell me I have to keep the henna hidden from Miles. I tuck my arm behind my back, careful not to smudge the design.

"Oh, it's girl stuff," I say. "You wouldn't get it."

"Try me." He moves closer. Dark circles frame his blue eyes, and his chin doubles when he looks down at me. Still, his good looks wrestle through—and that old softness for him tugs at my heart. We lock eyes, and a yearning zips through me like a bolt of lightning. Heat builds in my cheeks as I silently beg Poppy to save me.

And she does. "I was just telling Sami that she's not my

type."

Miles' face drops—a moment of surprise—and he recovers, blinking out of our eye contact. It's almost funny how he's so thrown off.

"You're not Sami's type, either." He tries for haughtiness but it falls flat. "I don't think."

"What are you doing here?" Poppy asks.

By the time he turns to me again, both my arms are tucked behind my back, which makes my boobs stick out. His eyes drop to my cleavage—*ick!*—and I will the henna paste to dry in record time so I don't have to stand like this for long. But it seems Miles is too irritated to bother wooing me.

"I've been looking all over for you. In just a few hours—"

"I know," I snap. "I'm ready. I told you we'd meet at five."

"Well, guess what? It's not all about you, Sami. Ms. Aleia and I have worked hard on this—"

"I bet you have." It comes out automatically.

Poppy throws me daggers. *Shoot.* My mouth has misbehaved.

"What's that supposed to mean?"

"Nothing, I just—I mean, we've all worked hard."

Miles eyes me through slits. "There are some things to go over. We need to meet sooner." He checks his watch. "An hour from now, be at her office."

My insides churn with anger. How dare he order me around like that? Behind my back, my birthmark is triggered. It feels like a bee sting. It takes incredible poise not to yelp in pain. I bite my lip, avoiding Miles' eyes.

"It's not a request," he commands. "Got it?"

concerto

I hate him. My nod is purely for self-preservation; my hand is torturing me.

He goes to leave and turns back at the doorway. The stupid bell on the door clanks over his next words: "And remember to wear red."

CHAPTER 42

His last comment pisses me off. He wants to control what I wear, for crying out loud? The last thing I want to do is comply. Unexpectedly, it's Poppy who talks me into wearing red. "If you don't wear red, they might dress you themselves—something laced with their evil magic or something." She gives me a piece from the shop: a cherry-red hemp sundress.

"Besides, the hemp may offer more protection. Because it's made from a plant, it's from Gaye's domain. Plus, it's naturally anti-microbial."

"Quite the sales pitch."

"Put it on. The henna's dry by now."

Why would I argue? Honestly, I can use all the help I can get. The fabric is breathable and softer than I'd expected. Comfy.

My nerves about performing with Miles and what might result from it have shut out all other emotions and thoughts of Jason. If I let myself hope he'll be in the audience tonight, the stress would paralyze me.

The corridor to Ms. Aleia's office goes on forever. Like when Miles kidnapped me, the school is mostly empty, the doors locked, the rooms dark. The only source of light comes from Ms. Aleia's office, and it makes a stark imprint on the tiles.

concerto

The Aquamarine pendant is on an extra long cord, falling inside my dress at my breastbone. A thin-knit cardigan hides some of my Mehndi, but a good amount of the design pokes through. It's not like I can wear gloves. They're going to have to see it at some point.

Breathe, Sami.

With each step, I steel myself for Ms. Aleia's wrath. My legs are numb, all the energy sucked out of them. My left hand is on fire, my birthmark overactive. Closer to the light, my mouth dries up, and my tongue feels swollen to preternatural size. I'll be lucky if I can get a word out. A few paces from her door, I hesitate, lingering in the last shadow.

"She's here," Ms. Aleia says.

I shudder. Did she hear me or sense my presence?

Miles steps from her office, his tan loafer putting a dark splotch in the lighted tile. He wears a red Polo shirt and white khaki pants. He smells of jasmine cologne.

"Sami. Hi." He sounds beseeching and apologetic, and my nerves go on high alert. He guides me into the office, giving me a final pull that I hadn't thought necessary until now. Ms. Aleia's office is too bright, making me squint. The door closes with an authoritative *thunk*, and I'm locked in with two evil people.

No. Three.

Posh Eichen is here, too.

And I thought I was nervous before.

"What the hell is that?" Posh says, waving a thick hand my way. He's clean-shaven, and his hair is slicked back with gel. He's reclining in one of Ms. Aleia's chairs. His gut peeks out from under his linen shirt—a visual reminder of our time at the beach. Thinking back to that day, which seemed so innocent, I almost can't believe he could be so evil. Almost.

He glares at Aleia. "I thought you said she was going to help us."

"She is. She is," Ms. Aleia says quickly. "We've already had a dry run."

"It wasn't completely dry." Miles chuckles.

"Oh, be quiet," Posh says. "This is no time for jokes. What's that on her hand?"

A gasp tears through the room, and I realize I've had my eyes squeezed shut. An awkward pause fills the space. Blinking at the three of them, I find my voice. "What's wrong?"

It's a dumb question. I don't know why I ask it.

"Samantha, why have you vandalized yourself again like that?" Ms. Aleia raises her voice. "I thought I told you the harmful effects of henna? Were you not listening?"

"I told you I found her at Henna on Newbury." It almost sounds like Miles is coming to my defense.

Ms. Aleia glares at him. "You didn't say anything about her doing henna."

"I didn't see it. But really, I don't think—"

"Can we get it off? Is there a way to . . . remove it?" Ms. Aleia flutters her hands near mine.

Sweat glistens on Posh's forehead as he reads from his smartphone: "There are a few ways. Toothpaste. Olive oil. The most thorough way seems to be with hydrogen peroxide. We'll need to soak a cotton ball with it and vigorously rub—"

"No," I say, and all eyes widen at me. "I'm not taking it off." I catch myself. *Play the role, Sami. You don't know anything.* "You guys are overreacting." I make my voice light. "It's not like this henna is going to affect my music.

concerto

That would be silly."

"It might—"

Miles saves me again. "Sami's right. It's not going to matter." He looks pointedly at his father. "It's not going to matter. I promise."

That makes me wonder: is he saving me . . . or just that sure of his own powers? For whatever reason, I'm grateful he's taken the attention off me for the moment.

"Why are we meeting early? What's this about?" I ask.

Ms. Aleia hands me staff paper with a musical composition penned in black Sharpie. My eyes scroll measure by measure from the time signature, the melody instinctively audible in my mind, reverberating between my ears, as if someone has turned on the music in there. It's complex and dynamic. The kind of music I'm drawn to. The kind of music I love to play. The kind of music I usually create myself.

"Who . . . wrote this?"

A look passes between Miles and Ms. Aleia. I study them both, but my eyes land on her. She smiles woodenly as Miles answers, "I did."

His tone is uncertain. I turn to him and can see it in his eyes. He's lying.

"You don't believe me?" His crooked smile torments me. "You don't think I'm capable?"

"It's not that, it's just—"

"We want you to play that," Posh says impatiently. "You can handle it, I trust?"

My eyes stay on Miles. "I thought we were going to improvise."

Miles huffs. "Think of this as a starting point, then." His voice gets soft, and his presence encircles me. "And we can take it wherever we want to go."

Ms. Aleia's voice stabs through. "Do you need to practice, Samantha?"

"She doesn't need to practice," Miles answers for me—with astonishing confidence. "She knows this piece."

Confusion swirls. "Me? I don't know what you're talking about. I've never seen this."

"Really?" Miles says, grinning sideways.

Oh, no. Whatever's happening is out of my control. *SLAM!* The door to my cage locks shut. I'm trapped.

I'm obliged to go along with their plan, whatever it is, however blindly. And somehow the sheet music I hold in my hand is the key ingredient. Their plan won't work without this music.

And I have a sinking feeling it's mine.

CHAPTER 43

Posh and Ms. Aleia are buzzing around backstage like a pair of flustered stagehands. Miles won't leave my side, and every few minutes I'm tempted to wave away the jasmine-y fumes coming off him. The second piano waits on wheels backstage, occupying too much space.

"I'll have someone wheel this out," Ms. Aleia says, oblivious to our plan.

Our plan. Will it even work anymore?

My grip on the original score—my composition?—is so tight, the pages are going damp beneath my fingers. Since Ms. Aleia handed me this sheet music, everything has come into question. I have no idea what will happen when I play. All that careful planning—for nothing. The pendant? The henna? No wonder Miles isn't worried. They've turned my greatest weapon against me: my music.

Despair drags me down like I'm wearing cement boots. It kills me to disappoint Gaye. And I can't give her forewarning, either. Not only will I not be able to stop them, I will be helping them.

How can I protect myself from me?

Hopelessness plagues me like a high fever. I've completely lost control.

The gears in my mind have been spinning since leaving Ms. Aleia's office, trying to figure out when I could have possibly written this piece. During my blackout? It must

concerto

have been then. Not only did I play during those six hours, I composed. Not only did we improvise, but we documented our melody on staff paper. I try to envision myself doing it, filling in the chords quickly to keep up with the tune looping in my mind.

But it doesn't seem right. Documenting my music like this is not something I usually do. I've composed ever since I can remember, but it's been a casual thing. I rarely put the notes down on paper. It simply becomes part of me . . . and it's always changing.

Now I'm questioning. Maybe it isn't mine?

Staring at the sheet music, running a finger over the notes, I force myself to switch gears. No more wallowing. There's got to be a Plan B. It's not going to be as easy as staying alert, dueling Miles at the piano. I need to flip the script on them. I need to gain control. But how?

Only ten minutes until show time.

Beyond the closed curtain, a crowd is forming in the audience. It's a much bigger crowd than normal. And I was impressed with the size of the crowd at Miles' first Showcase. His reputation precedes him. Mine, too? Despite the circumstances, nervous excitement tickles me, as it always does right before I perform. Sounds of overlapping conversation and laughter grow as minutes tick by—feeling like a countdown to a time bomb. It's distracting. Before I think better of it, I peek out from behind the curtain to see who's there.

Poppy's easy to spot with her spiky hair. Next to her is Gaye. On the other side of Gaye is—

My breath stops short. Jason is here.

Jason is here!

My fingertips go tingly. Butterflies swarm my insides.

He came! I can't believe he actually came. My grin is so big, I'm sure it shines on him. *Look up!* I want to say. *I'm right here!* But he's talking to someone seated opposite him. She's got long pale hair and—

A gasp escapes me. It's Lauren.

Lauren!

She's the same as I remember, pretty as ever. Her pale hair is gathered into an Elsa braid, a crown for her heart-shaped face. She looks like a musician, wearing a black cropped-neck top. Her signature gold pendant catches the ambient light of the auditorium. I feel my face relax into a joyful smile.

Lauren is here.

"What are you doing?" Miles says behind me. "You shouldn't peek. It's bad luck."

I can't help myself. "Miles, look. Look who's here."

He leans past me to see, and I watch his profile go from curiosity to shock. He rears back as if he's been slapped.

"What the hell?" He snaps the curtain closed. "Why is she here?" A flush of crimson travels up his neck. He sticks a finger in my face. "Did you invite her? Did you bring her here?"

His rage is a shock. "No. I'm just as surprised as you are." It's true. Despite my repeated efforts to contact Lauren, there was nothing but radio silence on her end. But she must have gotten my messages. She's here. But, gosh. Is that a good thing or a bad thing that she made the trip from New York? Is she here to help . . . or is it something else? Maybe a warning wasn't good enough. Maybe she feels she has to intervene . . .

No, I can't go there. It has to be a good thing. I can't freak myself out or the gig won't happen at all.

concerto

Miles' agitated behavior cuts into my thoughts. He paces the crowded space backstage, banging his fist on the second piano. "This is no good." He grits his teeth. "This isn't going to work for me. She's got to go. You have to get her out of here. There are three sets before us. There's time."

His reaction is baffling. His whole body clenches. Lauren's warning loops in my mind: *under no circumstances should you play music with him.* And now, Miles is freaking out that she's here. She's got to have some kind of power over him. I can't let Miles think she and I are in cahoots against him.

"Why me? I have nothing to do with her being here. It's not like we're super close anymore. You know that."

He bangs on the piano again just as the first act takes the stage. Sweat collects on his brow. He mumbles incoherently, staring at the floor. He's so weakened. Like he'll crack any moment. I latch onto it. "Miles, why do you care? What does it matter if Lauren is in the audience?"

The first act is well underway. Horns. It creates a jarring background to our argument. Instead of whispering, we almost have to shout over the noise. "Damn it, Sami. She's going to ruin everything. You don't get it."

He seems to crumble before my eyes. Hesitantly, I step toward him. "What's she going to ruin, Miles? Tell me."

"I can't play with her here. It's not going to work." He shudders. "She . . . gets in the way."

"What do you mean, 'she gets in the way?' "

Something shifts inside him, and he turns to me with the devil in his eyes. It chills me to ice. "Screw you," he says through clenched teeth. "You think you're so above me. You think you're untouchable." He moves in, I retreat. He moves in, I retreat—until I'm backed up to the brick wall near the curtain cord. "You think your piano is everything. You live in a small world, Sami."

Audience applause. First and second acts swap spots. Miles puts a cork in his temper, but it doesn't hold. As soon as the next act begins—a string quartet—he starts in again.

"No one knows what I'm going through—not my father, not Ms. Aleia—no one knows what it's like to be a demi. Stuck in the middle ground, like freaking purgatory. I don't belong anywhere." He backs away, stabbing the sky. "My human talents got tapped out when my godly talents kicked in, and everything went downhill from there. But guess what? I don't care about the godly stuff. I don't want the storms. I don't care if we get more water. I don't want what my dad wants. I want . . . I want—"

He catches himself. He's said too much. His words echo silently—*I don't care if we get more water. I don't want what my dad wants*—and he was about to confess more. He buries his face in his hands, hunching to my height. His shoulders quake gently. He's crying? My arm is stiff going around his shoulders. He sinks into me, vulnerable, with a childlike neediness. It's like I'm the grownup.

And I'm on the cusp of discovery.

"It's okay, Miles. Tell me. What do you want?"

He gazes at me through tears. "What do I want? It's nothing magical or anything. It's what everyone wants. Respect. Admiration. World fame. The whole shebang." He sigh-cries. "I want to be the absolute best in history."

"The best—what?"

His eyes are pools of hope. "The best musician."

concerto

Miles seems so sincere. So genuine. His goal is so innocuous, I'm almost ashamed for labeling him as evil.

As he tries to pull himself together, a tear rolls to his chin, and a bubble of empathy has enveloped us. If all he wants is the music part, we can let all the other stuff go. We can walk away from this whole mess and figure out how to strip the magic away and keep only the music. I can get him on our side. Maybe he can help us protect Gaye's land.

The third act takes the stage. A folksy three-piece band. Way too chipper for the mood du jour. We're up next.

I face Miles head on and wait for him to meet my eye. "You can be a great musician. You already are. It's in you. No one can take that away." I truly feel like I can help Miles now. I'm not faking it anymore.

"No, I can't, Sami. Not without"—he flicks his hand—"causing damage. There's no way around it. I can become powerful in the world, maybe. But in all the wrong ways. People will be scared. They might fear me, but they won't respect me."

"I don't think—"

"I can't even have a relationship that's not all . . . tangled up."

"What do you mean?" My shoulders tense. "Miles, tell me what happened with Lauren."

Miles tugs on his collar as if it's strangling him. Sweat beads on his forehead again. "Everything you loved about Lauren, I loved, too. We were perfectly simpatico, she and I. Evenly matched, if not challenging each other."

"Musically, you mean?"

"Yeah. But then when it started to change . . . when I started to change, and my music changed with me, she just kept going. Like, left me in the dust. She didn't support me at all. As a matter of fact, she went against me."

"What do you mean? How did she go against you?"

"If you asked her, she would pin it all on me. She would accuse me of horrible things. But it didn't go that way. She's the one who ruined everything."

"How did she—"

I'm interrupted by Ms. Aleia's whitewashed visage that appears like a sudden nightmare. She gives me a start.

"Showtime." She gives me a sterile, joyless grin. Worry is written all over her face. "Are you ready?" she asks Miles.

"Yup." He spins from me, leaving my unanswered questions lingering like noxious gas in the air. He trudges onto the stage and thuds onto the bench, his face twisted in despair. He pushes his dark hair off his shoulders and puffs his chest, feigning confidence. He looks at me expectantly, a glint of worry in his eyes.

I don't realize I'm hesitating until Ms. Aleia shoves me from behind. The curtain opens, and I'm caught center stage. Lights go up, bright and blinding. A hush falls over the audience. And I freeze.

Beyond the bright spotlight, Jason is there. Lauren, too. They're here for me. Gaye and Poppy—all my reinforcements. With their support, I know can do this. *I can do this!*

"Sami!" Miles' stage whisper bounces off the auditorium's acoustics.

Before I can respond, noise from offstage gets my attention. Some kind of commotion from where Ms. Aleia stands in the wings. She hisses fiercely at someone. A stifled argument. And then a glorious sound echoes across the stage and fills the whole vast space: wheels rolling over wood. And it's like chicken soup for my ears.

The second piano—my piano—is here.

concerto

My birthmark pulses as the henna floods my veins with energy. The pendant zings electric against my chest. What Miles has told me gives me hope—even if I don't know the entire story. If he was somehow vulnerable to Lauren's music, he won't have a chance against mine. My power is coming back. My steps are sure, my breath is steady.

I sit tall at the keyboard and meet Miles' confused gaze across the stage. He's beyond flustered. First, Lauren. Now, a second piano, positioned to attack. My lip curls in a wry grin. At once, I'm overwhelmed with respect for the instrument in front of me. This piano commands it. My fingers caress the keys to the middle C position.

I nod once.

Yes, Miles. I'm playing here. You're playing there. Are you ready?

Because I am.

CHAPTER 44

My hands begin working the keys as if coming home. It feels so natural and comfortable, and I revel in it for a moment. My gaze is locked on Miles, who tries to mask his uncertainty with a cocky grin. His piano movements are jerky, almost constipated. All through our opening, he looks beyond me, searching for answers in Ms. Aleia. Finding none, he throws a quick half-laugh into the audience, asking forgiveness, and I almost feel sorry for him.

At the bridge—the crescendo into a chorus—it becomes clear that this is my music. This is my creation, and no one is going to take it from me. Neither Miles nor Aleia nor anyone else. No one is going to steal it and use it for sick, evil purposes.

The energy has shifted. My people are here. Jason. Lauren. Aunt Gaye and Poppy—I can feel them boost me up. Their faith in me blocks the murky dark void I'd felt that time in the studio playing side by side with Miles.

Tonight, our pianos face each other. Like Poppy had described, it's a dueling piano arrangement. At the refrain, Miles gets it. He senses the shift in power. A flaccid anger changes his face. He's pissed. And ready to fight.

Through our music, we launch into an impassioned conversation. We fight to get the next word in, interrupting each other with the next note.

Chords build as my ballad evolves into a more complex,

concerto

layered piece. It shuts out whatever Miles is playing. I can hardly hear him play over me. My birthmark zings, fortified by the henna, and I go with it wherever it takes me, letting my fingers do the work. My hands are strong. More than capable. My heart lifts, my senses are on high alert. I can feel a vision coming on. I let my eyes close—*it's okay*—and allow my mind to soar . . .

Boston's skyline is as recognizable to me now as Jason's Skenesboro landscape painting. It appears under a dark cloud, the lights in the Prudential building blinking out, like the city is suffering a power surge. In my dreamlike state, I'm flying overtop the buildings, close to the imminent storm. Lightning flashes, illuminating the murky night sky. Thunder rumbles in the distance. At the next shock of lightning, I count—

Flash! One . . . two . . . three—*Boom!*

The storm's getting closer. It's almost directly overhead.

My hands run the length of the piano, blurring notes in succession like dominoes. Miles' music is faint but insistent. A nagging cough. I sit tall and proud, popping off the bench slightly with each chord . . .

Lightning strikes again. It's raining hard now. Boston is swathed in darkness. I zoom—super-fast-motion—toward Boston Harbor, past the financial district, hoping to get a sense of what's happening in the ocean.

Whitecaps trundle across the active waters. Yachts shudder into docks. Moored sailboats rock and tip like bath toys. Waves roar in an unceasing battle cry. They overlap, layer atop layer with no beginning and no end. A different kind of impassioned conversation, as if each wave is trying to get the last word.

The last note, the last chord . . .

Miles does something new—a staccato in a minor key. It's eerie and unfavorable to the ear. It sounds like a child tinkering clumsily on the keys, almost. But it's not awful, remarkably. It makes sense in an unexpected way. Still, why would he play like this? This is not what he'd planned. Can't be. I'm thrown off—my confidence shaken.

I zone back in on my vision, trying to see the end game. What are they trying to do?

Out past the Boston Harbor Islands, deep across the ocean, is a thundercloud. The distant storm is violent and disturbs the waters beneath, sending its energy to our shores. Wind whips, tousling my hair into my face, flapping my red hemp dress against my thighs. Wind screeches through the narrow alleys behind me—a siren. Gusts rip, and glass breaks somewhere nearby.

A hurricane? Is that what they were planning? Same as Newport? I should be able to stop—

Wait—what's this?

Below the storm cloud, out at sea, there's a sight so strange and frightening . . . and familiar. I can't believe my eyes. Huge red laser-like columns of light pour down out of the storm cloud.

Light against black. Neon red stripes cut through the darkness, falling in clumps from all corners of the sky. They last less than a second. A flash. Red light reflects off the shadowy clouds like a warning signal.

I've seen this before. In one of my first visions at the Berklee studio . . .

Red lightning. Falling in twos or threes. Grotesque giant jellyfish tentacles, swaying ominously in the dark sky. They grow in frequency and duration; the light lingers for more than a second now. They appear to be alive—or controlled somehow, clawing for something.

Wear red, Miles had insisted. My veins go cold, hearing his voice, seeing again his twisted grin. Was this part of his plan? Are these monstrous neon claws Aleia's secret weapon? Is our music summoning them somehow?

I watch in horror as the giant red claws stretch down toward the water. My breath is caught, waiting, knowing something terrible is about to happen.

No, no. I've got to stop it from hitting the water, but how—

The monstrous claws gouge the ocean's surface, and bright red light surges into the waters. It reflects off the clouds above as far as the eye can see. The sky, the water, the city seems to be on fire. Then, the light fades. The water, the sky go bloodshot.

It's over in a few seconds, but the effects are devastating. The ocean is tumultuous—a churning witch's brew. Steam radiates off the water, filling the gray sky with beady prisms that look like eyes. Millions of tiny eyes.

Fire has mixed with water and air, changing the chemistry of our world. Fire in the water, fire in the air—what's left?—fire on Earth. These monstrous red claws are going after Earth next?

The city is in peril. We are all in danger. There's not much time.

Eyes open. My music has stopped—abruptly cutting off with an ugly splatter of notes as my hands mash the keys. Miles keeps playing, intense, his face strained.

"Miles! What's going on?" I yell across the stage, not caring about the show. We'll all need to evacuate any moment if—

Miles ignores me. He's pounding away, masterfully performing a solo in what's supposed to be our piano duel. His music is aggressive and captivating and, I imagine, has the audience pinned to their seats in awe. He meets my eye for a millisecond, his eyebrow cocked in agony or victory— I can't tell. Desperate, I glance back to Ms. Aleia. She's there in all her whitewashed glory, arms folded, a triumphant grin plastered on her waxy face. I spin toward the audience, blinking against the harsh spotlight, trying to communicate with Gaye telepathically.

We're all in danger. We need to evacuate. Now!

Why don't I scream this aloud? Why don't I jump up and down and insist everyone get out, run to safety, save themselves?

Time seems to be suspended. Uncertainty clouds my judgment.

Then, I spot Lauren in the audience. A warm glow surrounds her. Her gold pendant shines like a beacon. Miles continues to play, but with difficulty. Sweat gleams on his brow. He leans upstage, away from the audience, cringing from some tormenting force. He seems to be in pain. Back and forth from him to Lauren: she's the cause. He struggles through a few more measures. I'm lost in the moment, witnessing the power she has over him. A hush falls over the auditorium. Miles' agony plays out on the keys—a somber, melancholy tune.

He continues to play, but in slow motion. Everything seems to have decelerated.

Overtaking him now is almost too easy.

In a moment, my spirit has renewed clarity. I know what I need to do. I spin back to my keyboard, shake out my hands, and dive in . . .

concerto

I'm at Boston's waterfront, in the Custom House Tower—inside the clock tower. The bell mechanism, *à la* Big Ben in London, chimes as a chilling accompaniment to Miles' music. It's toxic to my senses. Time seems to be running out. I'm trapped in this tower, its bells jarring my ears, drowning out the roar of the tumultuous ocean waves.

Yet when the last bell chimes, I feel Lauren's energy once again, in a warm, invigorating glow. As if she's here with me. Maybe it's the calming effect of her presence, but everything seems to slow down, giving me time to get a sense of what's happening.

My view out to the ocean is daunting. The red lightning is falling in sheets toward the water, closer to the shoreline this time. The flash of red is so bright, I'm blinded for a moment. Blinking into focus what must be the horizon, I do a double take.

What am I seeing?

The line where the sky and water meet is gone—or blended together. The next cruel flash of red shows me what it truly is: a towering wall of water, moving toward our city. Like a Mack truck thundering down the highway, there's no stopping it.

No way. A freaking tidal wave.

Its magenta glow surges from the depths of the ocean, as if lava from the Earth's core has fed the giant wave. Reds and magentas and violets and fuchsia. Images swirl with painful memories: Payne disappearing into the cave two years ago, Payne emerging as a spirit of light deep in the crevasse. The last shard of Aquamarine had been her gift—

Aquamarine!

The pendant! The storm—with its monstrous electric-red claws—is distracting me from my most powerful weapon.

From the innards of the clock tower, I push through the winds to the observation deck and shield my eyes from airborne sand and debris.

The surge of water is barely visible, but I can feel its approach. Still—it's all in slow motion. Time is on my side. My music is alive inside me; I can feel its vibration. My birthmark, the henna, are working—but it's not enough. Every muscle in my body tenses as I zone in on the Aquamarine at my heart-center. Its energy fills me, layering upon my music, delivering its power.

Pushing my shoulders back, I thrust out my chest. A scream escapes me—something shoots from my ribcage. An explosion of blue light bursts forth, and I'm thrown back against the clock tower. My skull knocks against the hard stone. The huge wave advances, relentless. Another flash of lightning and the tsunami is alight, bearing down . . . about to hit shore. The reclaimed waterfront of Boston—on such fragile footing—is about to be wiped out.

No!

I push forward, feeling my music come through me, feeling the Aquamarine magic flow through my veins. Again, I thrust out—super-hero style—against the giant wave.

Bright blue flashes into the red like laser bolts, neutralizing its power, tamping it down, sending it back where it came from. The waters are still raging, but the wall of water is no more.

"Impressive." Her voice more than carries over the wind. It *is* the wind.

Ms. Aleia.

Frantically, I search for her overhead, my music fading

into the background. All I see of her is her gown, white gossamer like cloud wisps streaking across the dark sky.

"But we still have my Red Sprites." Her laughter is thunder, echoing against the storm clouds. As if on cue, more red columns drop from the thundercloud, clawing at the water. Too many to count.

"Why?" I call to the sky. "Ms. Aleia, why are you doing this?"

Thunder shakes the tower as if in response. More jelly-fish tentacles drop down and seem to sting the ocean water. The light expires at the water's surface, now, and it looks like the ocean is a giant pool of blood. It gives me pause. It seems she's hurting Posh's domain, too. Her giant red claws—Red Sprites, as she calls them—are terrorizing all the elements of our world indiscriminately. Does Miles see this? Does he know what he's doing?

Or is Aleia now working alone?

"Aleia!" I call, blinded and burned by the red light. I can't open my eyes. My face feels like it's melting from the heat. "Stop! Please!"

Her white gossamer surrounds the clock tower, encircling me, shielding me from the scalding Red Sprites that fall from the thundercloud. Beyond her cloudy wisps, the sky is burning. I see her ghost-like visage fading in and out. The wind carries her words: "She who controls the wind, controls the skies. Lightning can defeat lightning—with my special luminous darts. And she who controls the skies, controls the heavens and all the gods."

All the gods? The wind is like acid on my skin. The sky—alight with fire—explodes in bursts over the sea. A single red bolt appears within the gossamer shield, like a spear, and Aleia's ghostly visage materializes, reflected in

322

ominous red light.

"My darlings, brought down from the mesosphere. Red Sprites are like an electric shock—zapping out those puny *triggered* lightning bolts he's so fond of." The spear of red light shoots down from the gossamer shield toward the water, and Aleia's sickening cackle echoes within the fog. "It's laughable! My lightning bolts are far more powerful than his."

"His lightning bolts?" I process her words, and they take me back to Ms. Galvin's class or with Aunt Gaye, being schooled in the ways of the Greek gods. She's not talking about Posh or Miles. She's talking about—

"You mean, Zeus?" I shout into the wind. "Are you crazy?"

More laughter. More thunder. And the shield of white gossamer dissipates into the violent storm, giving me a clear view of what's transpiring. More Red Sprites shoot down from the thundercloud. Hundreds. The sky is filled with them.

I can't believe it. Aleia's taking on Zeus—the god of all gods? Is it not enough to work with Posh to gain control of more land and inland waters? She wants to control the gods, too?

Miles' words echo in my mind: *You know what's cool? How the ocean affects the weather. Like, extreme weather.*

The only reason she's partnered with Posh is to use his oceans to bolster her storms. Does Posh know he's being used? Does Miles? Has Miles been working with her behind his father's back?

Tilting my gaze up to the heavens, I silently pray for Zeus' help. Perhaps, I realize with dread, he's already fighting. It's clear—there's blood in the water and the sky:

concerto

the war reaches far beyond the thunderclouds.

There's got to be something I can do.

My music is still here, running through me. My birthmark is on high volume, the henna flooding me with magic. My piano sounds over the storm. The pendant at my chest is more active than ever. I follow its pull and shut out the rest of the world, zoning in on the power of Aquamarine.

And then, it happens.

A burst of brilliant blue light shoots out from the clock tower like an arrow, a direct attack on one of the Red Sprites—zapping out one of the giant red claws. My music surges, and another burst shoots forth.

"What are you doing?" Aleia screeches in the wind.

Again and again, blue cones of laser light rocket toward the thundercloud, like shooting stars, destroying one red claw at a time.

"Blue Jets? How . . .? But you can't—you mustn't! This isn't supposed to happen. Your music was supposed to—"

"My music is mine and mine alone. And it will stop you from destroying this city." My voice is sure and strong. I clench my fists as a Blue Jet fires from the clock tower, zapping out yet another giant claw. "My music is more powerful than your winds, your Red Sprites, and your lightning."

Squeezing my eyes shut, I press on, leaning into the winds, feeling Miles' music drowning in the background, hearing my song play louder. And louder still.

"My sprites! Stop it! Now!" Ms. Aleia screams. "No! Don't do it."

Her voice is being sucked into a void. I open my eyes to a strange sight. A cottony-white mass swirling up toward the thundercloud. It's Ms. Aleia; I can see her figure within the gossamer vortex.

"My sprites!" she calls, her words lost in the helicopter chop of the air.

A buzzing from the pendant, and a final Blue Jet zooms to destroy the last monstrous claw—and Ms. Aleia's precious Red Sprites are gone.

The cyclone of white, a tornado in the sky, drills up through the darkness, up and up and up and up. It's like her own force turned against her, the wind shifting from pushing to pulling, a vacuum sucking her into the heavens.

"Wait! No . . ." Her screams are distant. Her last words fade out as the winds die away.

A sudden colorless calm falls over the waterfront. The air goes still and thick with silence. My back is pressed against the clock tower wall. The cold, hard stone is comforting—tethering me to the Earth. I run my hands along the rough surface, a tactile reminder of what all this is for. Protecting the Earth and all the precious minerals of Gaye's domain.

The storm is over. The Red Sprites have dissolved. And Ms. Aleia is gone.

Closing my eyes, I let myself slip away from the Clock Tower, fall back from the waterfront, and sink onto my piano bench at Berklee.

CHAPTER 45

Fingertips pressing on my neck. Checking for a pulse.

A voice, soft and intense. "Come back to me. Come back to me."

It's Jason. *Jason's here.*

My head's cradled in his lap. He's smoothing my hair and stroking my face with urgency. He mumbles something. I think I hear "sorry." It doesn't matter. Nothing matters. I could lie here in his lap all day, enveloped by his warmth.

"Go get some smelling salts or something." His voice is frantic now and cracks with emotion. "She's not waking up."

Waking up? What's he talking about?

OMG—my vision. The tsunami threatening Boston's waterfront. Ms. Aleia and her Red Sprites. Miles and our piano duel. Was it all a dream? Or am I really here?

"Hey bonehead." Poppy now, louder than usual. "You there?"

Leave it to Poppy to laugh me into consciousness. I blink Jason into focus; his relief is palpable.

"Sami, my gosh. You scared me!" Jason smothers me, hugging my neck. "You totally passed out. Dead to the world. Are you okay?"

"I'm okay." I don't know if it's true. Everything's fuzzy. We're on a wood floor next to a piano—on stage. So, it wasn't a dream. It really did happen. Poppy stands over us. The dinner-hour lighting tells me the curtain's closed,

concerto

thank goodness.

"How long have I been out?" I ask, panicked about losing time again, remembering my six-hour blackout.

"Not long," Poppy says, businesslike. "You're good."

"Where's Aunt Gaye?"

Jason sounds almost ticked now. "Don't worry about Aunt Gaye. She's at her gallery."

"She had to get back. She ducked out before the finale. Before the madness hit."

Madness? "What did you see?"

Poppy shakes her head. "It's not what we saw, it's what we felt."

"The entire auditorium shook." Jason's eyes go wide, and he clutches his chest. "Scared me half to death."

My insides quiver like they've been subjected to turbulence. I need to get my bearings. There's got to be evidence of our duel. Glancing around, nothing looks out of place. Still, that floaty, uneasy feeling won't quit.

Jason helps me up onto the bench, my back to the piano keys. "Did it work?" I ask Poppy. The images are still fresh: the glowing red of the ocean, the towering wall of water, the terrifying Red Sprites dropping from the thundercloud, the cyclone that vaporized Ms. Aleia. I shudder remembering it.

"Girl," Poppy says. "I have no idea what happened outside these walls. Gaye will have to report on that. But I will tell you this. There was a clear winner of the piano duel."

Jason folds his arms. "What are you guys even talking about? Something out of *Clash of the Titans* happened in this auditorium tonight. It was like you guys were literally fighting with music. But there was more to it than that, wasn't there?"

I take his hand. "Yes. Yes. There was a lot more to it

than that. It's hard to explain."

"Could you try?"

"I will. I will. I need to see Gaye first—" It hits me then; Ms. Aleia is nowhere in sight. "Wait. Where's Ms. Aleia? She was right there, standing in the wings."

Poppy shrugs. "Miles might know."

Following her shrug, I notice Miles arguing with someone backstage. His body language tells me he's apologetic—desperately so. Even before I see her, I know he's talking to Lauren. Her arms are shelved at her bosom—protective. With one hand, she slides her gold pendant back and forth on the chain. The look she gives him could cut glass. It's clear he still loves her. Maybe a few weeks ago that would have made me jealous, but right now it's like a load has been lifted from my shoulders.

Something's still not right, though. "Where's Miles' father?"

Jason hovers over me, as if to shield me from another storm. "Who cares about Miles or his father, Sami? I care about you. I'm not going to let you get into trouble again."

Jason doesn't get it. I can't blame him, though. But now isn't the time to fill him in. My anxiety reaches a new plateau. I leap up from the bench. "We have to find Aunt Gaye. We have to make sure it worked."

Jason looks from me to Poppy, who gives him one of her snarky grins. "Then we're going with you," he says.

"Good." But I hesitate and hope the next thing that comes out of my mouth doesn't sound like I'm putting him off. "Jason, I don't need you to protect me. And you need to understand . . . there still might be work I need to do."

All his worries over the last hour are released in a giant sigh. His shoulders slump with it.

concerto

"Okay. Fine. But promise me you won't leave me in the dark."

My answer is in the way I look at him, as if there's no one else more important in the world. Because, really, there isn't.

Poppy leads the way. We pass Miles and Lauren—still arguing—at stage right. Lauren shifts her attention to me easily, and Miles shuffles closer to her, desperation behind his every move.

In Lauren's smile, she's trying to tell me something. There's pride there, approval. And something else. She locks her gaze on mine and slowly opens her locket, revealing an old timey clock face—one that remarkably resembles Custom House Tower clock. It's ticking bridges the space between us, and happy tears come to my eyes. She's given me a gift. I ask her silently, "That was you?"

An almost imperceptible nod before Miles steps between us, blocking my view of her.

I could feel her presence. A warmth. She was with me in that clock tower as my vision played out. I wasn't alone. She was there.

Did it work, then? Is it truly over? So many questions.

Miles' odd behavior is puzzling. He doesn't acknowledge me at all. It doesn't bother me, but it's strange. He seems altogether uninterested—impassive, even—in our piano duel and is solely focused on winning Lauren's affections. My mind spins, wondering what that might mean. Does he truly not care, or has he won?

I keep my eyes on Miles, watching for a sign that he's lost, feeling a fresh sense of security with Jason by my side. But there's nothing in his space beyond Lauren. They're fighting like lovers. He keeps stroking her arm, as if trying to nudge his way into her good graces. I'm still studying them, my neck twisted back to see, when I literally bump into—

Posh Eichen.

I freeze. My throat dries in an instant, taking my voice. Posh looks past me to his son, but he isn't done with me yet. He jabs two fingers into my shoulders—*ouch!*—pushing me back until I'm level with Miles and Lauren. Over his shoulder, I see Jason clench his fists, ready to pounce. My eyes tell him no. I can handle this. But can I? Jason steps forward. "Hey—" But Poppy grabs his arm to hold him back.

"She's betrayed us, son," Posh's deep voice booms, filling the stage area all the way to the velvet curtain. "She's betrayed us!"

His words cut me to the core. They tell me two things: one, our plan worked. Two, he knows it was me who defeated them. *Oh, no.* My body is trembling all over.

My mouth drops open to speak. But nothing comes out. A bead of sweat rolls down my back. My only saving grace is that Posh's icy glare is not directed toward me at the moment, but at his son.

"What do you mean?" Miles says, visibly irritated at the interruption. To my astonishment, he points at Lauren. "It was her fault. I couldn't . . . perform. Not with her in the audience. It's like what happened before—"

"Stop that nonsense." Posh steps toward Miles, his footfalls quaking the stage beneath my feet. "It wasn't Lauren any more than it was,"—he waves a thick hand in my direction—"this slight thing."

Me? I'm the slight thing? It wasn't my fault? I'm too shocked to feel relief.

Then, Ms. Aleia's desperate words come back to me:

concerto

My sprites! They will give me control of the seas.

Posh isn't talking about me or my music or my magic. He's talking about—

"Aleia. We were wrong to trust her. And now she's a real threat to my domain. Come on. We have work to do." He places his large paw on his son's back, and Miles has no choice but to obey.

Miles truly looks miserable as he trudges beside his father. Tears start in his eyes as he whines like a child resisting bedtime. It makes me sad for him. He looks with longing at Lauren, pleading silently for another chance or forgiveness or maybe friendship.

Lauren, glowing with beauty and confidence, mouths one word in his direction: "Goodbye."

After they're gone, the four of us—Jason, Poppy, Lauren, and I—look at each other. Checking in. Taking a collective breath. But it's not time to rest. The way Jason's all wound up, I know he feels it too. But not for the same reason.

"Miles is lucky his daddy saved him," Jason says, scowling. "He wouldn't have two working legs if I had a shot at him."

"Relax, tough guy." Poppy grabs my arm. "Come on. Let's get to the gallery."

Desperate now to see Gaye, I take Jason by the hand, and we press on at a healthy clip.

Inside her gallery, Gaye stands in front of her landscape painting of Boston's waterfront, a hand cupping her chin thoughtfully. She doesn't move when we come through the door but senses our presence.

"Come and see, Sam," she says evenly, giving no hint about whether she's pleased or not.

The rest of the group waits at the conference table. It takes ages for me to cross the gallery to meet Gaye's line of vision. My shoulders are to my ears with nerves.

There it is. The Custom House Tower—its clock face looking like an old friend—and the other buildings that line the waterfront. The scenic Harbor Walk, the green parks that resulted from the Big Dig, the Summer Street Bridge that connects to Southie . . . And then, a handful of yachts sitting unscathed at the docks. Some cruise boats. Sailboats moored in the calm bay. All without a scratch. The Boston Harbor Islands are intact in the distance, a moody sky overhead. The waters are calm—more like a lake than the sea.

I search for a remnant of my battle with Aleia, not sure what to expect. Maybe there would be a trace of red in the water. Or a pink streak from the sky. But nothing seems off. Not only that, but there's no hint that anything's happened at all.

Turning to Gaye with a wrinkled brow, I say, "I don't understand. I don't see anything."

Gaye gives me a hearty side hug. "That's because you did it, Sam. I watched the whole thing." Tears shine in her eyes. "You stopped the wave. You stopped the Red Sprites."

"The henna, the Aquamarine, my music . . . it worked?"

"It seems you had some reinforcements beyond what we'd planned." Gaye's eyes are alight. "Were you aware of what you witnessed?"

A safe feeling envelopes me as I remember being in the Clock Tower—time seemed to be suspended, putting the tsunami in slow motion, giving me time to thwart it. It felt so natural at the time, but now that I think about it—

333

concerto

"Everything slowed down . . ."

Gaye gives a little hum. "I'm sure it seemed that way, but I'm talking about a more—authoritative assistance."

"Authoritative assistance?" I'm at a loss. "Are you speaking in code?"

Gaye blows out a breath and sings a high note with it. Her cheeks pink up. She looks simply delighted. "I've never seen anything like it. Sam, you have to know what a gift you've been given. An honor! He wouldn't waste his time helping a human being unless he deemed her worthy."

"Who are you talking about?"

"Zeus, my child."

Zeus? THE Zeus?

My mind reaches back. In the Clock Tower, after the tsunami quelled, the Red Sprites were still attacking the sea. Blood filled the sky. The war raged in the heavens. It was true; Zeus was battling Aeolus.

"Zeus heard my prayer."

"You alerted him to a dire situation."

Those blue spears of light that shot down the Red Sprites? "He was the one who fired the Blue Jets," I say.

"Oh no, child. That was all you. That was Dion."

"Then how—"

She winks. "He created the vortex . . ."

The vortex—the vacuum that sucked Ms. Aleia up into space. A hand floats to my mouth; I'm feeling a little faint. "He took Aleia. What happened to her?"

"Oh, they'll deal with that on Olympus." Gaye flicks her hand skyward. Once again, I have to quell my astonishment. There really is such a thing as Mount Olympus?

Gaye doesn't register my pause. She claps her hands, elated. "You have something to be proud of. You dissolved the Red Sprites. You took on Aleia—and won."

A cry of gratitude escapes me.

"You did it," Gaye says again, and we're both crying.

CHAPTER 46

Hello, Skene Mountain, old friend.

My shoes know this trail so well by now, they nearly walk themselves. The path is cleared of branches. No more cobwebs to fight through. It's like the hill has rolled out the red carpet for me and Jason on what we both know will be our last day together for quite a while. Tomorrow, he returns to RISD. In a few weeks, my senior year at Skenesboro begins. That school will feel so empty without him.

We walk hand in hand, which feels so right I have a hard time remembering ever feeling distant from him.

But I did, this summer. And it almost ruined everything. We haven't talked about why he ghosted me for so long. We've avoided any mention of Miles . . . or Sydney. Now that our five-week plan has come to a close, we'll need a new one. With everything that's happened in the last forty-eight hours—at Showcase—our relationship is a topic that seems almost immaterial. Or, too fragile for words.

Can he sense my struggle through my silence? Part of me wishes we didn't need to have another talk. Part of me knows we have to—and I'm terrified this may be our last date ever.

We pause, short of breath from the hike. A shock of longing grips me as Jason releases my hand to take some water. I grasp a spindly branch that's grown into the path. I caress pine needles and some come out in my hand. Sap

concerto

sticks to my fingers. It's relentless, so I'll be sticky for the duration. It's irony at its best—these fingers that harnessed a magic more powerful than the gods . . . are now covered in sap.

After the final Showcase, my program at Berklee was essentially over. Jason helped me pack my things. To my surprise, he offered to escort me home to Skenesboro. Although I think Gaye had a hand there, worried about my mental state after battling the weather gods. It did kind of suck the life out of me.

I don't remember the last couple days in Boston. The ride home was a blur—albeit a comforting one. I let the wholesome, pastoral scenery wash over me as we drove through the mountains and farmlands. Only when we arrived in Skenesboro did I feel a semblance of my old self.

Thank goodness for Jason. Even though we're technically still fighting, he's by my side. If only we could have kept this feeling intact when there was distance between us. I know it's possible; other people have long-distance relationships that work out just fine. Is there a magic formula? Or some map we can follow so we don't grow apart again? I can't make all the effort, though. He has to want it, too.

He offers me water. As I drink, I'm over-aware that his lips touched the same spot on the bottle. It's the closest thing to a kiss we've had since I visited Rhode Island at the very beginning of my program.

I was the one who suggested we do this hike today. I needed to see the cave—or chasm—or whatever it is now. The scar is still visible from downtown, but part of me hopes I'll see signs of regrowth in the clearing. Part of me needs to see green there.

That pungent smell of soil here at the clearing first

hinted that my magic was coming back—and that it had something to do with healing the Earth. Did I do it? Did I do enough? I'd hoped to help the environment. I'd wanted to rebuild to make up for what I'd destroyed two and a half years ago. I'd wanted to find a solution, not just prevent environmental disasters. And although Gaye insists my efforts were more than successful, I'd hoped to do more.

Hope. What a flimsy emotion. Yet it's my source of strength to reach the top of this hill, to face what's left of the cave, and to find the courage to have that difficult talk with Jason and accept what our future will be.

We approach the last bit of undergrowth before the clearing, and I hesitate. Jason seems to understand and nudges me. "Go ahead. You first."

On reflex, I do a 180—putting my back to it. My eyes pinch shut. "I don't want to see it."

Jason half-laughs. "What do you mean? I thought—"

"What if it looks the same?"

"Then . . . it looks the same."

"That would mean my music did nothing to rebuild it. It would mean I failed."

"You didn't fail. Far from it. Gaye even said—"

"But I wanted to fix this mountain; it's, like, a symbol for the entire Earth. I want that scar to go away. And if I don't look, I can still hope . . ." My words trail off as my heart breaks in two. Because today I'm hoping for more than healing the scar.

Jason gently places my hands around his neck and hugs my waist—a middle school slow dance. His smile is tender. "Sami, it's okay. You don't need to put that kind of pressure on yourself. No one expects you to save the world."

I quirk an eyebrow. "Oh, really?"

concerto

"Well, maybe Gaye kinda does. And you did! Don't diminish what you did in Boston."

"I know. I just . . ."

"You just—what?"

He pulls me close, and the crown of my head rests on his shoulder. As he holds me, my line of vision tunnels down our bodies, dances past our knees, and swirls to where we stand. Under our feet, the ground is firm, dry soil speckled with dead leaves and rock. Go a bit deeper and the soil is rich and moist and alive with tree roots and crawling bugs and microscopic seeds. I silently thank Gaye for this gift. The Earth is our platform and our promise. It connects us in a way that will never change. It gives me courage.

"Jason, we need to talk."

He hugs me tighter, and the tunnel closes. "I know."

I breathe him in. He smells like cedar and pine and all the things I love about the outdoors. "What are we going to do?"

He hugs me hard and then lets go abruptly. He marches past me into the clearing as if on a mission of his own. Is he angry?

"Jason."

His shoulders are rigid, unwelcoming, yet I reach for him anyway. But before we touch, something stops me.

Jason's framed by it. We're here. We're at the clearing. What's left of it. It steals all my attention. I take in the washed out, destitute state of the clearing and hope seeps from me as if from a pinhole.

Despair blankets me.

It's not so much how the space looks; the feel of it is altogether different. Before, it held an energy. It was charged. After all my experiences up here, with Aquamarine and Payne's spirit and channeling my magic, I had come to expect it—depend on it, even. That energy, I now realize, fed me. It inspired me. It helped me find my magic.

But this—what this place feels like now? . . . is death.

It reminds me of a website I once saw that showed a town that had been deserted during the Holocaust. It had become a ghost town. The buildings and cars were overcome by the elements. Ash and sand. Everything gray. Depressing as anything.

Not a hint of green. Not even a weed.

"Oh, Jason." I can't help myself. "It's worse. I didn't think that was possible."

"What is?" His glare is jarring.

"This—this space."

He turns to me, his eyebrows darting together. "You know what? I don't really care about this space. I don't think you should either."

I blink at him.

"We never really finished our talk." He stares at his feet, bitterness tainting his voice. "When you told me about Miles."

My shoulders fall from my ears. "Miles is a non-issue. You saw that for yourself this weekend."

"I'm not talking about Miles, really. I mean, it's not about him." He picks up a stone from the ash and tosses it like he's skipping rocks. It hits a tree; the hollow *thunk* is huge in the quiet.

"Sami, there's a reason you didn't tell me he was there with you in the program. And your questions about Sydney. I mean, I like hanging out with her and part of me feels like that should be okay. I don't know. There's a lack of trust or something. I mean, do you trust me?"

concerto

"Do you trust me?"

Big sigh. "See. If both of us have to ask, something's not right. I've thought a lot about it, and I just think . . ."

"What?"

"It's not fair to either of us to struggle through this thing. It should be easy. It shouldn't be . . ."

"It's not. Whatever you were going to say, it's not."

"It shouldn't be hard."

"Well, sometimes it is!" My voice carries through the clearing. "Sometimes, relationships are hard. Sometimes, we do have to work at them."

"I don't know. We shouldn't have to force it."

"Force it? Jason, you totally iced me out. At the start of the program, too."

"There was a lot going on. You know that."

"Yes, I know that. There was a lot going on in my world, too. Believe me."

His gives me a sideways grin. "Miles."

"Not just Miles. Stuff I wanted to share with you. I tried to share with you."

"Whatever." He's got an ugly look on his face. I hardly recognize him.

"Really? Are you giving up? Just like that?"

"I'm no quitter. You're the one who gave up on us just because I didn't call you all the time."

"How about: you never called me! You totally hung me out to dry. I had no idea what was going on."

"That's not true."

I whip out my phone. "Look. Look at all my texts. Look how many times I called and you never picked up. I have it all here—and it was a one-way street. Relationships can never work that way."

"Come on, Sami. You should always know how I feel. I shouldn't have to tell you all the time. You should just know it."

"So you do your thing in Rhody, and I'll do mine in Beantown. And I'll never know what's happening with you, and you'll never know what's happening with me. And if I ever really need you, I'll just tell myself 'Oh, Sami, it's okay. You know he loves you.' And that's it? That's supposed to be enough? What's the point in that? Why would we even be together if we're always alone?"

An edge of pain changes his face. "If that's how you feel."

In my voice, I hear tears. "No, it's not how I feel. I want to be together. I want to be a real part of your life. I want you in mine. I want this to work, but you have to want it, too."

"I do want it," he almost whispers.

"Do you?"

The next stone he throws falls to the ground with hardly a sound. The fight has left him. That hard edge to his features has softened. My Jason is back.

"I'm sorry. I've never done this before."

"I haven't either." My next words take longer to come out. "I'm sorry, too."

"And I'm sorry for icing you out. Honestly, sometimes it hurt more to hear from you than to just . . . wait."

"Wait for what?"

"For the next time I saw you? I know it sounds silly now. It's not easy to wait." He softens all over. Makes me want to kiss him. He tosses another stone before taking my hands again.

I choke out my next words. "Just—don't tell me it's too hard. Don't tell me it's not worth working on."

concerto

He pauses, and a flicker of confusion crosses his face. "I'm not." A smile, tender and warm. "That would be the biggest mistake of my life." He thumbs away a tear. "Sami, I believe this is worth fighting for. Us. We're worth fighting for."

"Well, I know it's going to be work. I'm not sure it will be a fight—"

"It will. We're going to have to fight off all the Mileses and the Sydneys that might come along. Because there will be more—"

"Not if I can help it there won't."

He throws his head back laughing. "Oh, really? You don't think anyone else is ever going to try?"

No, this won't do. We're not going to sit back and allow outsiders to meddle with our love. We need a plan that makes temptation impossible. I sniff back my tears. "Okay, listen. That stuff won't matter if things between us are solid. We need to commit to each other in a different way."

He gives me an exaggerated wink. "Are you proposing?"

"I'm not joking around. I need a promise from you. I mean, we need to make a promise to each other to connect every day. And not just through texts."

We start a slow trek down the trail. Jason stays just a half step behind me. "I'm sorry about the phone calls. You know, we never talked on the phone here. You lived right across the street. I saw you all the time. But then when I was at RISD—I dunno—it felt funny. And I always felt like Tiko was listening."

"I know what you mean. I'd rather see you in person, too. But at least for the next year we're going to have to do something to fill in the time between visits. There are other

344

JD SPERO

things, you know. Like, hello: FaceTime? We can have a set time every night before bed, say. It'll be like a standing date in our PJs."

He stops me on the trail. "Will you promise to wear those cute polka dot ones?"

That makes me laugh. "You remember those?"

"My favorite. And you're right. FaceTime would be so much better."

"And you can't ignore my texts, Jason. Send me an emoji or something. Let me know you're alive, for crying out loud."

"All right. All right. I will." He moves closer. My breath stops. "Hey, I don't want you to worry about this scar anymore." He flicks his hand toward the clearing. "It's not what matters." He takes my hands and presses them one atop the other against his chest, over his heart. A surge goes through me. "It's this. This is the scar we need to heal."

I go to laugh, and he leans in for a kiss. My pulse races as if we'd never kissed before. His lips feel like home—slightly chapped and perfectly sweet. He draws me closer so there's no space between us at all. A yearning for him plunges deep in my belly. I want to dive inside him. We sink deeper into the kiss, and my whole body tingles. Fireworks dazzle behind my eyelids. My heart expands to fill my chest. I lose track of where we are—until a bird calls overhead. A slight breeze flaps at my hair.

We're both grinning as we pull away.

A gentleman's kiss on my hand. I playfully slap his shoulder. "When did you get so sappy?"

He wrinkles his nose. "You should talk. Your hand is full of it."

"That's it. You're stuck." I lace my fingers into his. "No

345

concerto

getting away from me now."

"I could think of worse things."

"Me, too." I'm so buoyed by happiness, I'm floating.

Jason's right. I don't have to worry about the clearing or the cave. Maybe it's time to worry about normal teenage things for a while. I can already feel the scar between me and Jason starting to heal.

All my cares turn to dust, swirling away with the wind, as we continue down the path toward home.

~ THE END ~

Continue reading for a sneak peek of book 3 of the *Forte* series, *Cadence*, coming in 2018.

Cadence

Lauren's story
PROLOGUE

Hot pink. Neon, almost. A happy color—perfect for pedis. My fingers I always leave bare. Wouldn't want it to distract the judges during my cello audition. But my toes are a different story. Since last fall, it's a matter of survival. Anything that brings me the slightest sliver of happiness—anything that keeps me in the present moment, appreciating the here and now—is a priority. And it's a fact: you can't not smile looking at hot pink toenails.

Fuh. It's been quite the year.

I'm putting on the second coat when Sami calls.

It's such a surprise to see her name light up on my screen, my bottle of polish almost tips over as I reach to answer. My pendant swings on its chain and smacks against the counter. A premonition?

"Sami?" For a moment, it's like we're little kids again. Maybe it's the hot pink coming through. But I hear my voice lift with a childlike eagerness I thought had been lost forever.

About six months ago, I got an email from her—Sami. It was pretty boring stuff. It took me forever to summon an awkward-at-best response. It's not like we're going to reconnect over cyberspace. Too much has happened. For reals. I never liked email, anyway.

"Oh, Lauren. You answered." She laughs. "How are you?"

"Good. Good." That innocent perkiness is still there but now it sounds plasticky. It's like it belongs to an alien. I turn on my old me, the one Sami used to know. "How are you? It's been a long time."

"I know. Too long. And I'm so glad you're . . . good. Really glad. And I can't wait to hear all about everything. But there's a reason I'm calling—"

Her tone shifts to a minor key. She's businesslike and staid. All those childlike vibes go out the wazoo. What did I expect? Even the hot pink nail polish seems sadly optimistic.

I twist the little brush back into the bottle and hide my feet under the table. Is it care or curiosity that makes me ask: "Is everything all right?"

"Yes. Well, I think so. It's that . . . Hey, did you know I'm in Boston? I'm doing the summer program at Berklee School of Music?"

"Oh, really?"

Hold up. Berklee School of Music? She's there with Miles? What the—

My heart climbs up my chest, pushing on my lungs. Everything goes dark—despite my silly hot pink. "I-i-i-i-e-e think I know why you're calling."

"You do?"

"Miles Eichen. He's there, too."

"Yes, he is."

What do I tell her? After all that went down? I can't just blurt it out. She would think she called the loony bin.

"Sami, I know it's been a long time. It would take hours for me to fill you in. You know, Miles and I dated for quite a while."

"I know."

If I could put the relationship in a bottle and send it away, out to sea, I would. Details of *us* need no repeating. "It ended kinda ugly." Understatement of the century.

"It did?"

Holy Hogwarts, she sounds so naïve. Now I'm starting to worry. A twist in my gut tells me it's happening again—or on the verge. "Sami, he's not the kid we knew and loved growing up. He's . . . different."

"I'm getting that sense."

There's an intimacy implied. It's like a kick in the gut. "Are you guys . . . ?"

"No! No, we're not dating. I have a boyfriend from back home. But, Miles and I . . . we're kind of hanging out. Just—you know . . . like, friends. But things have gotten a little bizarre."

Bizarre. Ha! If she only knew . . .

A murky fog rolls in, threatening to suffocate me. I grip my pendant, pressing my eyes closed. I serve up a prayer: *I don't want to relive it. What's in the past is in the past. Please. Don't make me.*

Sami's still talking. "I mean, I think I might know what you're talking about—Miles being different . . . He took me up to his father's beach house. The past two Saturdays, we've been at the beach up there. Spending time near the ocean. And with his dad."

"Oh." If I say anything more, I'll barf.

"And music. Well, you know as well as I do how much he loves music. But it means more now. It seems to have a certain power now. Does that sound nuts?"

She has no idea. "No, Sami. I know exactly what you mean." She keeps talking while my mind rewinds of its own accord, fast-playing all we went through, me and Miles. It's nauseating.

"So, I wanted to call you to see if you could tell me anything about Miles I should know?"

I have to warn her or something. But if I go there right now, here on the phone, I'll crack directly in half. Crack open like a freaking egg.

She goes on, oblivious. "I know you were in a pretty serious relationship and your breakup was probably hard and you must still have feelings—"

"No, that's not it." I get it out, word-vomit-style. Deep breath. From the bottom of my spine, anger rises up unexpectedly. My next words are sharp. "The only feeling I have for him is—well, it's complicated. There are many feelings. None are good."

"I'm sorry for that."

She wants more. Of course she does. Sorry, Charlie. Not getting it. "Well, it's certainly nothing for you to be sorry for. But Sami, you will be sorry if—" The mere thought makes me woozy. "Listen, I'm not sure if this is why you called. And I don't know how to say this without just coming out and saying it, so . . ."

"Go ahead. Say it."

"You really need to stay away from him. Miles, I mean. He's not a good person." There, I said it. Fuh. Let me go now.

"Like, how do you mean?"

Barf is traveling up my esophagus—a river of hot pink. "Let me put it this way. He will make you do things you don't want to do."

"Like, what kind of things?"

Oh, my little friend, must we get into specifics? "It's

going to sound weird."

"Trust me. It's not going to sound weird."

No. It's the stuff of nightmares. It would take preternatural willing suspension of disbelief on her part. "I really don't like talking about it. Especially by phone. And it's been so long since I've seen you. It's like you're a stranger."

"Lauren, please. I wouldn't be calling you if it weren't important. I'm meeting him in fifteen minutes and I'm not sure what he's planning."

Suddenly, I feel him here with me. The little hairs on the back of my neck rise to a high pitch. My voice drops low so he won't hear. "Are you going to be . . . making music?"

"Yeah. Think so."

A cry of panic bursts out before I can get my hand over my mouth. It takes a few beats for the bile to settle.

"Listen to me very carefully." Can she hear the urgency in my voice? "Under no circumstances should you play music with him. Period."

"But, he's expecting me in, like, twenty minutes. We have a rehearsal planned. I can't just not show up."

"Don't play music, then."

"Lauren, what the heck? That's kind of the point of the whole meeting."

Oh, Miles, you demon. What in the world are you planning now? I'm at a loss. At once, I can't find it in me to intervene. Sami's got to figure this out on her own. Like I did.

"Tell you what, if you have to play, then play. But make sure you stay alert. And keep track of time. Can you do that?"

"Yeah, sure. I can do that." She's got more questions.

"Then you should be fine." Without thinking, I open my

pendant watch and stare at the clock face. My prayer's been ignored, apparently. I'm going back to relive it all, I can feel it happening. I swallow a thick lump that's formed in my throat, resigned. Maybe it's a necessary path to help Sami. I'll do it for her. For the friendship we once had.

Is she still on the line?

"I need to go. Sorry."

And I thought hot pink would save me. I should know by now. Nothing will.

ABOUT JD SPERO

Johannah Davies Spero, award-winning author of *Forte* and *Catcher's Keeper*, has pursued her love of narrative through degrees in English, Russian, and teaching. In winters, she splits her time between her writing studio and the yoga studio. In summers, she splits her time between Lake George, New York and Salisbury Beach, Massachusetts. She met her husband while living in the great city of Boston and two of her three sons were born on the North Shore.

AUTHOR'S WORD & ACKNOWLEDGEMENTS

Years ago, I watched a documentary about polar bears that made me cry. With their habitat melting away, the problem seems insurmountable. And that's just one example. Climate change. Global warming. Beyond these buzz words in the political arena, when I think about the kind of environmental problems we are passing on to the next generation, my mama-tiger claws come out. But then, despair hits. What can I, a writer, possibly do?

Write this book.

There are other things we can all do to help heal our planet. Looking for a to-do list? Visit http://science.howstuffworks.com/environmental/green-science/save-earth-top-ten.htm

In my twenties, I lived in Boston right near Berklee School of Music. On a warm day with my windows open, I could hear musicians practicing. Whatever I was doing in my apartment, I would stop, be still, and listen. Although I'm not a musician, I've always loved music, and I believe in its power.

In any work of fiction is always some truth.

Boston borders are mostly man-made and were expanded in the 1640s. The Esplanade is dredged land from the Charles River. Most of the financial district and Faneuil Hall is made up of borrowed land from Needham—where glacier-made hills were transferred to what is now Boston's waterfront. Bunker Hill was another source for borrowed land.

To see a map similar to what Gaye shows Sami in chapter 40, go to www.bostongeology.com

Want to witness thundersnow? Search the Weather Channel's video featuring Jim Cantore covering the 2015 winter storm Neptune on YouTube. Other rare weather events such as Red Sprites and Blue Jets actually exist, although they remain a mystery to many weather experts. Red Sprites and Blue Jets are types of lightning called Transient Luminous Events (TLEs). Both appear above thunderclouds for only a few seconds. Blue Jets have been reportedly witnessed by airplane pilots, but Red Sprites can only be seen with special cameras. For more information, visit http://www.nssl.noaa.gov/

This book would not be possible without some amazing people. First and foremost: Thank you to the fans of *Forte*. For reading, reviewing, and passing it on, you have given me an author's greatest gift. Thanks especially to Ms. Georgianna Bull, who invited me into her classroom multiple times to speak to her students and is currently on a mission to make *Forte* into a movie (and claims dibs on the role of Mom). Thanks to all the educators who championed *Forte* in their schools—Kristina Peterson, Denise Troelstra, Mark Allen, Morgan Smythe, Antoinette Donohue, Jen Cornell, Sarah Olson, Bill Elder, and Beth Wright.

Awards from Adirondack Center for Writing (2015 winner), National Indie Excellence Awards (2016 Finalist), and Book Excellence Awards (2016 Finalist) helped put a spotlight on *Forte*. Thanks to Rhonda Triller and Cathy DeDe for giving *Forte* a splash in the local press. It was one of the most exciting author moments when Jessica Curtis and Tonya J. Powers interviewed me on FOX News Radio.

Penny Freeman's casual question—*Where's the sequel?*—got me thinking one was possible. After finishing *Forte*, my friend Sandra wanted more about Miles, and thus a love triangle was born. My brother Jim Davies and his wife Vanessa helped me brainstorm early on and helped shape the magic dynamic in the story. Thanks for "throwing spitballs" with me. My husband and always-first beta reader, Anthony, shared his fascination with weather patterns and also his company's expertise on music therapy. My friend and son's piano teacher, Juliet Scott, was my resident piano consultant. Chris Reed Jr. from Glens Falls Music Academy set me straight on drumming terminology. Shout out to *Henna by Heather* in Boston, MA for accurate henna references. Smart and talented Isabel Denise helped me keep it real for my teen readers.

My parents, Jim and Janet Davies, continue to amaze me with their generosity and unwavering support. I hope I show my boys the same level of respect when they are adults. My son Adam Henry is responsible for bringing music into our home with, first, his obsession with the game *My Singing Monsters* and, second, his insistence on drum lessons. And Chazzy, my little guy, gave me hugs whenever I needed them. Turns out, writers need lots.

My oldest son, AJ, reread *Forte* in the midst of all his other fifth-grade homework and responsibilities so he could be a well-informed beta reader for this book. His feedback—delivered on an index card at my bedside table—was most valuable and will be cherished forever: "I loved your book so much! I loved the description, and I felt like I could really feel the characters. I loved the combination of music, magic, and mythology. Definitely one of the best books I've ever read! – AJ <3"

Trillions of thanks to Penny and the rest of my X-team: MeriLyn, Jessica, and Anne-Marie. Shout out to my #JaNoWriMo partner-in-crime and fellow Xchyler author Russell A. Smith (half this book was written in one month—January, 2017—thanks to my 1000-word-a-day month-long writing challenge).

Thanks to my in-laws. Judith Basile has the coolest green eyes with specks of brown and green, like little planet Earths. My father-in-law, Mike Spero (and Robin!), lives on one of the most beautiful beaches in the world just an hour north of Boston. Sending writing power to Aly, Michelle, Betsy, and Sandra. Love to my "lifer" friends and constant cheerleaders Carrie, Wendy, and Erika. I'm grateful for my cherished writer *and* lifer friend, the accomplished Anika Denise, who is also my go-to for all book-related musings and my domestic and overseas writing retreat partner. (Scotland, here we come!)

And, finally—once is not enough—Anthony Spero, you are my muse and my magic. You are my world.

ABOUT XCHYLER PUBLISHING:

Xchyler Publishing, an imprint of Hamilton Springs Press, proudly presents CONCERTO by JD Spero. Follow the author online at www.jdspero.com, @jdspero, www.facebook.com/jdspero/.

Xchyler Publishing strives to bring intelligent, engaging speculative fiction from emerging authors to discriminating readers. While we specialize in fantasy, Steampunk, and paranormal genres, we are also expanding into more general fiction categories, including several manuscripts in the developmental phase. We believe that "family friendly" books don't have to be boring or inane. We exert our best creative efforts to expand the horizons of our readers with imaginative worlds and thought-provoking content.

OTHER YA SERIES YOU MAY ENJOY FROM XCHYLER PUBLISHING:

Forte by JD Spero
Forte, Concerto, Cadence—coming 2018
Vivatera by Candace J. Thomas
Vivatera, Conjectrix, Everstar
Vanguard Legacy by Joanne Kershaw
Foretold, Reflected, Fated
The Bookminder by M. K. Wiseman
The Bookminder, The Kithseeker—coming early 2018